CAN'T FIGHT THIS

CAN'T FIGHT THIS

A RESISTING TEMPTATION NOVEL

MARLEY GIBSON

eISBN: 978-1-937776-39-8
ISBN: 978-1-937776-73-2

Praise for the Resisting Temptation Series

"Marley Gibson takes one smart, sassy heroine and an instantly loveable heartthrob, throws in the perfect amount of humor and spice, mixes up some heart-tugging emotion and delivers one utterly irresistible temptation of a series. Prepare to be addicted!"

– *New York Times* bestselling author Roxanne St. Claire

READ THESE OTHER BOOKS BY MARLEY GIBSON

Ghost Huntress Series - Young Adult/Paranormal

Ghost Huntress: The Awakening
Ghost Huntress: The Guidance
Ghost Huntress: The Reason
Ghost Huntress: The Counseling
Ghost Huntress: The Discovery
Ghost Huntress: The Journey
Ghost Huntress: The Tidings, A Christmas Novella

Other Young Adult Books

Radiate

Non-Fiction

The Other Side: A Teen's Guide to Ghost Hunting
and the Paranormal with Patrick Burns

New Adult Books

Poser

Books for Adults

Can't Touch This (Resisting Temptation series)
Can't Fight This (Resisting Temptation series)

CHAPTER ONE

I walk into the room full of party goers and tamp down my jealousy. This should be *my* engagement party.

But it's not. Not yet.

I move deeper inside Alibi, the restaurant in the Liberty Hotel, and cut a straight path through the crowded room to one of the guests of honor. My best friend, Vanessa Virtue.

"That's the biggest diamond ring I've ever seen!" I hear our friend Marina Baye say way too loudly.

Of course, I've already seen the brand new, sparkly two-carat engagement ring— in the platinum setting with baguette diamond accents on either side of the larger stone. Yes, I checked out the details online. Major dime spent.

"Kyle really blew me away with it," a blushing Vanessa says. Her vibrant smile speaks volumes about her over-whelming joy.

I snag a cold glass of golden champagne from a passing waiter and tip it in my friend's direction. Vanessa's eyes light up and she waves me over.

"Griz! You finally made it." She hugs me to her.

Griz is the ridiculous nickname Vanessa dubbed me when I'd confessed my obsession with the musical "Cats." I can't explain it. It's just a story I've always adored. My idol is Grizabella the Glamour Cat, the downtrodden soul who

1

rose to a new life. Isabella Perry, my real name, is way too close to Grizabella, so the nickname stuck.

"Sorry, Double V," I explain and then take a sip of the bubbly. "I had to work late and it took forever to get over here on the T."

Vanessa's brows furrow. "I thought Rick was bringing you over?"

I shrug. "Guess he got caught up at work, too."

Marina gushes more over Vanessa's new jewelry and relationship status. "I can't believe you're *finally* engaged. I called last week when I saw that you'd changed your relationship status on Facebook, but you never answered the phone."

A blush crosses Vanessa's cheeks. "Kyle and I were sort of, umm, occupied."

I down more champagne as my face heats at the thought of Vanessa and Kyle *in flagrante*. It's been so long since I've had anything *in fla-me* that I think I've forgotten how to do it.

As Marina and Vanessa keep chatting, I glance around the restaurant in search of my other half, Rick Churchman. Over in the corner, I see Vanessa's boyfriend—now fiancé—laughing it up with a group of his friends. Rick is conspicuously absent, I note. Probably stuck on the Red Line like I had been. Of course, I know people here at the party are talking. Things they won't say to my face, rather what they're thinking. Rick and I've been dating longer than Vanessa and Kyle and our collective group of friends assumed that Rick and I would take the plunge first.

So did I.

I swallow the lump in my throat as I watch Vanessa flitting through the room. It's as though she's floating over the hardwood floor in her happiness haze. My emotional overload has nothing to do with jealousy of Vanessa and Kyle's situation. However, I do envy the hell out of my friend's amazing piece of jewelry and what it symbolizes: *commitment.*

Vanessa comes up behind me and places her bejeweled hand on my arm. "You're next, Griz. I just know it. Rick's crazy about you."

Laughing nervously, I stare out the window at the sparkling snow. A fire crackles away filling the room with warmth and glow… or maybe that's just coming from Vanessa.

I stretch my neck toward the door, wondering where Rick is. He should be here by now.

"Griz! Did you hear what I said?" Vanessa asks. "Next thing you know, Rick will be buying you a diamond."

If Rick and I were having one-third of the sex that Kyle and Vanessa were, I might agree with her. However, Rick and I have been working too hard, too late, too long, and haven't been the couple we used to be. Hell, we don't even live together. He lives with a friend of his from high school and I live in Vanessa's old apartment with our fabulously gay best friend, William McEwan. How can we commit to each other when we can't even sign a lease together?

I shuck off the internal conflict swirling through my brain and turn to my friend. "Tonight's about you and Kyle," I remind her, trying to deflect the conversation. Vanessa's not having any of it, though.

Vanessa scowls at me. "Come on, you and Rick have been together for two years. It's the next natural step."

I glance at my empty champagne glass. "The next natural step for me is finding that waiter with the bubbly stuff."

Vanessa shrugs and rolls her eyes. "Fine. Avoid the subject."

"It's what I do best," I say with a laugh. Not thinking about the fact that Rick and I haven't had sex in five months keeps me from going stark raving mad. Or crying like a baby in a green-monstered jealousy fit that my best friend is beating me to the altar. Of course I want to get married to Rick. I wouldn't have spent the last two years of my life with him if I didn't think it was going somewhere or he wasn't The One.

Vanessa lifts another flute from the drink tray and passes it over to me. "Tell me what's going on with Rick and you."

I steady my breath. Okay, she went there. "Look, Rick and I haven't exactly been intimate lately." My cheeks warm at the admission. Vanessa and I don't normally dish details of our sex lives—although I did hear about how she and Kyle first did it on an airplane—however, right now, I feel compelled to confess. "It's been almost five months," I say barely above a whisper.

"Five months since what?"

I blow out the breath I've been holding. "Since Rick and I've, *you know*. Had sex."

Vanessa's eyes widen and she gasps dramatically. "That doesn't seem feasible. We're still young and no one's saving themselves these days."

I flatten my lips, wishing I hadn't told my friend the truth. "It's feasible… and it's my life."

"Oh Griz!" Vanessa's eyes grow sympathetic of my plight. "Why haven't you told me?"

"It's not something I want to brag about over cocktails," I say, sipping mine.

Vanessa lowers her voice and asks, "How the hell do you survive? Do you service yourself weekly?"

"Vanessa, stop sounding like a guy! I don't need this right now." Not from Queen Get-a-Lot'a (whom I love) and her kazillion dollar engagement ring. And her mapped out future.

"I'm sorry, Griz. I'm just trying to help," she says and then turns to hug someone who just arrived at the party.

Standing there, I feel like I'm going to black out as little ants seem to be crawling over my field of vision.

It hits me. Hard.

Oh. My. God.

Vanessa and Kyle are getting married.

Then, the next thing I know, they'll have a mortgage on a house in the 'burbs and pets and children and a minivan. The lump returns to my throat, threatening me to choke on the reality that is my life. I work twelve hour days, I eat frozen Lean Cuisines, and I barely see the man who's supposed to be in love with me. I suddenly feel all alone, as if the pairing off of the human species is a new thing and I should be surprised.

Vanessa turns back to me. "That was Kyle's cousin who works out at Boston College." Then she pauses. "All couples are different. You and Rick are simply going through a dry spell. It happens to everyone."

I stare up at her through my blurred vision. "Have you and Kyle had a dry spell?"

Her silence is a dead giveaway.

"See."

"Look, everything will be okay," she assures me. "You two are meant for each other."

Just then Kyle steps through the crowd, moving in our direction. His gorgeous face lights up when he sees Vanessa. Like she's the only woman—the only person—not only in the room, but in the entire world.

My heart skips a beat watching her rush into his arms for an affectionate kiss. Yeah, I want that, too. Happily ever after *has* to be in the cards for me, too. I just know it. Rick and I just need to reconnect. We can't let life's busy-ness get in the way of our love. Tonight, I'm going to make sure that changes.

"What's with the water works, Isabella?" Kyle asks.

"I'm just amazingly happy for you guys," I say honestly.

Kyle wraps his arm around Vanessa and stares over my shoulder. "Hey, look who finally decided to show his ugly mug!"

I turn to see Rick shucking off his coat at the door. His usually short blond hair has grown out a bit lately and really sets off his green eyes. Eyes that seem a bit too tired and weary for someone who is only thirty years old. He's got a stern jaw, chiseled features, and a body for sin—from what I remember. My chest aches in delicious memories as I gawk at him and think of the possibilities. I can so see me married to a gorgeous man like Rick Churchman.

Mrs. Rick Churchman.

Isabella Perry Churchman.

Maybe I'll drop my maiden name.

We will have *the most* adorable children, too. Despite all of my freckles. Rick's classic manly features often have women staring and giving him the eye. But he's mine. And I plan on reminding him of that once we're alone.

Rick waves and winks at me and I experience that delightful roller coaster dip in the pit of my stomach like I did when we first started dating.

"Hey, babe," Rick says a bit out of breath and then kisses me on the cheek.

"It's about time, man," Kyle says, clapping him on the shoulder. "We're going to do the toast now."

Vanessa beams a radiant smile and moves off to the front with Kyle. Rick returns from the bar and I lean back against the exposed brick wall. This chic Boston hotel used to be the city jail. Now, it's the perfect location for Vanessa and Kyle to be bound together. Rick lifts a cold Sam Adams and downs a few gulps instead of talking to me. There's so much left unsaid between the two of us. We seem to be in a relationship penitentiary ourselves. I gaze at his handsome features and his clear eyes wishing I could read his mind.

"Griz!" I hear shouted out. "There you are!"

My roommate, William McEwan pushes his way through the people to get to me.

"William, what's wrong?"

He waves his hand in front of his face in great frustration. "Bitch, you took *my* cell phone when you left the apartment this morning." Then he laughs.

I reach into my purse and retrieve the Android phone that exactly matches William's since we got them together in a two-for deal that saved us *beaucoup dinero*. "Sorry about that, I—"

William's lips flatten. "Some ass-hat has been calling all day for you. Some lawyer with a messed up name who says it's 'imperative' he speak with you. I thought I was going insane until I really looked at the phone and saw the screen-saver picture of you and Rick instead of the one of Kirk's bare chest."

I snicker at the thought of William expecting to see his latest boy toy on the screen, but instead was greeted by the snapshot of Rick and me on our Vermont apple picking trip two months ago.

William shoves the cellular device my way and I hand him his. He huffs off into a corner to listen to his voice mail messages. I take the opportunity to do the same, wondering what some lawyer could possibly want from me.

I punch in my voice mail code and listen. "Ms. Perry. My name is Westin Esterhazy, Esquire. Attorney for Stella Hardwick." I furrow my brows at the phone thinking this guy obviously has a wrong number. Yet the message continues. "Stella Hardwick. Your father's aunt on his mother's

side. I regret to inform you that Ms. Hardwick died yesterday. Since you are the executor of her estate, as well as her
heir, it's imperative that you come to Alabama immediately
and take responsibility for business matters that need your
attention. Please call me back at 251-555—"

What? Who? Huh?

Estate? Executor? Me? I'm an heiress?

There's obviously been a *big* misunderstanding. I've
never heard of Stella Hardwick in my life!

I start to dial my father's cell phone number, but Kyle's
laughter over the microphone drowns out my intentions.
As he and Vanessa thank everyone for being here tonight,
I try to process this information from that Westerhazy
guy's voice mail. My hand finds my temple and I close
my eyes to the light-headed dizziness as the room closes
in around me. It's probably the champagne. I guzzled it
way too fast, plus I haven't eaten anything all day. Claudia
Coldren, a.k.a Boss from Hell, has been riding me like a
Kentucky Derby filly for the past week and a half to make
sure my graphics and web designs are ready for our new
product launch. If she had her way, I'd be marrying the
company and not Rick Churchman who would take me
away from my job.

"—and then there's Rick and Isabella," Kyle says, grabbing my attention.

Who... us? All eyes in the room turn to us. Rick slides
in behind me, fresh beer in hand, and is just as surprised as
I am.

Kyle's relentless as he presses forward with the mic in his
hand. "Rick and Isabella mean the world to us. Wouldn't it
be great if the four of us have a double wedding ceremony?"
Our crowd of friends goes crazy hooting and hollering. "Of
course, Churchman, that would entail you getting down on

one knee and popping the question to your lady, right here, right now."

"Is he fucking kidding me?" I hear Rick mutter.

"Oh, my God." I want the floor to swallow me whole as my entire body bursts into flames. The crowd loves it, though, and everyone is clapping and egging us on. Rick laughs nervously and shifts from one foot to the other.

"Come on, Churchman," Kyle yells out. "If you don't do it, Isabella's going to tell you to 'shit or get off the pot.'"

"I wouldn't do that," I mutter back. My skin itches, though, at the prospect of Rick dropping to his knee in front of all of our friends.

The entire room echoes with laughter like some sick Adult Swim cartoon. Faces and bodies morph in and out of shape to me as the champagne hits rock bottom in my empty stomach. I sway backwards into Rick's chest and he wraps his arm around my waist to steady me. "Come with me," he whispers softly.

As he hustles me through the crowd, there are more cat calls, cheering, and clapping. Thank heavens Rick knows me well enough to get me out of the embarrassing situation. He turns down the hallway and presses open the door that reads "Ladies."

"You can't come in here," I say to him with a girlish giggle. Maybe he just wants privacy so he can do this right. I bite my tongue to keep my excitement tamped down. Does he have a ring in his pocket? Did he and Kyle orchestrate this?

"Don't worry about it," Rick says.

Once inside, he looks under the stalls to make sure we're alone and then he locks the door. My heart races in anticipation. Not the most romantic location for a proposal, but certainly memorable.

"Issy," he begins.

I don't let him finish, though. Before he says the words that will surely change our lives, I want to have a little fun. My drought period of pent-up desire, emotion, and wanting comes to a frothy cappuccino-like head. I want him. I want him *now*. I rush forward and wrap my arms around him. My lips, hungry from five months of fasting, attack his full ones, ravishing him with my kiss. He's hesitant at first, then his mouth opens over mine like it's the very first time. Our tongues meet in an epic battle for control, stroking, smoothing, and licking. I groan a little when I feel his hands move into my hair. He moans a lot when my fingers find the zipper to his Joseph A. Banks slacks. Kissing and feeling, tugging and burning, I back us up until we're in the handicapped stall. I sit down on the porcelain seat and deftly pull his stiffening erection out into my hands. Rick's breath hitches and I sense him shiver.

It's been too long. Way too long.

For both of us.

I place my tongue on his firmness and test out his resolve.

"Oh Issy..." he hisses out. "This isn't—"

"I know, baby," I say, my eyes shining up at him. "It's not the best place. It'll do, though."

"It's not that, it's that Kyle said—"

His words stop immediately when my mouth encompasses him whole.

"Oh God..." he says with a long sigh. "How do I say this with your mouth on me like that?"

Ask me to marry you.

He leans forward with his hands on my shoulders. Kneading my skin and... pushing me away.

"Rick! What's wrong?" I ask as my hand flies to my mouth.

He presses Little Ricky back into his pants and stares at me. "Be serious for a minute. It's what Kyle said in there."

I don't want to be serious. I want to be lovers, like we used to be. "It's okay," I say, smiling in what I hope is a mischievous way. "I just want to be with you."

Rick hangs his head. "That's just it, Isabella. Kyle's right. I should have done this a long time ago. It's not right to keep you hanging on for so long."

My breathing stops momentarily as I await the words every girl longs to hear.

I promise to say "yes."

"Isabella." His face morphs into serious regard. "I'm getting off the pot."

"You're wh-wh-what?"

"Yeah. It's time we moved on."

Stung, as if slapped in the face, I gasp. Hard.

I don't believe this. I don't fucking *believe this.*

Before I can utter a word, Rick turns and walks out of the bathroom.

My life has just turned to shit.

CHAPTER TWO

Sunday morning at o'dark-thirty, I haul my travel-weary body off of the 727 parked at the gate at the Pensacola Regional Airport. I'd opted to get the hell out of Boston promptly to avoid Rick, Kyle, Vanessa, William, Marina, everyone, all of them. The world.

Against my better judgment, I called back the attorney, Westin Esterhazy, got the scoop on this long-lost relative who left me her estate, packed my bags, and left town. Nothing like a week in the countryside of Alabama to give me some time to tend to my wounds and think things through.

Vanessa thought I was crazy to react to the call of Stella Hardwick's attorney like I did thinking it was like one of those e-mail scams you get saying you have inherited money from a relative in Kenya and they need you to send thousands of dollars to get it. I Googled the lawyer and he's legit. Besides, Vanessa has her man, her future, and her plans. I have nothing except a stack of bills and a job that sucks the life out of me. Speaking of work, I left Claudia a voice mail telling her I needed time off for an emergency family matter. I'm sure she'll have plenty to say about it, but right now, I don't care.

The hell with her.

The hell with all of them!

It's high time for me to take care of Isabella Perry.

No man's going to do it. In fact, I don't need a man to do it. I'm a single, independent woman who now, apparently, owns property. I'll deal with what I need to with the lawyer and this estate in Alabama, spend a little time re-grouping, and then figure out my next step.

My dad is of no help in all of this. He and Mom are off on a month-long missionary trip to Israel and getting hold of him is nearly next to impossible. Great time for the 'rents to go informationally AWOL on me. I'm literally flying into this situation blind as a bat.

Unfortunately, Westin Esterhazy, Esquire, didn't give me much information about what I'm headed into. He said we'd "talk in person." His pressing demand was to get to Dilligus Flats, Alabama, *ASAP*. William and I looked up the place on Google Maps, but all we found was a reference to the annual Dilligus Flats Watermelon Seed Spitting Contest.

So, here I am.

And not for the seed spitting contest.

I pac through the concourse and out through security at the Pensacola airport. Around me, military men are greeted by wives and children with hugs, kisses, and waving flags. Grandparents carry packages meant to spoil the grandchildren who've met them here in the terminal. Couples are reunited and business affiliates clap each other on the backs and shake hands. I glance around for a sign of the driver Esterhazy said he'd send to "fetch" me. No Italian-suit-wearing limo drivers with dark glasses here like at Boston's Logan Airport.

Instead, everyone seems to have paired or grouped off, making their way to the escalator that descends to the baggage claim area. I'm alone. Trying to figure out where the hell to go.

Suddenly, I feel eyes on me and I shift to see what I can only describe as a hunk and a half of a man standing at the bar to the right, sliding down the last few sips of his coffee. His eyes are watching me. Unthinkingly, I run my hand through my airplane hair and suck in my stomach. I smooth my hand down the front of my Lucky Seven jeans and try not to stare back at the gorgeous man. A smile hitches on one corner of his mouth as if he knows a secret about me and isn't telling. My broken heart stitches together momentarily at the flirtatious nature of such a stunning stranger. Sure, he's wearing dirty jeans, a work shirt, dusty boots, and a leather jacket, but his body position says he's built for sin. Pure and simple.

Unable to break the eye contact, I move forward toward the escalator and then nearly fall when a little girl has squatted down on the floor to play with her dolly.

"Oh my!" I shout. "That's not a good place to sit, sweetie."

"Watch where you're going," her mother snaps at me.

"I'm sorry, but she just stopped in front of me."

The woman presses her lips tightly together and then says, "She's just a baby."

Yeah, just a baby who's rolling around on the floor in a public airport blocking the entrance to the escalator. Ewww…and she's putting her dropped pacifier back into her mouth and her mother doesn't seem to care.

I sigh hard.

The woman snags up the little girl and heads down the escalator.

I pull my hands through my sandy-colored hair again in frustration and take a peek back behind me at the bar. Disappointment coats me when I see that Hunky Boy is no longer there. Ah well, he's probably there to pick up his girlfriend and tell her how he's going to marry her instead of "getting off the pot."

Rick the Bastard.

I clunk down the escalator—that's barely moving—and try to imagine the property I've inherited. I'll admit my heart flutters a little at the thought of getting an inheritance. It's so grown up. So responsible. I envision an elegant, sprawling antebellum mansion on rolling green hills, Tennessee Walkers gracing the white fenced orchard, hound dogs roaming the immaculately trimmed front yard and me, in a rocking chair sipping a mint julep and eating the best fried chicken ever.

I close my eyes wondering what's in store for me. Yesterday my life had so much hope, and now... Another sigh escapes me when I realize I need to practice what I preach. For eons I've told Vanessa, William, and others to "go with the flow." I guess it's time to take my own advice. It's just this sense of total upheaval in my world—as of yesterday—that's freaking me out. I breathe in deeply. I have to stop making everything into a big deal.

It's all about attitude.

I'm an executor and an heiress.

That has to mean something.

One more sigh out of me that's so intense that the lady with the squirming baby glares at me. She clutches her child like I'm going to snatch it from her. "You know, sighing invites Satan in," she says to me.

My mouth drops open at her forwardness. "You know, honey. My mother lives in Chicago. When I want to be told what to do, I call her. Why don't you take care of your own kid who's sucking on God knows what kind of germs on that binky."

With that, I slip around her on the escalator and exit off to the right toward baggage claim.

Probably not the kindest way I could have handled that. However, that woman has no idea what I've been through. And what I have to face.

I can handle it, though.

Dealing with Stella Hardwick's business affairs is something to block out my thoughts of being dumped by my boyfriend. Something to distract me from the fact that I'm starting to wonder if my life is one big, completely unfixable muck up.

Something to—hey, it's Hunky Boy again standing next to the luggage claim for my flight. This time, I get a luscious view of his backside that's gloved into those too-too tight jeans of his. His hair is a bit long in the back like he doesn't care. Yet, when he turns and meets my stare, it's obvious he does care.

In his hand is a white sign with black lettering that reads, "I. Perry."

Holy shit! He's here for me.

I jump at the blaring of the horn announcing the arrival of the bags. The luggage belt moans and groans and begins to puke out the various suitcases from on my plane. I see one of mine; however, I let it go as I force my feet to walk toward Mr. Hotty.

I clear my throat as I stand before him. "I'm Isabella Perry."

His dazzling smile is damn near heartbreaking. "I know you are."

Taken aback, "You do?"

"Sure, you're Stella Hardwick's relative. I see the family resemblance."

I shrug at this stranger who knows more about my great-aunt than I do or ever will. "And you are?" I ask with a bit of city-girl attitude.

He drops the card to one side and extends his right hand. "Jake Hansen at your service."

My eyes dance up and down him, thinking about all the things I need servicing. My heart. My mind. My body…

every nook and cranny of my body. Not the time, though. My libido is still recovering from Rick's metaphorical drive-by shooting.

I take Jake's offered hand in mine and squeeze in a business-like manner. Though there's nothing professional about the tingly feel of his hand against mine. The beat of his pulse through his fingers and the heat from his body is palpable. The intense stare from his blazing eyes has me almost believing he can decipher the color of my underwear through my winter coat and street clothes.

I pull my hand away, breaking the contact, and try to organize my thoughts. "Who are you now?"

His laugh is deep and rolling like an ocean wave. "I was asked to come get you and drive you to Dilligus Flats." Then he looks down at his attire. "Sorry I'm so sweaty and dirty. I was up early working and didn't get a chance to shower before I drove over here."

I'm not complaining. There's something hearty and earthy about a man who does physical labor early in the morning. Like he's working hard so he can enjoy the rest of his day. "That's okay."

Even though I pull my two bags from the conveyer, Jake hoists them together and manhandles them for me. He cocks his head to the right, his long bangs falling into his eyes, and then he slips a pair of dark sunglasses over his blue orbs. "This way."

I follow obediently and take a deep breath as I step out into the remarkably warm November day in Florida's panhandle. (Pensacola is the closest airport to this Dilligus Flats place.) I hope I packed appropriate clothes for this adventure: T-shirts, jeans, a couple of dressy outfits for meetings with the lawyer.

I tag along behind Jake and my bags as we cross the street and then weave through the parking deck. Jake stops at spot D-40 and tosses my bags into the back of the most God-awful, beat-up, red mud-caked beige—or at least at some point in its life it was beige—Chevy pickup.

"*This* is your mode of transport?"

"Not my usual ride, but it's your chariot, Ms. Perry," he says with a grin.

"You've got to be kidding me."

Jake doesn't move to open the passenger door for me— not that I should have expected it or anything—so I climb up into the pickup using one of the handles inside the truck. Jake bends down and pulls a Folgers coffee can out from under the seat with the keys in it.

"People sure are trusting here," I say incredulously.

"Who'd want to steal this piece of shit?" Jake asks. He's got a point.

I glance into the back and see my very pregnant-looking rolling bag and large black duffel sitting in the dirt encased pickup bed. Good thing I brought my discount suitcase instead of William's Louis Vuitton he offered for me to use. Inside the cab, the bench seat isn't much cleaner. Torn and tattered from wear, the dingy Styrofoam is busting through in a perfect Gluteus Maximus pattern of the former driver.

"Why Aunt Stella... baby had back."

Jake chuckles and then slides in behind the wheel. "Yes, she did."

Dust covers the dashboard and instruments and I can see that the radio is a push-button AM/FM only. So much for plugging my phone into the auxiliary port to charge. I sneeze once. Twice. Three times, feeling the tickles of filth and grime attacking my sensitive nasal cavities. And me without my Allegra.

"Bless you," Jake says.

The beast of a truck cranks reluctantly and I pray to God to get me to Dilligus Flats safe and sound. He's probably laughing at me. God, not this Jake person, although Jake's laughed at me, too. I'm laughing at myself. At my situation. At my lot in life suddenly.

Jake puts the truck in reverse, exits the parking deck, and points us west on I-10 toward the Alabama state line. Heaven only knows what awaits me over the border.

CHAPTER THREE

The forty-five minute ride is the longest of my life.

Jake is easy on the eyes, but he is *not* a conversationalist.

He's one of those quiet and pensive types.

You have to watch out for them.

I notice there's no ring on his left hand or any sort of indentation to show he may have once worn a ring. Although, I have no business assessing his ring status. It's just idle curiosity.

As is my wanting to know his exact role in this little masterpiece theater of my life.

The air conditioner I insisted on turning on heaves a blast of red, dusty air and I break into hysterical sneezing. Jake tries to hand me a Hardee's napkin to help out with my allergies and then swears when he nearly misses the turn for County Road 42, which will apparently take us to "downtown" Dilligus Flats.

"Bless you," he says gruffly.

"Did I do something wrong?" I ask.

"No."

Then silence again.

I finally see that I have enough bars on my phone to check my voice mail. There's a message from William. "Hey Griz, your dad called with the 411 on your mysterious Stella. I could barely hear him since he was at some sort of revival.

I wrote it all down. He vaguely remembers her. Says she kept to herself. Never traveled. Sort of the black sheep of the family. Said no one talked about her much. But she was on the list for the Perry end-of-year newsletter."

"Ugh," I moan, wiping my itchy nose with my palm. I hate those frickin' family newsletters giving people a dissertation of your life for the past year, like they care. Apparently Aunt Stella cared since she willed me her property. I just hope the demise of Rick isn't one of this year's feature articles.

I click "end" and toss the cell phone to the dirty seat. Jake's eyes follow the movement, but he doesn't comment. Moments later, we pass into what has to be "town center."

"Welcome to Dilligus Flats," he announces. "Don't sneeze again or else you'll miss it."

A police station on the corner of Main and Truancy Streets. A flashing yellow light. Pike's Drug Store on the left, Willie's Gas and Fluff on the right. We turn onto Truancy and, ironically, pass Dilligus Flats High School.

"You're not from here," I say more than ask.

His smile hitches with his one word answer. "Nope."

Clearly getting any background information from this guy is going to be worse than a tooth extraction with no Novocain. A mile down the road, the sporadically spaced single-family houses turn into pecan orchards and cow pastures.

"Are we getting close?" I ask.

"Yep."

"So, do you work for Esterhazy?" I ask, unable to take the silence anymore.

"That jerk? Hell no," he says firmly. "I don't work for anyone."

Ohhhh-kay. That doesn't help.

"Do you work on the farm?" I press.

Jake chuckles. "No. I don't."

Who is this guy?

"Did you just come to—"

Jake interrupts. "Look, Isabella. I was asked to come get you, so I did. It's nothing personal, but can we leave it at that? This week has been a bitch and I'm totally wiped."

I know when to quit talking, even though my questions don't go away. He stares ahead, focused on driving and nothing else. Someone must have hurt him awfully bad for him to be this closed off. I'm an affable person—even though I've had my own heart stomped—and didn't think just trying to get to know a new person would be met with such resistance.

The road narrows and I see a fence under repair on both sides of the road, which bends hard to the right up ahead. Jake slows the truck and signals, then he turns into the dirt drive. Through the tall oak trees I can see a hint of a house. The truck bounces along on the uneven path and Jake hits the brake.

Then, I gasp.

My jaw drops and my heart sinks.

"What a fricking dump!"

"What did you expect? A McMansion?" He plops a First National Bank fob with two keys on it into the palm of my hand. "She's all yours."

I stare down at the keys until I can no longer focus on them.

Jake quietly hops out, gets my bags, and places them on the rickety front porch.

I get out of the truck and walk around the expansive yard. Before me is a huge, white, dilapidated farmhouse that seems to be listing slightly to the left. In the back yard, there's a light blue mobile home with a motorcycle next to it parked lazily on its kickstand.

"Oh, that trailer's going to be the first thing to go."

I have no idea what I've stumbled into. The stereotypes of the south surround me and I listen up for the inevitable banjo music to start playing.

This must be some sort of cruel joke. Where are the rolling hills? Where are the Tennessee Walkers? Where's that mint julep? I don't smell fried chicken. In fact, I smell... *eww*.

The orchard to my right is full of broken tree branches, abandoned farm equipment, and rolls of hay overgrown with weeds. In the distance, two long barns stretch out with a silo between them. I wonder what they're for, although I have no desire to walk out there to see for myself. All in good time, I suppose, as this disastrous plot of earth is now my responsibility.

My airway seems blocked and I feel I might pass out from disappointment. Tears stain my vision as I glance to my left at the too-tall grass that desperately needs mowing, the paint peeling from the baseboards of the house, and the menacing looking fire ant mounds that dot in the front yard like land mines for trespassers. I don't want this Jake person to see me cry... wait, where is he?

I spin around in psychotic fashion. Jake is nowhere in sight. Neither is the pickup truck I rode in. Did I imagine him? Is he a ghost? A dream? An illusion of a perfectly handsome, yet unattainable man to help me get over Rick?

Maybe he's just a rude son of a bitch who was doing a job and left without saying goodbye.

Either way, I'm sick of men. They're all a big old disappointment.

Rick especially.

I don't understand why he dumped me like he did. Just like that... in the blink of an eye and the snap of a finger.

Could he have picked a more awkward time? We didn't talk about anything. We didn't discuss our time together and our possible future. *Snip!* He just cut the cord. While I was trying to heat up our sex life! He had to get off the pot. Hell, I should have flushed him down it.

As I take this all in, the soft chug of another pickup truck, slowing to a near halt on the county road, catches my attention. When I turn to see who it is, I notice there's a chubby man in a big hat behind the wheel. He eyeballs me and then continues down the road at a slow pace while craning his neck.

"Take a picture, it'll last longer," I say in a very sixth grade manner.

I ignore the onlooker and venture toward the house. Okay, so it's not Tara, but perhaps it's not a complete loss, either. Sure, I'm bummed that it's not a plantation—that would get a more lucrative selling price—but I've got to get a better look at the inside. Outside, the neglect sings out in the form of unkempt bushes, trees that need trimming, and a weed-strewn front lawn. The clapboards could use a strong re-nailing and the place would benefit from a fresh coat of Sherwin Williams. Hopefully there's running water and electricity.

I wonder what could have caused this property to fall into such disarray. Was Stella sick and bed-ridden? Too old and fragile to trim the hedges? I mean, Esterhazy told me she'd "died suddenly working the farm" so I would have thought the place would have been in better condition. Maybe she was too busy taking care of the other acres to tend to her own personal living quarters.

I sniff the air. Clean. Grassy. A slight whiff of manure coming from somewhere. My body cringes and I choke back a gag. That's disgusting.

I carefully pick my way through the weeds and fire ant mounds—I learned when I was at Clemson to steer clear of these suckers—as I make my way to the house. Walking up to the porch, I'm not exactly confident the groaning planks beneath will hold my one hundred and twenty five pounds. I brace myself on a joist and I lean forward to put the key in the lock.

This is an effort in futility because the door is unlocked. What's the point of a set of keys? Hesitantly, I step into the house that smells of mothballs and Oil of Olay. I'm quite surprised to see the insides so well kept, totally unlike the outside. To the right is a parlor full of beautiful, antique Victorian furniture. A grandfather clock sings out the morning hour and causes my heart to skitter away at the loud bonging. On the left is a bedroom with a tattered quilt draped over the high double bed. A Boston rocker sits in the corner with a dingy lace antimacassar. This must have been Stella's room. Suddenly, I envision the scene in *Little Women* where Beth died and I'm totally creeped out.

"I'm so not sleeping in there."

I turn down the hallway, which opens into an expansive Great Room decorated only in an Oriental rug and oil portraits of rolling hills, horses, and windmills on the wall. I crouch down and flip up the end of the runner, hoping was done by hand and therefore, the real thing. Nope. Machine sewn. Can't get a big sell-off in the estate sale.

A hinge squeaks and I almost fall over as my pulse freaks out. Off this main room, there are three doors on the right. The middle one is cracked open and I swear I hear running water.

"Hello?" I call out.

A black cat appears from the opening and bounds over to me, purring as it rubs on my ankle. I scoop up the kitty and start rubbing its bunny-soft fur.

"Who are you?" I ask. The kitty blinks with yellow-gold eyes and reaches out to pap at my nose. A collar around her neck identifies her. "Well, hello, Puddy Tat. Looks like I inherited you, too."

A noise in the middle room causes the cat to squirm. She jumps from my arms and rushes back to the cracked open door.

When a second loud noise comes from the middle room, I know that the cat and I aren't the only people here.

The question is... who *is*?

CHAPTER FOUR

Crap, that kick boxing class Vanessa and I signed up for was just an excuse to go out to dinner on Wednesday nights. Now I wish I had actually attended the sessions.

Quickening my step in time with my frantic heartbeat, I peel off to the left into the large kitchen. I grab a cast-iron skillet from the pot rack over the stove and head into the Great Room, poised in front of the middle door. There's a rustle signifying something much larger than Puddy Tat is in there.

My hands shake, but I raise the skillet high over my head with my left; I dial "911" on my cell phone with the right and put my finger on the "Send" key. A deep breath for fortification and I call out, "Whoever you are, I'm armed. You better get the hell out of here... or else... "

The door creaks and Puddy Tat bolts from the room. Steam swirls through the opening and I realize it's a bathroom.

"I'm serious! Get out here, whoever you are."

"No need to get testy," the deep voice calls out.

I swallow hard at what appears before me.

Jake.

Dripping wet, with steam rising off his skin.

Wearing nothing but a smile... and a towel.

Blood rushes to my head and I fear I might black out from seeing his amazingly hot body in front of me... naked.

Okay, well *nearly naked.* Either way, it's more manly flesh than I've seen in the last five months—except for in the bathroom at Alibi, which so doesn't count.

He clutches a worn white towel around his narrow hips and holds a hand up at me. "Don't shoot... err... rather don't cook?"

I pull my hand out of the air and hide the idiotic frying pan behind my back. I hope I'm not drooling noticeably at him. No, I can't be when my mouth is completely arid. "How the hell did you get in here?"

"Up the back steps. In through the back door," he says with a slight cockiness coating his tone.

His wet hair—way too long and sexy in the front—is dripping beads of water down his muscular jaw. I'm overtaken with the urge to step forward and lick the liquid off his cheek, his neck, his throat, his...

Dammit, girl! Get a grip!

Dear God, I've been without the sins of the flesh way too long.

Oh, but Jake's chest. It's so not like me to pick a guy apart like this, but his chest is something women only dream about. His nipples are tight from the cold air of the house. He is a solid rack of muscles with a broad, muscular, tanned, taut torso, and not a hair in sight. Well, except for the smattering of dusty gold trailing down the hardened indentation of his stomach that disappears into the—

Stop it!

This is my property. I'm in charge here. I have to *take* charge.

"This is my house, Jake, and you're trespassing."

His eyes light up and he laughs. "Come on, Isabella, you'd think you'd never seen a man step out of the shower before. Surely you're not *that* rattled." His voice is rough and dark, like he's spent many a nights imbibing on whiskey. Not the cheap stuff either. Since this is pretty much the most he's said to me, I notice there's no drawl in his voice, rather, his words are distinct and sharp.

I really shouldn't care about his accent at this particular moment. Not should I care about his state of undress. Both have me a bit unnerved and off my game. I furrow my brow. "I really don't understand your role in all of this. You pick me up at the airport, you disappear, and now you're in my shower? Who *are* you, Jake Hansen?"

He peers up through the saturated hair covering his eyes and then sweeps it back with his tanned fingers. His eyes—deep, dark blue—sparkle with recognition and he begins to laugh. "I ask myself the same question pretty much every day."

My nerves are beyond shot. Not because I'm mad at Jake for slipping into the house for a quick shower. I'm annoyed at him for being so goddamned handsome, hot, and sexy. And for making me look. "Then what is it you exactly do, if you don't mind my asking."

"My, we're irritable," he shoots back teasingly.

"That's another thing," I say. "We rode in practical silence in the truck over here and now you're getting cutesy with me?"

"Like I said, I was hot, sweaty, and tired from working this morning. Now I'm clean and… fresh."

Definitely fresh.

I stand straight and tuck my cell phone in the back pocket of my jeans. No need for 911 anymore unless it's to alert the fire department that I'm about to burst into flames. "Look, I came down from Boston to get matters in order and get back to my life. I can't do that if I don't know everything I'm dealing with." There, that sounded good.

Professional. "I didn't plan on encountering someone in your state of undress."

He doesn't flinch at all from the scrutiny of my eyes. Nor does he move to find clothing or cover himself. He just stands there with a cocky grin on his face.

Clothes don't do this man's body justice. I allow myself an extended evaluation of his model-esque physique. However, my eyes stop when upon closer inspection, I notice a long, shiny, thick white scar on his right shoulder. It appears to be fresh and still healing.

Jake catches me looking at the injury and reaches inside the bathroom door for another towel that he drapes around his neck to cover the wound. As though sensing my assessment, he shifts his weight from one leg to the other, drawing my attention to the well-formed, muscular calves and perfectly sculpted feet and toes.

This guy can't be for real.

No normal person is this gorgeous. This sexy.

"Can you just put some clothes on?" I say, finally turning away from him. I spin back around when I hear his muffled laugh.

A crucifying grin spreads across his face and sets his eyes afire. His straight, white teeth appear from underneath full lips and he cracks up.

He's laughing at me?

"What is your deal?" I demand.

He tosses his head back. "You're acting like I'm some male prostitute who's been hired to service you."

My brow lifts as I spin around. "Excuse me?"

Jake waves me off. "The water pipes in the trailer are inconsistent and spew out more red mud than anything, so I shower in here sometimes."

I point out back. "*You* live in the trailer?"

"Yeah, I do. I'd appreciate it if you don't get rid of it until I move out."

"Oh. Sorry. I thought you were... well, I don't know what I thought. You're not exactly an open book." I feel like a complete idiot.

"You're awfully cute when you're flustered," he says very matter-of-fact.

I drop the cast-iron pan onto the kitchen counter and cover my face. My ears ring in tune with the pang of the skillet. Breathe. Breathe. Calm down. Act cool.

He reaches out to me. "Are you okay?"

I pull my hands down and look at his outstretched one close to me. *Don't touch him.* Don't. Touch. Him.

"I'm fine. No one said you'd be here, Jake. Strike that. No one told me much of anything."

I place my hand in his and am floored by how small it looks wrapped in his large, tanned one. A current of static shoots up the length of my arm and all the way down to the tips of my toes. That hasn't happened to me in a long time. Not since my first date with Rick. I don't want to think about Rick. Not when this Hunk of Muscles stands before me. Jake. Nice manly name. And boy is he all man. Hey, just because I believe all men suck ass these days and should be avoided at all cost, I can still appreciate a work of art when I see it. Besides, I'm not being disloyal to anyone by checking him out. I'm the dumped, not the dumper. I'm a free agent and can look all I want.

Jake gives me a sidelong glance, squeezes my hand in a friendly manner, and then drops the contact, breaking the connection or whatever it is that just passed between us.

Whoa. I wonder if he felt it too. An ache low in my belly tells me this man spells d-a-n-g-e-r with a capital "D."

I lift my eyes to Jake's and bite through my nerves to smile. "Maybe we can work out a bathroom schedule while I'm here. You know, to give us both some privacy."

His head tilts towards the bathroom. "Sure thing. Stella never minded, but I don't want to make you uncomfortable."

"Oh, yeah, sure. Whatever." I try not to stare anymore at the sinewy expanses of skin not hidden by the towel. Or imagine what attributes *are* hidden by said towel. "Umm. Okay." I've suddenly lost my ability to make words.

"She was a hell of a lady," Jake says wistfully. He stares past me in remembrance. "I'm going to miss her. A lot."

A lot?

For a split-second, I wonder if there was a little some-thing-something going on between Great Aunt Stella and this hunky Jake person. I shake away the image of an older lady and thirty-something Jake going at it. That's just too much daytime television in my life of late. "Double the Age, Double the Love" on the next Anderson Cooper 360 .

Jake smiles, that heart-piercing one again, and then motions to the bathroom. "I'll just... you know... finish get-ting dressed."

I wipe my hands down the sides of my jeans and bounce in place. "Yeah. You do that."

He stops and turns. "If you're hungry, there might be a casserole in the fridge from what the church people brought over after the funeral."

Wow, so the whole town knows about Stella and Jake. Or so I'm assuming. I do have way too much of an over-active imagination. Maybe I need to quit making rash judgments. Stella could've been a hottie (with a big ass) as far as I know.

"The kitchen's basically bare," he says.

Like you, buddy boy.

No. No. No. I need to stop looking at him like he's on display in the window of Macy's and I want to add him to my charge card. He needs to go dress. I need distance.

"Why don't I run to the store?" I offer, trying not to watch the curve of his well-toned arm as he holds onto the door jamb.

"Go see Willie."

"I beg your pardon?"

"Up the road," he says with a laugh. "Willie at the Gas and Fluff. They've got everything you need up there."

When Jake goes into the bathroom, I let out a satanic sigh (well, satanic according to that woman at the Pensacola airport) and try *not* to think that everything I need is standing naked behind that door.

I mean, Esterhazy said I was getting a farm, but he didn't mention anything about the side of beef.

CHAPTER FIVE

"**D**'ain't I see'd you down Hardwick's?" a loud, lazy accent hollers out to me.

Oh no...is that man talking to me?

At the Gas and Fluff, I try to hide behind a cardboard display of some NASCAR star hawking Nacho Cheese-flavored Doritos. But the shouting farmer advances on me. I stuff a pouch of the fat-laden snack into my basket and head around the corner. I don't feel the need to talk to the local color yet or get to know people until I can get my bearings. Or at least talk to Esterhazy.

However, the loud man isn't giving up.

Peering between the Pop Tarts and Moon Pies, I get a good look at him. Sure enough, it's the pudgy guy from the pickup that slowed down to watch me at Aunt Stella's. The man's wearing overalls, a blue jean work shirt, and a dingy undershirt showing at the collar. On his head is a well-worn John Deere cap. Tufts of curly brown and gray hair stick out from the rim above his flopped-over ears. His portly face and small set eyes bring out his most prominent feature: a large, pug nose. I blink hard because I can't get over how incredibly much he looks like a pig.

He's a pig man!

My face surely shows my astonishment. His beady eyes zero in on me with targeted recognition and I try to look away without being caught staring. Too late though as I've backed myself into a corner of the store. And Pig Man is advancing.

"D'ain't I see'd you down Hardwick's?" he asks again.

On the front pocket of his overalls is a weathered circle in the shape of a tin of snuff or tobacco. His smile shows tiny flecks of the product on his bottom teeth. I think I'm going to gag.

"I'm sorry?" It's like this guy's speaking another language. Pig Latin? No. No. No. I need to stop using that label. I'm sure he's nice person with feelings that can easily be hurt. I can't let my bitterness about the world right now lead me astray. "What did you say?" I ask politely.

He leans in. "Hardwick's. I see'd you at her house. That was you a little while ago."

Perhaps he's the head of the welcome committee from the Chamber of Commerce for all I know. "Yes, I'm staying at Stella's farm." Like it's any of his business. Although, I have to remind myself that this is a small town and he probably *does* think it's his business.

He tugs off his John Deere cap and runs his meaty hand through greasy curls. "You look like her. You her kin?"

No, dude, I'm her taxidermist. Wait. Strike that. From the looks of this town, Stella might have *had* a taxidermist.

I need to check the city attitude at the door and mind my manners.

"I'm Stella's great niece. Isabella Perry," I say in my most friendly voice. I feel badly judging him so harshly. Must not do that moving forward. I contemplate offering him my hand, but it doesn't look like he's seen a bar of soap in many years, so I grip the shopping basket instead.

"Oh yeah, you're the one who inherited the place." He reaches for a can of some undistinguishable meat product and adds it to the loaf of Wonder bread and Miracle Whip in his basket. "I'm Jimmie."

Since his hand is now extended, I can't be rude. His skin looks rough and in severe need of moisturizing treatment. I don't think Aveda Hand Relief cream has exactly made it to Dilligus Flats. "Nice to meet you," I say with my best grin.

"Name's James Ford Hemi. The name my momma gave me. But everyone 'round here calls me Jimmie."

Jimmie Hemi. Like the truck ads? Like "it's got a Hemi?" I stifle a laugh and pull my hand back.

He presses on. "I'm supposed to be helping you."

"Helping me? How so?"

"With them there chickens."

Strange. I hadn't seen any chickens. I figure there are lots of surprises waiting to be discovered on Aunt Stella's farm, though I hope a freshly showered hottie in nothing but a towel will be the biggest shock I'll have to deal with. "Oh, I'm sure I can handle a few chickens, Mr. Hemi," I murmur, hoping he doesn't call me out on my blush.

"My daddy was Mr. Hemi. I'm Jimmie."

Okay. Now that I'm on a first name basis with Pig Man, I mustn't think of him that way anymore. He's Jimmie. "Aunt Stella's lawyer said I was only needed for some unfinished business, so I'm sure I'll be okay in the meantime."

"I don't mean no disrespect, but what's a pretty little thing like you know about running a chicken ranch?"

"Ranch? I thought it was more like a farm."

Ranch sounds so grandiose.

So imposing.

So Texan.

"With all them chickens being delivered in a few days, you can rightly call it 'bout anything you want," Jimmie says.

I shake my head. "I'm not sure I understand. There aren't any chickens on the property already? And what do you mean 'all them?' Mr. Esterhazy said—"

"Lordy, little lady. D'ain't it the funniest thing. You done inherited fifteen thousand chickens."

I think I'm seriously going to pass out this time.

"I inherited *what?*" My heart leaps to my throat and nausea coats me instantaneously. Did he just say I'd inherited *fifteen thousand* chickens? Not merely a few hens and roosters. This is unfathomable.

My stomach roils and I brace on the cooler door to let this soak in. Fifteen thousand. It might as well be fifteen million for that matter. Images of feathers, beaks and shells galore color my vision in some sort of sadistic Easter egg hunt. I'm not sure what I've gotten myself into. Somehow I want to point the finger of blame in Rick's direction. This has to be his fault. Has. To. Be.

"I reckon that fancy lawyer of Stella's didn't tell you that?"

I swallow hard. "No, Jimmie. I reckon he didn't." The slime ball lawyer hasn't told me a whole hell of a lot. Period.

I don't know the first freaking thing about running a chicken operation. Do I gather the eggs? Hatch the chicks? Or will my chickens get turned into boneless breasts for Purdue or Tyson? The closest I've come to a chicken is the ones packaged up at the meat counter at Stop 'n Shop.

Focus. On. Breathing.

"Hon, you're turning green," Jimmie says. "Didja eat yet? Something other than that airplane food?"

"No, sir, I haven't had anything other than a Diet Sprite on my flight from Boston." Maybe that's my problem. Even Jake picked up on this and sent me here to get food. Or maybe it was just to get me out of the house. I shake away the image of the sexy man in a towel and stare down into my basket that holds a liter of Diet Coke and a bag of Doritos.

Jimmie puts his chubby paw on my shoulder and steers me around the NASCAR display. "You let old Jimmie take care of everything. We'll go to Stella's, I'll make some sandwiches and we'll talk. Don't you worry, missy. Jimmie's here to help."

I peek into his basket at the items he's gathered and shudder. No comment on the pork rinds sticking out of the top. It seems cannibalistic of him.

Be afraid.

Be very afraid.

CHAPTER SIX

Fifteen minutes later, I ask, "What *are* you making?"

Bread, mayo, and some sort of meat from a can are spread out on the butcher block in the middle of Stella's kitchen while Jimmie reaches into the middle drawer and nabs a knife. He certainly seems at home here. Just like Jake. It makes me think Stella's house was some sort of community gathering center.

"Vienna sausage sandwich. Ain't you never had one?"

I screw up my nose at the thought of eating this pressed-formed-chopped meat. "No, sir. Can't say I have."

I reach for the small pop-top can full of short, white, hot doggish items. I sniff. Okay, not too bad. Smells okay. I tip the can and read the ingredients: *made with chicken and pork in a beef broth.* Not exactly physician approved. Get me some Zocor because my arteries are clogging up being in the same room with these things. Twelve grams of fat doesn't set well with me, but there's only one gram of carbs. Okay, so it's Atkins friendly.

After washing his hands thoroughly (thank heavens!), Jimmie slices the round Vienna sausages into planks and spreads them out on the white bread, topped with a generous dollop of mayo (which isn't low fat in any way, form or fashion). I know he's trying to be nice, but dare I eat this concoction? I fear my rumbling stomach answers for me.

Jimmie reaches in the cabinet for a plate with a picture of a red rooster on it. Then, he lays the sandwich in the middle of it and pushes it toward me.

Just as he chomps down on his snack, there's a knock on the back door. Jimmie pulls the sandwich away from his portly face, mayo dotting the corners of his mouth, and says, "Must be Jake."

Aside from the disgusting fact that Jimmie's talking with his mouth full, my heart trips along at the thought of seeing Jake again and finding out who exactly what he's doing here on this farm.

"Anyone here?" Jake calls out.

"We're in the kitchen," Jimmie answers through another bite of food.

I sit up on the stool and tug at my tight black top. Unconsciously, I foof my hair and await his entrance.

"Hey there, Jimmie," the whiskey-like voice says behind me.

Jimmie lifts his hat in greeting and then dives back into his meal. The sandwich never stood a chance. "You met Isabella yet?"

"Picked her up at the airport," Jake reports.

I swivel on the stool and my knees nearly knock Jake in the crotch. *Way to go, idiot!* He puts his hands out defensively and they brush against my fabric-covered skin. The heat from his fingers burns through my jeans and I damn near lose my balance. I take back what I said earlier. He *does* look even hotter in clean clothes. As if that's even possible.

He smiles and crosses his arms across his muscular chest. A white Henley shirt—straight from the L.L. Bean catalogue—is tucked into yet another pair of snug-fitting—in all of the right places—faded jeans. The three buttons at his neck are open, revealing his bronzed throat. My throat goes dry again. Parched like it's been ages since I've had water.

"Sorry about that," I mutter. Then, I turn back to the counter and pick up the mystery meat sandwich. I need something to occupy my mind so I don't sit here lusting over this stranger.

Jake comes around the butcher block. "Can I have one, Jimmie?"

"Sure thing." Jimmie slaps together the bread and Vienna sausages and hands the sandwich over to Jake.

I take a bite, tentatively at first, and am surprised by how edible this actually is. Wow. Parts is parts, but this isn't half bad. I swallow down and try not to imagine the twelve grams of fat going straight to my hips. But hey, I'm on a farm, there's bound to be a lot of walking/exercise to work this off. I wipe my mouth with a checkered napkin—old, worn and hand-sewn—retrieved from a basket in the middle of the butcher block. I peer at Jake as he chews.

I can't resist any longer.

"Jake Hansen. So, are you like, a cousin or something?"

Jake laughs and grabs the Diet Coke bottle sitting on the counter. He walks to the cabinet and removes a glass like he's done it a thousand times before. Mr. Tight Jeans seems as at home in Aunt Stella's kitchen as he was in her bathroom. There has to be an explanation.

"No. I'm definitely *not* your cousin," he says to me.

Good. That makes my fantasies of him and that towel a little less white trash-ish. Course, here I am fantasizing about a guy who I think has had a fling with a lonely old woman.

I press, "So, what exactly is your deal?"

He drags his hand through his hair, the corner of his mouth lifting. "What's my deal? Good question." He says it like he's looking for the reason himself.

"Jake's a handyman," Jimmie says, cramming the last bit of his sandwich into his mouth.

"A handyman?" I echo.

Jake's brow lifts. "These days I am. I'm sort of taking a break from my life for a while." He pours the soda up to the rim, watching the frothy brown foam recede before adding a little more. "I was driving through here a couple of months ago when my bike crapped out on me. Stella gave me a lift to the service station. She gave me room and board in exchange for me repairing her fence line. So, I've been working on it ever since."

Okay, so maybe it was a noble arrangement and Jake wasn't diddling an old lady. Relief cascades off of me.

"And is your bike repaired?" My silly pulse triples and I wonder if he's ready to leave town. Secretly, I hope not.

I stare at him. His hair—now dry—flows over his fore-head in a cascade of golden brown, highlighted by the sun's touch, more so than when I met him at the airport. It looks incredibly soft and I have to sit on my hand to keep from reaching out. As if reading my mind, Jake rakes his fingers through the thick strands again, setting them away from his face momentarily before they fall back into place.

"Bike's fine now," he says flatly. His eyes don't leave mine as he takes a sip from his glass.

Sure, I should be thinking about these chickens and meeting with Esterhazy and everything farm related, but Jake's too much of a temptation standing in front of me. I shouldn't care about guys at all after what Rick did to me, but still, I'm intrigued and I take the bait. "Where were you driving through from?"

Jake shrugs. "Lots of places. Nowhere in particular."

Evasive response. There's no trace of a Southern accent, so I know he's not from around here. Okay, I won't push this time. However, I swear I make out a distinct pain behind his dark blue eyes. Not the time to pry. I've barely been around the guy. Besides, I'm not here to flirt or get to know the "handyman." Although, with hands like those... *Enough!* I'm here to settle Aunt Stella's estate.

"So, Jimmie," I say, returning the conversation to the here and now. "What else can you tell me about the farm?"

Jimmie starts laughing and snorting like a pig. "Why, little lady, I know everything there is to know 'bout this here farm. I used to be the overseer."

Overseer? Like that Yankee Wilkerson in *Gone With the Wind* who hooked up with that white-trash Slattery? I didn't know that term existed post-Civil War.

"Why 'used to be'?" I can't help but ask.

Jimmie pulls a red and white bandana from his hip pocket and blows his nose into it. Returning the used hankie to his pocket, Jimmie says, "Old Hardwick and I had a falling out two weeks ago. I said something to the old gal and she reacted by shoving me off the farm. Then she up and kicked the bucket on me."

Maybe she didn't appreciate being called "old."

Then I hear him sniff and it seems that Jimmie Hemi is on the verge of tears. Nooooo... I cannot handle his tears. Old men crying always break my heart. "Jimmie, shi—, err, I mean, things happen. I'm sure Aunt Stella knew whatever happened between you wasn't—"

What do I know? I'm completely talking out of my ass. I sigh deeply (yes, more of letting Satan in) and turn my attention back to my half-eaten sandwich.

"Things were good for us again, you know? Until I done went and pissed her off. That Stella. She had a temper."

"You can say that again," Jake agrees. "Most women do."

"I don't," I snap, realizing I sounded angry even saying that.

"Remains to be seen," Jake teases.

It's weird sitting in a room with two total strangers talking about a third stranger who left you her frickin' estate. This has got to be some sort of weird hallucination. Maybe that's all this is. Some sort of mucked up dream. Perhaps there was something potent—hallucinogenic—in the champagne at Alibi the other night. I passed out and went into a coma that's making me think this up. Rick didn't actually break up with me in the bathroom during our best friends' engagement party. I didn't get a random call from a lawyer with a screwed up name. And, I'm not eating the most bizarre lunch of my lifetime with a Hunk of Muscles and a man who resembles a pig.

I squeeze my eyes shut and count to five.

Wake up, Griz!

Slowly, I peel my left eyelid open.

Jimmie's peering at with me with great concern. "You okay there? Do I need to call a doctor?"

I sit up tall and gulp hard.

It's real.

I'm in Alabama. I'm single. I'm a fish out of water. A stranger in a strange land.

And, apparently, an heiress to a chicken farm.

"Yes sir, I'm fine," I manage to say. "Just thinking."

Jimmie nods. "Like I said, whatever you need to know 'bout this place, I can tell you. I know it like the back of my hand."

Jake sets his plate on the butcher block and then goes to wash his hands in the large white double-sink.

"What about you?" I call out. "Are you going to be any help to me?"

Jake turns back and his face breaks into a impish grin. He leans on the counter and connects his blue stare with my eyes. "My deal with Stella was the fence. I've got to finish the roadside and then clear brush off the fence down by the lake. Then I'll be done with my debt to Stella's kindness. If you'd like me off the property before, I understand."

I jump to my feet. Crap, first I almost make Jimmie cry and now I've offended Jake. "No, no, that's fine. I didn't mean... That's great that you'll finish the fence. I don't want to go against any promise Aunt Stella made to you. Heck, you guys knew her, not me. I'd never heard of her until Esterhazy called me." I hang my head, my shoulder-length hair falling forward. "I don't get why she left all of this to me."

"Y'all excuse me a minute," Jimmie says. "Nature calls." Yet another man who's comfortable navigating the landscape of Aunt Stella's house.

I shift my eyes over to Jake and wonder what I should say.

He takes the initiative. "Look, I'll help out where I can, Isabella. It's the least I can do for all Stella did for me at a time when I—well, when I needed someone."

I want to press, but it's obvious he doesn't want to share more information.

"You'll help with all these chickens?" I ask. After all, that's the main issue at hand. Something I've got to accept and deal with for the time being. Isabella Perry, Phi Beta Kappa, Magna Cum Laude, Graphic Designer. *Chicken Farmer?*

Jake shakes his head. "Jimmie's your man to help with the chickens. Not part of my deal."

"What if we make a new deal?"

"I don't know how long I'll be sticking around."

I feel a surge of disappointment ripple through me, wondering if I'll wake up tomorrow and Jake will be gone.

But so what? He means nothing to me. He's just a guy. With thick, inviting hair, eyes to drown in and... oh my God, is that a cleft in his chin, a la Kirk Douglas in *Spartacus*. Why hadn't I noticed that earlier? Vanessa and I share the weakness for facial dents. She's a dimple gal. And it got her a man, a ring, and an upcoming commitment ceremony.

I shake the cobwebbed thoughts from my head. "That's cool, Jake. This farm isn't your problem," I say in defeat. Apparently, it's mine.

"I think you'll do fine, Isabella," Jake says. "Stella obviously thought so, too." His confidence in me is inspiring and gives me a tingly feeling all over.

He must feel the electricity sizzling between the two of us because he moves away from me deftly. "And just so you know, I'm not looking for a relationship or anything," he states so firmly.

My eyes widen to mirror my shock. "Who said anything about a relationship?"

Jake dips his head. "I see how you look at me, Isabella. Like you're hungry for a man."

"Why you..." I stand and stab my hands to my hips. "I'll have you know that I have a *very* serious boyfriend back in Boston. We'll probably get married, too. *He's* the only man I'm hungry for." Yes, it's completely a lie, but I don't want to give Jake the satisfaction of being in on the humiliation of the "get off the pot" announcement. What he doesn't know won't hurt me.

He smiles and nods. "Good to know."

He nabs what's left of his sandwich, salutes me with it and pops out the door. I slump in defeat. Just like a man to walk away when you need him the most.

Just like Rick.

Jimmie rushes back into the kitchen. "That lawyer said he'd be up here this evening for you to sign some papers. For now, let's take you down to the chicken house so we can get started. You'll need to change outta your city clothes. Jeans and boots'll do." He looks back. "Y'all did bring boots?"

I gnaw on my lip. "Sure, I brought boots." Though they're not exactly the trashed work boots like he's wearing.

I hear Jake pound down the rear stairs. Through the large back windows, I see him disappear into the trailer. So far, he's the only person I've seen in Dilligus Flats that's even remotely near my age. And even though he's taken any kind of fraternization off the table, maybe we can at least be friends. Perhaps he can be of some use to me, like telling me where I can get a good cocktail. I'm sure I'll need one before this day is over, although I'm convinced Vox Raspberry hasn't made it to these parts yet. At any rate, some kind of alcohol will definitely need to factor into this equation.

While Jimmie waits, I scoot to the bedroom where I stashed my things and unzip my suitcase. There are a variety of clothes stacked in neat piles. I quickly pull on my worn Levi 501's and a Toronto Maple Leaf t-shirt that used to belong to Rick. I guess this will do as farm attire for now. It'll have to.

Besides, I'm only here for a week to get the estate wrapped up, signed off, and sold. Then it's back to Boston to start all over.

For now, I'll take the bull by the horns. Err...or the chickens by the beak.

Nothing's going to stop me.

CHAPTER SEVEN

Well, nothing's going to stop me except maybe a thirty-ton pile of chicken shit.

Damn that Esterhazy. I can't wait until my meeting with him tonight to give him a piece of my mind.

"What the hell are we supposed to do with this?" I look at the unhitched trailer full of the bird excrement and try to breathe through my mouth. Oh God, I'm going to be sick. This is disgusting. This is worse than a downtown Boston T station that reeks of urine.

"Homer Shuckabee bought it for his peanut field," Jimmie reports, wiping his chubby fist across his bottom lip. A fine line of tobacco sits in his bottom lip and he munches on it. Obviously the vociferous ammonia and sulfur odor emanating from the mountain of chicken crap doesn't faze him one bit. "See here, the chicken shit's used for fertilizer. Nature's best. Homer pays twenty-five dollars a ton for it."

I don't want to think about someone spreading chicken ick over their peanut field. I won't be able to look at a Planters canister ever again knowing their dirty little secrets.

I clear my throat. "So, how much do we get for the, umm, waste?"

"Seven hundred and fifty."

I suppose I should be impressed that for seven hundred fifty bucks, some farmer will take away this mountain of chicken poo. Wait a sec, this is *my* farm now, so that money belongs to me. I can so see me using seven hundred bucks for a stopover in New York on the way home and a Barney's shopping spree or to pay off some of those bills that have been piling up. Okay, maybe this isn't so bad. But, damn, if I want to talk about manure and entrails anymore.

"Should I be doing any of this before I talk to Mr. Esterhazy about the terms of the will and the details of what I've inherited?"

Jimmie scratches his head. "Lord, Isabella. You're in the country, not the big city. Things'll work out when they're supposed to. Esterhazy said he'll be 'round here this evening. But this farm work don't wait for no one."

I suppose he's right... although I'd really like more details than to let things unfold as they may.

"Come on now," Jimmie says with a smile. "Let old Jimmie help you out."

I step back from the trailer and glance to my left at the long, white buildings. Two of them, identical and parallel connect to each other with a small walkway and shed. "So, these are the chicken houses?"

"Yep. Each houses 'bout seventy-five hundred chickens that'll be here in two days. It's like crop rotation. The chickens don't stay here forever. We get fresh batches of twenty-two week old birds."

"Can't we send them back?"

Jimmie scowls at me with a definitive "nope."

"Why not?"

He spits again. "They's contracted."

I so need to talk to Esterhazy to understand what the hell is going on here.

"And how long do they stay here?" I ask, like this is Club Med and it's our responsibility to entertain the fowl with golf lessons, spa treatments, and five-star dining.

Jimmie pulls the cap from his head and scratches with his fingers. "I reckon 'bout six months."

The loud crank of a tractor echoes within the long chicken house on the left, sputtering like a semi running out of gas.

"Hold on there, little lady," Jimmie says.

As he walks away, I glance out into the distance—a couple hundred yards—through the veil of the pecan trees in the orchard to where Jake's motorcycle—I should've known the bike was his—is parked and he's working on the fence line. Even from this far, I can see he's pulled his shirt off to handle the task at hand. He's attacking the weeds growing along the fence line like he's got a score to settle with them. He seems to have a lot of pent-up anger and I wonder if it has anything to do what that gnarly scar on his otherwise perfect body. The dedication to the promise he made to Stella is noble and admirable, but I'd a lot rather have him over here helping me with whatever the hell is going on here with these houses. I'm supposed to be getting acrylic nails and shopping on Newbury Street, not playing in chicken manure.

Jake stops what he's doing and peers through the orchard as though he sensed me watching him. I wave out to him, trying not to feel stupid that he caught me ogling him, yet again. He nods his head and raises his hand back non-chalantly. He grins, devilishly, almost, as though he's getting a kick out of seeing the city girl so out of her element. I raise my chin up a bit haughty. I'll show him.

I walk over and join Jimmie. He's at the end of the house and slides the moveable wall. It reveals a cavernous inside with two metal nesting areas—so Jimmie tells me—on each side. Chugging down the middle is a red tractor with Massey Ferguson written on the side. It's dragging a long blade behind it, cleaning up the last remnants of the nastiness from the floor.

"Dwayne! You 'bout done here?" Jimmie calls out.

"Yeah, Jimmie," this Dwayne fellow yells over the noise of the tractor. "All's left to do is put down the chemicals and then toss out the pine shavings."

Jimmie holds his hand up in an "okay" sign and walks back towards me.

"Does Dwayne work here?"

"Nah," Jimmie says. "He's just the contractor from Double C. They's the ones we contract the chickens with."

Right. The chickens. I wonder for a moment who's been "overseeing" the place since Stella booted Jimmie out of here, but then I remember it's only been about a week since that happened *and* there aren't exactly chickens to oversee yet. But there will be soon. That means Stella's staff will come back when the chickens are here. I've got to get a handle on all of this. "So, what—"

Jimmie interrupts. "We need to get right at the chemicals. Hope you don't mind getting' dirty, Isabella."

Actually, I do. I have this thing about wallowing around in dirt and chicken poo. "I'll go back up to the house and unpack while you take care of things here."

"No ma'am," Jimmie says, followed by a spit. "You're needed here."

"Jimmie, I'm a girl."

He smiles. "A mighty pretty one."

I feel my cheeks heat. "Thanks, Jimmie."

"That don't mean you're getting out of work. This is *your* farm now," he says to me with a bit of a smirk. Is he resentful that Stella left me her property and her business when it's clear he's the one who's been working the land with her for years? I'm not exactly sure. Jimmie seems nice enough—a southern good old boy—yet I can't help but wonder.

My pulse picks up and my breathing hitches. I'm going to pass out. The stench alone is making my eyes water, but my stomach is starting to fight back against the quickly eaten Vienna sausages. But what's most overpowering is the fact that this isn't some sort of Tara run by paid employees, farm workers, and overseers. It's a working business. Hands on. Toil with the soil. Roll up your sleeves and apply the proverbial elbow grease. There go my fingernails.

This isn't what I bargained for. Esterhazy never told me about tons of chicken excrement, selling it as fertilizer, stacks of nests as far as the eye can see, and cleaning out a facility with special chemicals. I have a Bachelor in Art, for Christ's sake. I know nothing about animal husbandry. I went to Clemson, not Auburn!

I need to breathe. Eww, no, I don't want to breathe. I cough when I inhale the noxious odor of the chicken muck the tractor drags past me. I wasn't made be one with nature other than spending a day at the beach and communing with the ocean. I like zippy computers, happening martini bars, and strappy sandals.

"Look, Jimmie. I think there's been a huge mistake. I'm not here to work the land. I'm here to deal with whatever Esterhazy needs me for and then get back to my life."

He looks me up one side and down the other. The flab of his double chin wobbles back and forth like a turkey wattle. "I reckon there is a misunderstanding, little lady. This here's your farm now. Your operation. It's your responsibility to keep Hardwick Poultry in business."

I spread my arms wide toward the empty chicken house. "How can this be a 'business' when there aren't any chickens? I was told I was needed for paperwork. Nothing more." My plan is to sell this albatross as soon as I can and put the much-needed money to good use back home to pay off credit card and student debt and to save, save, save now since I don't have any future husband that's going to take care of me.

"Esterhazy didn't fill you in?"

I feel my nostrils flare. "On what?"

"Lord, d'ain't I look like a fool. Here I thought you knew everything."

I put my hands on my hips and face him. "What aren't you telling me, Jimmie?"

He hocks up a mouthful of nastiness and chucks it behind him, across the yard. Then, he wipes his hand across his mouth and sighs deeply. (See, he's letting Satan in, as well.)

I raise my eyebrows at him in a "what the hell" manner, impatiently tapping my booted foot.

"Just 'cause the old gal died, don't mean this farm ain't still running. These here chicken houses are under contract with Double C Farms. They're the biggest chicken producers in the country and they're real bastards—excuse my French—about their business. And in two days, they'll be delivering a whole new flock of birds to these here houses. As per the contract."

I don't want to hear this. No one's going to tell me I have to honor the contract of a dead woman. "Call them. Tell them not to come. Tell them we're out of the chicken business."

"D'ain't that simple, Isabella. Signed contracts are signed contracts. This farm is a corporation. Double C still expects things to go as agreed to. A death don't matter. You're the new CEO, so it's business as usual. That's why Esterhazy done told you to get down here," Jimmie says in an exhausted breath. "You've got to take care of everything."

"I can't! I'm just here on family leave. You know, time off from work for bereavement. I only have two weeks of vacation. I can't just walk away from my job in Boston and all the responsibilities at work. We've got a new product launch in three weeks and then there's all of the sales PowerPoint presentations I have to convert to web docs and—"

"But Stella left this to you, Isabella. She trusted you to run her business."

"Why not *you?*" I nearly beg of him.

He kicks at the dirt and his face drops into what I can only describe as a heartbroken expression. He really does miss Stella, even if they did have "tiffs" with each other. "You're Stella's family. I was just..." he trails off for a moment and kicks the ground again. "I was just a friend."

My breathing quickens as though I've just rushed to catch the train. "Can't you just run it?"

"I don't work here," Jimmie says, scratching his head. "I'm just here to help you get started."

"But..."

"Like I said, Stella was a one-woman show running this operation. Now it's you, Isabella."

Thanks a lot, Stella.

What did I ever do to her to deserve this?

The wind whips my hair into my eyes. I push the strands behind my ears as Jimmie's words sink in. This isn't a joke. I really *did* inherit a chicken farm. Stella must have known what an utter, naïve flake I'd be about this. She's probably laughing at me from heaven.

Or up from hell, the evil wench.

I glance up at Jimmie and sense there's more to the story from the way his eyes won't look right at me.

"What else aren't you telling me? Come on. Lay all of the cards on the table," I say emphatically.

He's distracted by Dwayne now hauling in canisters of chemicals and backpacks that look like what the Orkin Man wears.

"Jimmie! Talk to me!"

He lets out a deep breath and then settles his ample girth on the tailgate of his beat up Dodge Ram that drove us from the house, through the pecan orchard, and down to the chicken houses.

"Hardwick Poultry ain't doing too good. And everybody knows it."

I feel the smirk cross my face and throw my hands up in the air. "Well of course it isn't doing well." Considering the luck I've had of late, of course it stands to reason that I would inherit an albatross. "How bad?"

"We done got a poor flock last time 'round. Sickly bunch. We didn't get our bonus from Double C Farms. Hell, Stella hadn't paid me in months."

Blood rushes throughout my head as I try to comprehend the reality of my situation. "Do I have money in a bank account to pay you, Jimmie?"

"Nah, I don't need your money. If we can get the egg production numbers up, you can give me a little something, that's what Stella usually did. I gots other things on the side that keep me in the lifestyle I'm accustomed to."

I don't exactly understand this arrangement Stella and Jimmie had, but I won't balk at it right now. Not until I comprehend everything around me. I lift a brow. "So these chickens lay the eggs that go to the grocery store." I'm still unclear on exactly what this alleged chicken business does.

"No, these here chickens produce fertilized eggs," he says. He must be able to read my face because he continues. "Houses have 'bout one rooster for every ten hens. The eggs get taken away twice a week to another farm for hatching. Other farms in the Double C system turn them into the parts you buy at the grocery store."

So, let me get this straight. These houses—these two long buildings the length of a football field—are a breeding ground. A boink-fest for these roosters to have their way with the hens of their choice. This seriously isn't real.

No wonder Jake was laughing at me earlier.

No wonder he's clear across the orchard right now staying out of this.

Why do I care what Jake thinks? I just met the guy.

And since he isn't helping me, I don't need to think about him.

But there's so much I *have* to think about.

Things I have no idea how to handle.

I crouch into a squat, my elbows on my knees and my fingers kneading my aching thoughts.

"Isabella?" Jimmie seems genuinely concerned. He should be since he helped put me in this panic. Him and that conniving, deceitful lawyer, Westin Esterhazy—whom I'm starting to doubt even exists… country lawyer, my ass. And Aunt Stella.

This isn't some well-meaning inheritance, but rather a bullshit pass off of a company going in the crapper. Sure, let's give it to Isabella. She doesn't have enough pressure in her life.

I can't hold back. I am officially ready to fly off the handle. I straighten up. "I don't want this! I don't need this!"

"Whoa now, little lady."

I lunge at him; the tears spout from my eyes, like Niagara Falls on acid, and roll down my cheeks. "Don't 'little lady' me! This isn't what I bargained for. I'm not some sort of migrant farm worker. Where are the people who are supposed to work here? Where are the rocking chairs and plates of fried chicken, okra, and cornbread? Where are the damned mint juleps?"

Jimmie looks confused. "Are you still hungry? I could make you some—"

I grab my hair and spin around. "Aaaaaarrrrgggghhhh!"

The roar of a motorcycle engine interrupts my tirade. I look from Jimmie's wide eyes to see Jake Hansen, poised on the leather and chrome bike like a GQ-on-the-farm cover model. *Damn him!* Damn him for showing up. Damn him for looking so sexy. Damn him for seeing me like this. Stupid non-waterproof makeup.

He swings a tight-jeaned leg off the bike and steps towards me. There's an incredible smirk on his face. Am I entertaining him? It seems he's here to laugh at my misfortune and to rub my face in the fact that I've inherited debt and chicken crap.

I shouldn't give a shit what he—or anyone else—thinks.

Apparently I do, though, since my chest heaving like I just ran Heartbreak Hill of the Boston Marathon.

Oh... my... God... I reach for something to steady me, but nothing's within reach.

Jake's eyes widen and he yells out, "She's blacking out!"

I feel his arms come around me, clutching me tight. Wow, that feels sort of nice.

Then nausea over takes me. My vision is getting fuzzy like a TV station gone dark.

And my ears are ringing. I can't breathe.

I'm totally screwed.

CHAPTER EIGHT

When I come to, drenched in a heavy sweat, I'm seated on the ground with my head between my knees and someone's hand is rubbing my neck.

It must be Rick. I've awakened from the nightmare that's become my life. Everything's okay. Everything's just as it was before Kyle and Vanessa's engagement party.

I focus on the green grass before me and I realize that, nope, I'm still on the farm. Still alone. Still hopeless.

"This one here's from Piggly Wiggly," I hear Jimmie say above the rustle of a paper bag. "Got it outta the truck."

"It doesn't matter where the bag's from, Jimmie," Jake says with a commanding voice. "I've got to get her to breathe into it."

Oh, that's Jake behind me. Jake's hand is in my hair. Soothing. Calming.

Ahh, that feels nice.

I sit up and try to concentrate on the here and now.

"There you go, Isabella. Long, slow breaths," Jake says in an authoritative, yet gentle tone. Like he's done this before. Like he's negotiated with a crazy person in the past. Like he's talked someone off the ledge of a building. "That'a girl."

"Whhhuh happpuned?" I mutter into the paper sack.

"You freaked."

"I freaked?"

"Saw it with my own two eyes," he assures me.

Jake continues to rub my back. My breathing has returned to normal, but it won't stay that way if he keeps touching me.

"I'm not coming on to you," he tells me. "I'm just trying to help. No need to report me to your boyfriend."

"Thanks, Jake," I manage to get out. If Rick were here, he'd be laughing his ass off at me.

I look over my shoulder into Jake's warm, blue eyes and for a moment, I feel like everything will be okay. Jake's smile is heartbreaking. And literally cover model potential. Straight white teeth that probably never needed braces or white strips. His golden hair is falling forward in an "I don't care" kind of way that makes me want to dog pile on him and roll around in the wet grass. If only I weren't so weak … and he hadn't laid down the "there will be no relationship" law. I really need to get a grip on reality. I'm the heir to Stella's misfortune. I have to wise up, get control and make the best of this.

I'm not alone. Jimmie's trying to help. And Jake? Jake's a lovely distraction even though he's made it clear he's not interested in any… entanglements. He's an easy rider. No attachments. No roots. Nothing to hold him back.

Besides, he thinks I'm still with Rick.

"So, what happened there?" Jake asks.

I pull the bag down and let out a long gust of air. "I freaked because I'm not very good dealing with stress. You should have seen me when I got laid off from my job a few years ago. Nearly puked on the HR Director." Looking back, perhaps I should have. "And this bitch of a boss I have now. If I even tab over to a screen on my computer that doesn't look like the graphic or web files I'm supposed to be working on, she has a conniption fit. I have to eat lunch at my desk. I'm a slave to the cube. She's going to go ballistic tomorrow morning when she gets my voice mail that I'm not going to be at work."

He puts his hand on my shoulder. "It's just a job, Isabella."

"Easy for you to say. You apparently don't have one," I snap. See, I'm not the best person when I'm stressed out.

As if he's been burned by my words, Jake removes his touch. "You don't know me well enough to make that sort of assessment."

I lower my eyes. "Yeah, that's right. But it's not that I haven't tried. I ask questions, and you just shrug them off with 'nopes' and 'yups'. Really, Jake, I'm trying. I'm trying but you're not making this any easier!"

"I know and I'm sorry. We all deal with our own shit, Isabella. I'm just working through it the best I can."

Vague, yet informative at the same time. I nod at him.

He stands and offers me his large hand. I slip mine into his and let him tug me good off the ground. He turns me around, my back facing him, and starts smacking at my rear.

I stand straight and tense up. "Are you getting fresh with me?" I shouldn't be enjoying it so much. It's because I haven't been touched like this in ages. I'm sure he has no idea how this is affecting me with tiny tingles everywhere.

His chuckle is a low, sexy growl. "No, I'm getting the grass off your ass. That is unless you'd like for it to stay there."

"Oh." I'm so embarrassed. But, I brush away Jake's hand—that seems a little more roving than helpful—and sweep the remainder of dirt off my backside. I don't want to admit that his hand on my ass makes my nerve endings sit up and take notice. Not the time to explore this option.

Jimmie comes to my side and puts a tentative hand on my elbow. "This here's been one hell of a day for you. Maybe we should let you go up to the house while we—"

"No. Jimmie. That's okay," I say, mustering up my most mature, professional demeanor. "I'm sorry for the way I reacted and what I said. I had no right taking my frustrations out on you. You've been nothing but wicked nice to me."

"D'ain't that the truth," he says with a grin that accentuates his turned up nose. "Not like I'm on the payroll."

Bless him, he's here out of the goodness of his heart or some displaced loyalty to Stella which I don't fully understand. Either way, I'll take the help.

"I'm here, too," Jake speaks up. "Seriously. I was rude not to help, considering the circumstances. I'm at your service." His hands are on his hips and his stance looks almost cop-like. Like he's ready to do detail or direct traffic.

"Thanks guys." Why they'll help a fledgling like me, I don't understand, but I appreciate it all the same.

Dwayne comes out of the chicken house lugging a tank of chemicals behind him. "Y'all 'bout ready to get going on this?"

I screw up my face and look to Jimmie.

"This here's the cleaning chemical I was telling you 'bout," he explains.

I bob my head up and down in recognition as I listen. "Then what?"

Jimmie moves to take a tank from Dwayne. "We spray the place down, let it set overnight and then tomorrow we come spread the pine shavings so the place is ready for our new batch of chickens on Wednesday."

"Wednesday," I confirm and take a huge sip of air. "When the chickens arrive."

"Yes ma'am. A fresh flock." Jimmie seems relieved that I've become a team player.

"And they stay for six months."

"Yes ma'am."

"I can't be here that long, Jimmie. But I'll do my best to learn what I have to do and keep this farm afloat." Hopefully my meeting with Esterhazy tonight will include talk of a potential buyer. With so many farmers around here, someone's bound to want this acreage.

Jimmie reaches his beefy hand out to shake on it. I can see he's pleased. This farm obviously means a lot more to him than he's letting on. Why else would he be here when he could be doing his own activities elsewhere? I'll have to buy him a steak dinner—or a side of beef—to thank him.

And what will I get Jake?

Maybe a side of me.

No... no... no... Guys suck. Ignore him. For now, I'll put his drop-dead gorgeous appearance out of my thoughts and look at him like someone who's helping. That's all. I know I'm single now, but I've got too many other things to think about than Jake Hansen. Besides, he could never be more to me than just a rebound guy and I don't want to go there. Not my style.

Dwayne hauls the chemical cleaning agent pack onto my back and straps it around my waist like some sort of psychotic scuba gear. I move into the chicken house to begin sweeping the designated area with the cleaner, as directed by Dwayne. A hand on my shoulder stops me, though.

Those intense blue eyes are right there.

"You sure you're okay?" Jake asks.

"Fine. Totally fine."

He smiles, a breath-stealing grin, and looks down at my shoes. "You should probably change into something more appropriate before getting to work."

"What do you mean?" I look at my feet. Esterhazy told me to pack boots, so I did. I damn sure wasn't packing my

Italian leather knee-highs from Aldo that I'd bought on Newbury Street a year ago, so I grabbed the only other pair in the back of my closet.

"Are you planning on herding some goats later?" Jake asks. "Or are you participating in the Iditarod?"

I glance at my tan UGGs with ivory sheepskin around the ankles. "These are worn on farms in Australia; surely they'll work in Alabama." Vanessa gave them to me for Christmas forever ago when they were all the rage. They're absolutely the warmest things I've ever put on my feet, even if they are out of fashion now and *trés* fugly.

Jake laughs again. "They're not exactly appropriate."

"I'll have you know there used to be a waiting list to get these. It took my friend four months to get them in my size. They're not cheap, either. They—"

As soon as the words leave my lips, I bite down on my tongue. I'm a complete idiot. Who wears a hundred eighty-five dollar designer boots in a chicken house? I smack myself on the forehead with my palm, like the doofus that I am. "What am I doing?"

Jake hauls his tank up onto his shoulder and cocks his head to the left. "We'll go over to Wal-Mart later and get you some real work boots. Maybe some work clothes, too."

I flash him what I hope to be my most dazzling, appreciative smile. Wow, he's cute *and* he doesn't mind shopping? (Okay, he's offering me Wal-Mart, not the Galleria, but still...) If I had more time to stay down here and try to chisel down the brick wall Jake's built up around him, he might be the perfect man for me. Oh well.

I turn to sweep the area with the chemical, willing my heart to calm the hell down and telling myself I can settle everything once I talk to Esterhazy. Yes, good old Westin will help me out of this asinine contract so I can unload this place.

Or so I hope.

Chapter Nine

"Ugh...I hurt all over."

Jake follows Jimmie and me into the house, watching my every move.

"I'm okay, Jake," I tell him and rub at my sore shoulder.

"Like hell you are," he says striding over to me. "Sit down."

I ease onto one of the kitchen stools and let out a big sigh when Jake's large hands settle on my sore muscles. His fingers knead deeply into my skin, attacking the ache of a long day's work. He rubs his hands over me like a professional masseuse. Not like I've been to one in the last year because my work hours have been so insane. I totally miss my Swedish rubs. Or maybe I just miss having a man's hands on me, period.

A contented moan escapes my lips and I hear Jake snicker.

"Feel good?"

"You have no idea," I say, lolling my head back a bit.

"I think I do," he says huskily. "Doesn't your boyfriend do this for you?"

I tense up at Jake's words. Then I remember my charade and clear my throat. "Oh, sure. We've both just been working late hours, so we haven't had time."

"I see," Jake says quietly. "I know what it's like being with a workaholic."

"You do? Girlfriend back home?" I ask, not really wanting him to say "yes."

"I don't want to talk about it. Now relax."

The pressure in Jake's hands changes from therapeutic to sensual almost. He's no longer kneading at my muscles; rather he's trailing his hand across my back. Through the thinness of the old T-shirt, I feel the warmth emanating off of him. I lean back into him, lost in the moment and relishing the human touch I've gone so long without. He pulls his hands down my sides, dangerously close to the swell of my breasts, before he moves them to the center of my back and rubs even harder at the tender muscles.

Strong fingers trip over my shoulders, teasing and tantalizing me with the sturdy touch. I close my eyes to the pressure of his kneading and the gravity of my own needing. How could Rick have denied me his touch for so long? If you love someone, you show them through physical contact. And not just sex. Guys never get that. It's not all about the actual act of intercourse. It's about touching and feeling, cuddling and hugging, kissing and being together.

Breaths mingled. Gazes seared to each other.

Lives tangled together. Two people blending in a loving mixture.

Fingers entwined. Legs wrapped together. Hands on skin.

Just like this.

Not thinking, I say, "Oh Jake… that feels sooooo amazing."

Immediately, he tenses up and removes his hands away from me.

I spin around to face him and see that his cheeks are flushed and the vein in his neck is protruding as if he's clenching his jaw.

He coughs nervously. "You should, ah, take a long, hot shower tonight. It'll do you good."

Our eyes meet for a moment and then he looks away. "Umm, okay. Thanks."

"See ya later," he says and then he bolts out of the house.

If my heart is tripping this fast at a mere massage, image if—

Jimmie bounds into the room, knocking me out of my thoughts. He goes to wash his hands at the sink. "Esterhazy'll be up 'round after dinner," he says.

Finally, some clarification on thing from the infamous Mr. Westin Esterhazy. Crafty, S.O.B. lawyer. Or is that an onomatopoeia?

"Oh, there's something I was supposed to show you earlier, but I forgot," Jimmie says. He goes into the dining room and rummages through a drawer like it's his house.

I shift my tired weight from one leg to the other. I so want to collapse on a bed—any bed—and sleep like the dead. But I need to change clothes and get ready for my meeting with the lawyer. I've also got to check my work e-mail, and see if I have any texts from William and Vanessa. I wonder, too, if Rick called and left a message, begging my forgiveness and saying he'd gone totally mental when he broke up with me.

"Here you go," Jimmie says. "This here's for you."

I take the large manila envelope he's offering. "What is it?"

"It's from Old Hardwick herself."

"From Aunt Stella?" Finally, a clue. Perhaps an answer.

Jimmie stares at me with an air of sadness around him and then leads me through the great room. Off the back of the larger room is a spacious den, complete with a well-worn Barcalounger, a quilt-covered couch, and a television set that looks as if it's never seen the likes of a cable connection.

"Sit yourself down here. I'm going to the store and fetch us some supper. I'll make you a home cooked Southern meal."

"Thanks, Jimmie." I don't deserve all this nice attention, especially after being such a spasmodic pain in the ass earlier today. But I could certainly go for a plate of food. Something substantial. Something not out of a can and mixed with mayonnaise.

I settle into the chair that smells faintly of Ivory soap and coffee. Aunt Stella must have sat here each morning with her java, staring out at the vivid green grass and pecan trees filling her back yard. I take in the view momentarily; the sunset lying lazily on the horizon of the hay field over the way. It really is pretty here. Not in a city-pretty way that I prefer; rather in its own back-to-nature manner. I favor the hustle and bustle of city life, skyscrapers, wall-to-wall people, packed commuter trains, and plenty of bars and restaurants to choose from. Excitement and action. However, I do understand there are people who are happy in existences like this. Like Aunt Stella, Jimmie... and evidently Jake.

Jake.

Jake Hansen.

Handyman. Motorcycle driver.

Complete mystery and totally out of place in Dilligus Flats, Alabama.

I know he's withholding some pertinent information from me. I wonder what drove him away from wherever he came from. Those brooding types are always running from something. It more than likely has something to do with that scar on his shoulder. Probably a woman too, although I'll bet he'd never admit it.

Of course, that's none of my concern right now. I need to focus on the task at hand and not on the hot man across the yard. Good-looking guys are nothing but trouble.

Opening the sealed envelope, I see something cardboard, as well as a white envelope. I tug it out. Sealed and dated two weeks ago with a notary's signature, it reads "For Isabella."

I tear open the flap and pull out a letter. A finely penned, cursive written letter—a lost art. Goose bumps dance across my arms in anticipation. Taking a deep breath, I read:

My dearest Isabella...

I know you don't know me from Adam's house cat, but I'm your great aunt Stella. Eddie—your daddy—visited the farm when he was a little boy. I caught him standing up on a hay bale preaching to the cats and dogs. I always knew he had a Higher calling.

You're probably wondering what this has to do with you. See, I took it upon myself to be your secret Godmother. I never married or had children, so I decided to adopt a relative in spirit and watch their progression through the years. Well, sugar, that was you.

I'm sorry we never met, but I've been a bit of a homebody. I never attended family reunions or traveled too far. Most of the family considered me a "kook." Your parents sent those nice yearly updates and I learned all about your cheerleading and church choir and sorority days at Clemson. You remind me so much of myself—in my earlier days. We share an unspoken connection. Or at least, I've felt it.

That's why I know you'll love my farm. It needs some TLC. Sure, I have regrets—we all do—and I probably could have made some better decisions in my life, but this farm has been a touchstone for me. I hope it will enrich your life as well.

Be good to yourself. Look carefully for the answers to life's questions. They may be right under your nose.

Love,

Aunt Stella

My hands tremble slightly as I let Aunt Stella's words sink in. Tears sting the back of my eyes as I regret never meeting this person who followed my life's progression. Family reunions and get-togethers with the cousins were never a big deal growing up in Chicago. I can't even name half of my cousins or where they live for that matter. My three sisters and I keep in touch through e-mails and phone calls, but we haven't seen each other since last Christmas.

I look at the letter again. It's like Stella is here, hugging me with her written expressions. The heaviness in my chest is overwhelming as I realize Stella watched my life from afar. And her letter... she *gets* me. It's hard to fathom that someone I never met understood me so fully when my piece of shit boyfriend flushed away our happiness like it didn't matter.

I clench my fists at the thought of him, nearly crumpling Stella's letter to me.

I have to stop thinking about Rick and how he hurt me. He's in the past.

There's a new future ahead for me. I'm not sure what it is, but I'm willing to take the journey. One that starts here in Dilligus Flats. One that will prepare me for the next phase. One where I'll be confident and certain of everything.

Aunt Stella had faith in me.

I look back at her letter. Oh, wait, there's more:

P.S. Enclosed is a portrait of me at age thirty.

I drill my fingers on the large envelope, eager to get a look at my benefactor. I slide out the old five-by-seven photograph, turning it around to face me. It takes a millisecond for it to comprehend what I'm looking at.

The image stares up at me. Into my eyes. Into my soul.

A whispered scream gathers at the base of my throat and
I think I'm going to choke on it.
    Breathing is a labor.
    Understanding is a chore.
    It's like I'm looking in a mirror.

CHAPTER TEN

"That is *such* a Brady Bunch moment," Vanessa says over the static-y phone connection after I relay my revelation.

I've made camp in one of the guest bedrooms and called home to Boston to talk to my best friend. With my head in my hands, I ask her, "What do you mean a Brady Bunch moment?"

While Vanessa laughs, I adjust on the four-poster iron bed that's covered with homemade green and white quilts that smell slightly of mothballs. I don't know how to interpret this look-alike in my life. It's like the photograph is a hidden message. Some clue to solve the ridiculous riddle of my future.

"You remember the episode, don't you?" Vanessa starts. "The one where they're cleaning the garage and Jan finds this old-timey picture of herself. Only, it's not her, but Aunt Jenny."

Rubbing my fingers under my eyes, I find this to be vaguely familiar from my many afternoons of watching Nickelodeon, since I have nothing better to do. "Is that the one where the woman shows up and she's butt ugly?"

"Yeah! Exactly."

"And what does this have to do with me?"

Vanessa scoffs. "It's your subconscious talking to you. Get it? You're afraid you're going to end up like your Aunt Stella."

"You mean dead? We're all going to die one day, Vanessa."

Vanessa ignores me and, instead, continues to get all psychological on my ass. "You look exactly alike at the same period in your lives. So, it's only natural that you might wonder where your future's headed. What's destined for you?"

"I know where my future is headed. No-frickin'-where." I sigh, expelling Satan for like the ninth time today.

"Griz. Don't be like that. I know you're still upset about what happened with Rick, and you should—"

"Stop right there. I told you before I left to come here that I don't want to talk about Rick getting off the pot." Just because I'm obsessing over it in my head doesn't mean it deems further discussion with my best friend. Besides, she'll just tell Kyle what I said and it would get back to Rick. I don't want him knowing that I'm thinking of him at all.

Vanessa sighs. "Sorry."

"Really, Double V. I'm going to be okay. I have other fish to fry or chickens, rather." Although, I have a feeling after this adventure, I may never want to eat poultry again.

I fling back onto the fluffy mattress and give her the rundown on the past twelve hours.

"How are you supposed to manage a chicken operation?" she asks. "You can't even keep your closet organized."

"Oh, like *you* can!" I say teasingly. "And no worries. Jimmie's helping me."

I can visualize Vanessa's expressions shifting, even though we're thousands of miles apart. "Oooo! Who's Jimmie? Is he cute?"

"No! He's this old, fat country man. He knew my Aunt Stella. He's a sweetheart and is really trying to show me the ropes."

"Any cute guys around?" Vanessa asks with a lift in her voice.

I almost dish the dirt on my close encounter of the Nearly-Naked Jake kind, but I don't want to discuss this now. I've got to get ready for dinner, whatever that might consist of—heaven only knows. And, I have to prepare myself for that conniving bastard lawyer (another onomatopoeia) Esterhazy's visit.

"This isn't a singles-only cruise, Vanessa. I'm here as executor to disperse the estate."

"I know," she says with disappointment lacing her voice. "It's not every day you inherit property and animals from someone you've never met."

"Tell me something I don't know." I tug my fingers through my hair while I grip my cell phone to my ear. "Maybe I needed this." The beginning of the post-Rick era.

"How long are *you* going to be there?" Vanessa asks.

I walk towards the window and peel back the lace curtain. I sure wasted a beautiful day working in the chicken houses. I probably could have gone apple picking in the orchard or something to enjoy the crisp fall air. But that's not what I'm here for. "I'm hoping I can fly home Saturday night, if that's enough time to get everything done," I say. "The lawyer is coming over with papers for me to sign in a little bit." I drop the curtain and think for a moment.

"Good."

"Why?"

"Because..." Vanessa pauses for a second. "Kyle and I've decided not to have a long engagement or plan a Kardashian-type mega wedding. I don't want to turn into Bridezilla or worry about seating charts, rubber chicken meals, or whether to do 'The Electric Slide or 'The Macarena.'"

Thank God. I nearly snort. "What do you have in mind?"

"William found this charming seaman's chapel on the New Hampshire shore. It'll be a simple ceremony with friends and family, and then we're going to have a small reception at a hotel. Nothing fancy. Just friends and family."

This is *soooooo* Vanessa and Kyle. And so the type of wedding I've always wanted to attend... and wanted to have myself. The one I thought Rick and I would share. That's not going to happen now. Instead, I'll swallow my self-pity and stand up at the altar with my best friends and ignore that Rick's the best man.

Obviously not for me, though.

"And since you're an event planner, I'm sure it'll be perfect. I can't wait."

"Thanks," she says. "I hope I can pull it off in a month and a half. What do you think about a Christmas wedding?"

My mouth drops and I nearly do the same with the phone. "Did you say a month and a half?"

"Yeah. That's why I wanted to know if you'd be back."

"Of course I'll be back." I don't understand how she's going to execute the one day every woman dreams of in six short weeks. My mouth goes dry at the thought of possibly facing Rick as he stands next to Kyle at the altar as the best man. (Best man, my ass!) So soon. I swallow hard as my hand reflexively creeps up my throat. The tight sensation threatens to overwhelm me, although I will it away. No. I won't let Rick's cruel "I'm getting off the pot" hurt me anymore. I won't let it consume me. We're finished. Kaput. I won't let it ruin Vanessa and Kyle's day.

She continues. "It's not like Kyle and I just met, you know. We've been living together almost two years."

I shrug, aware that she can't see me. "It's a formality at this point."

"I think that's great, hon."

"And Griz? I want you to be my maid of honor."

My chest tightens over the lovely sentiment. "I'd be honored," I say though my choked breath.

"Don't worry," she tells me. "I'm not making you get one of those ugly, never-to-be-worn again orange taffeta bridesmaid's dresses. It's going to be an all-white wedding and I'm letting everyone get their own dress. I totally trust your taste."

This is cool. A simple wedding ceremony to start their lives off together. And who knows, maybe if I make money off of the farm, I might stop off in New York, hit Barney's and buy myself a designer dress. Something from Versace, Michael Kors or Marc Jacobs. I deserve it. Come to think of it, I deserve a lot of things. Especially a good looking guy with amazing hands to tumble around with.

No, no, not the time to think about Jake. Wet. In a towel.

I cough to rid the image from my mind.

"Excellent, V," I say. "Rest assured, there's nothing—and I mean *nothing*—that will keep me on this farm."

CHAPTER ELEVEN

But an ironclad contract might have something to say about my wanting to leave this farm any time soon.

A contract written in stone, signed in the blood of my dead relative.

An agreement with a corporate entity so grandiose that they would sue their own grandmother for breaching it.

I twist my hands together in my lap as I try to comprehend this.

The old country lawyer pins his gaze on me. "Do you have any questions, Ms. Perry?"

I look out the dining room window at the yard outside, darkened now from the setting sun. Turning back to the table, I glare at Westin Esterhazy, Esquire, in his blue and white seersucker suit and white dress shoes. In November! He looks like a Baptist preacher sitting there. And I should know because my father has the same get-up for his fire and brimstone Sunday sermons.

I do everything I can to calm myself and not verbally attack this messenger.

"Mr. Esterhazy, I've got a hell of a lot of questions," I say after I expel the breath I've been holding. "First off, if this farm operation is in such dire straits, why didn't you advise Stella to file for bankruptcy?"

"Oh, well, people 'round these parts don't do things like that," he says, a weak argument. He opens his mouth to say more, but I stop him with my hand.

"Secondly, how am I supposed to honor this unbreakable contract with Double C Farms when I only have"—I pick up the bank statement he'd handed me earlier—"$920.57 in the corporate bank account?"

I slam the paper onto the tabletop for emphasis. So much for being an heiress.

He adjusts his wire rim glasses. "Ms. Perry, I understand—"

"No, Mr. Esterhazy, I don't think you *do* understand. I have a nine-room farmhouse that's mortgaged to the gills to pay the debt on the construction of those chicken houses out there. I have a contract with a poultry producer who's expecting me to deliver a gazillion eggs over of the life of the flock, with me handling it on my own. I have no monies to hire a staff and am expected to stay here and honor this contract at not only the executor, but the inheritor."

He adjusts his wire glasses. "I'm sure it's not all that complicated to—"

Still, I keep going. "All I know about eggs is checking the carton at the grocery store to make sure none of them are broken before I buy them. I don't have time for this." I sip in deeply for confidence and try to calm my boiling frustration. "Look, I have a job that I have to get back to, deadlines and responsibilities at work that no one else can do. I'm also the maid of honor in my best friend's wedding in six weeks and you tell me I can't walk away from this farm? You think you understand what's going on with me?"

I decide to leave out the part about getting dumped by Rick, in case either Jimmie or Jake have come back into the house and are listening in. Jimmie was so nice to make fried chicken—probably the last time I'll eat it—steamed okra, and cornbread for me and then clean up while I meet with the lawyer in the front parlor.

Esterhazy adjusts in the uncomfortable gentleman's chair covered in aged gold material. The mahogany set resembles something from Victorian days that somehow made its way across the Atlantic and then got passed from generation to generation until it ended up with Aunt Stella.

With me.

"You do have options," the lawyer tells me.

"Do tell," I snark off.

"You could sell, although not to anyone local. Don't know many in these parts who can afford to pay what the land's worth or what will cover the debt. You'd have to place ads in trade journals, list the property on websites and wait for a bite from the outside world. The Japanese are always looking for American lands to purchase."

If I had the time, I could design a kick-ass website with pictures of the property. Photoshop out the peeling paint and make the place look spiffy. However, this isn't a work project. This is my life. I groan out loud. "And how long will that take?"

"Months... years. Who knows?"

I want to vomit.

"However, Ms. Perry, I can't stress enough your fiduciary responsibility and obligation to fulfill Double C's contract as Stella Hardwick's heir." Esterhazy ignores that I've probably gone green on him and continues. "Even if you sell, you'll likely take a loss on the business. Any profit you make will have to go to pay off the mortgage on the chicken houses."

"How much is the land worth?" I ask.

He takes off his glasses, and cleans them with a white handkerchief he drew out of his pocket. "It's worth almost thirty-five hundred an acre around these parts. You know, they're not making land anymore, so if you've got it, you're potentially sitting on a goldmine."

"*If* you can find a buyer," I say with a resigned sigh. Dilligus Flats is obviously economically depressed just from what I've seen riding through town. No one here has that kind of money to ante up for this farm, especially one with debts and mortgages and contractual obligations. Of course, like he said, maybe there's some foreign businessman who's interested in farm-living and turning this place around. I could put an ad on Craigslist or eBay.

I prop my elbows up on the table and put my head in my hands. Okay, so I can't inherit someone else's debt, but I sure as shit have to manage it. "What else?"

He clears his throat in a high-pitched whine that makes me want to crawl under the table. Come to think of it, that doesn't sound like a bad idea. Fetal position. Like a cat curled up thinking about its Jellical name, like T. S. Eliot and Andrew Lloyd Webber wrote about. There I go thinking like Grizabella the Glamour Cat again. But like her, I'm tattered and torn, downtrodden and hopeless. I wish there was some greater being out there who would come take me to a better life.

Just then, Jake walks into the house and stares at me sitting at the dining room table. I convey my desperation with my eyes. For a moment, it seems as though Jake want so join me in the meeting and be my alpha wolf. Then, to my disappointment, he nods at me and steers clear.

"Ms. Perry? Are you with me?"

I snap out of it. "Sorry, Mr. Esterhazy. You were saying?"

He glowers at me. "I said the best thing to do is to get this new flock into the houses in a couple of days, work hard at producing as many eggs as possible, finish your contract, and pay off as much of the loan payments as you can with any profits you make. I recommend putting some feelers out there to sell the place, provided the houses have a better reputation than they've had in the last couple of years."

So it's come to this. I'm between the proverbial rock and a hard place. I have no earthly idea how I'm going to do all of that in the span of a week. Hopefully, I can convince Jimmie to come back on board to run things despite the rue with Stella. I'll have to find a way to pay him, even if it means cashing out some of my 401(k) from work. There's no way I'm staying here in Dilligus Flats.

I sit up straight and stare for a moment at the gray-haired Esterhazy. "Since it seems like I have no other choice, Mr. Esterhazy, I'll do it what I can."

"Stella would be proud of you, Isabella."

Maybe she would. Perhaps this was some sort of test she left for me. "So, the chickens will be here Wednesday and Stella's staff will come back to work then?"

His bushy eyebrows lower enough to nearly touch his eyelashes. "What staff?"

I don't need to be messed with right now. "The staff Stella had helping her."

Esterhazy's guffaw turns into a cough. "Stella had no staff."

There goes my blood pressure again. "No staff? But Jimmie said it wasn't him or that Dwayne guy, that—"

"—Stella did all the work herself," Esterhazy says. "Three shifts a day. Sometimes four. Seven days a week. Animals don't take vacation, Miss Perry.

"You mean—" The reality of his words pierces me on skewers of disbelief.

"It all falls on you, Isabella. You're it."

Head in hands, I say, "I need a drink."

CHAPTER TWELVE

There's like one bar in Dilligus Flats. One! I should have known when the city limits sign read "1,435 citizens; 8 churches."

The bar I found is out on the highway. ("The highway" meaning it has more than two lanes, can hold eighteen-wheelers, and actually leads somewhere, to real cities, i.e. civilization.) According to the hand-painted sign on the front of the cinderblock building, the Twin Twigs Lounge claims to have "soul food and soul action." Looking at all the pickup trucks with gun racks in the back, I'm afraid I'm not their target audience. They probably wouldn't take too kindly to some city chick waltzing in and asking for a Vox raspberry martini.

After driving around Dilligus Flats for a good half hour, searching in vain for at least a package store—or ABC store as they call them here in Alabama—I return to the farm in a cloud of dust caused by my disregard for the posted thirty-five mile per hour speed limit.

I hop out of Stella's truck and stop dead in my tracks. Jake's sitting on the front porch, lit by one solitary light, with a beer in one hand and his other spread across Puddy Tat's belly. She's upside down, sprawled out (have some dignity, would you?) and couldn't be happier that the handyman's rubbing her.

"Little slut," I mutter under my breath and then head to the porch. I point to his brewsky. "You have another one of those? Or twenty?"

His shakes his head. "Sorry. Last one. I can run to the Gas and Fluff for you, if you'd like."

Frickin' Gas and Fluff has everything under the sun. Why didn't I think of checking there? They probably only sell Bud and Boone's Farm Strawberry Hill, or worse, Colt 45 and Mad Dog 20/20. I'd gladly drown my sorrows in moonshine right now, quite frankly.

Turning my attention to Jake, I say, "That's okay. Wouldn't want to interrupt here." I put my hands on my hips and look over at the stroking scene going on with Jake and "another woman."

He pats Puddy on her stomach several times. She flips over, yawns in a lazy, satiated way, and then bounds down the steps into the bushes.

"Just like a woman," he says with a light tone in his voice. "Pay attention to her, make her feel like she's the only one, and she runs away." He takes a long swig of his beer.

"Are you referring to the cat?" I suck in my stomach as I stand before him, hoping I don't look like the farm skank that I feel like.

"She's the only woman in my life," Jake says. "Until you walked in here today, that is."

God, this guy's got charm oozing out his ears and doesn't even know it.

"Why don't I believe you, Jake?"

"Because you're smart," he says.

I walk past him up into the house. My house. My mortgaged house. I look at my watch. 9:45 p.m. Truly the day from hell. I want to take a bath and wash this entire, asinine day off of me. So it can all start again tomorrow.

I can already hear the furious voice mail I'll get from Claudia, bitching me out for not being at work, like I could control a relative dying and leaving me responsible for her earthly mess.

I stop in the doorway and look at Jake silhouetted by the full moon light. It's so something out of a romance novel. Dark, brooding, contemplative hero; desperate, rejected, hopeless heroine. I shake my head at the cliché.

But I'm no more Jake's heroine than he is my hero. He's made it perfectly clear that he's not interested in me. And I don't need to be interested in him or anyone else. It's only been three days since Rick dumped me.

Jake stands up and wipes his hands on his jeans. Then, he picks up the empty beer bottle. He faces me so that I can make out a slight smile on his handsome face. "Everything's going to be all right, Isabella."

I turn my head. "Why do you say that?"

"Intuition," he says.

"Well, Jake," I start. "Unless you want to tell me your life story, I'm going to—as they say here in the country—hit the hay."

His laughter fills the night air and I can't help but giggle along with him. "Not tonight, Isabella. Maybe tomorrow," he says with a slight wink. Guys who wink typically unnerve me, but it's usually the miscreants on the train who do it to me. Not a droolingly sexy guy like Jake Hansen, who might just mean it.

As I'm about to close the screen, he steps up onto the porch and puts his hand on the door. "Isabella?"

"Yeah?"

"I know you're this strong chick from the big city. But, if you need anything, just give me a yell. Sound really carries out here, so if you call out, I'll answer."

My heart lurches at his sweet words, dipping down to my toes and back into place. An unfamiliar ache settles low in my belly and my skin itches to touch him. To hug him. To thank him. This guy doesn't know diddlysquat about me, yet he's made me feel at home in a strange situation since I stepped foot on the farm earlier today.

"That means a lot to me, Jake."

My hair slips forward into my lashes. His hand reaches out, but before he can make contact, I sweep the wayward locks back. His eyes search my face and it looks like he's going to say something serious. I'm not sure I can handle close contact with him. I'm obviously not in my right mind. My hormones are out of whack and surely I'm on the rebound. Not a good place to be.

"I, umm, you'll want to turn the radio on or something as you're going to sleep," he says.

That wasn't what I was expecting. "Why's that?"

"You're probably used to city sounds. It can get deathly quiet out here. To the point of paranoia. Trust me."

Only an urban dweller would understand being lulled to sleep by the sound of cabs, trains, and street noise. Who *is* this guy?

"Thanks. I'll keep that in mind."

He steps back. "Well, good night."

"Night."

I close the door between us and breathe for the first time in several minutes. My skin feels tight around me and there's an alien twinge in my Southern hemisphere. Something I haven't experienced in, oh, say, five months. My hands shake at the effect this man—this beautiful, sensitive man—has on my entire system. In only a day.

My body is one gushy mess.

I'm so horny it's ridiculous.

I can't have this. I can't handle this.

I run to the bathroom, strip off my smelly clothes and plunge myself under the brutal reality of the cold showerhead.

Jake was right. The silence here *is* maddening.

After my ice-cold shower, I dry off, dress in my blue and white KKΓ tank top and Red Sox shorts and crawl into the high, fluffy iron bed.

With the Pandora Ambient station playing, I lie back and wait for sleep to come.

I toss.

I turn.

I flip.

I flop.

I replay the scene with Rick in the ladies room. I should have said something. I should have reacted differently. I should have bitten his dick off! You always think of the *right* thing to say once you're past a situation. Flashes of disappointment. Stickered and highlighted to point out my weaknesses and failure. Then, as I always do, I recount all of the horrible things that have ever happened in my lifetime, going back to losing my teddy bear on vacation in Virginia Beach at age six, chipping my tooth on a tree branch in third grade, to my sorority formal date making out with another girl in the elevator and, of course, the day I got laid off from my old job, and being too damn scared at this one that I let my bitch of a boss walk all over me. I shake my head into the pillow trying to toss off the negativity and remembrance. I can't change any of it and it just churns up emotions I don't need to spend right now.

The stillness of my surroundings resonates with loud, white noise. I can actually hear the wind tickling the outside of the house. My eyes shift in the darkness wondering what's lurking out there. A twig snaps. Probably Puddy Tat on nightly prowl. A cricket chirps. Annoying little bugger.

And in the hush, my heartbeat echoes in my head. Pounding out a steady rhythm against my temples, reverberating to my toes.

I honestly don't know how anyone can sleep in such utter silence.

Maybe I should do that mental body scan thing Vanessa taught me after she had her stress reduction class. That thing where you imagine you're in each body part, making it breathe. Okay, I'm game. Anything to put me to sleep.

I start at my toes... then I move to my feet. *Breathe.* Okay, this is working. I'm relaxing. On to my ankles... up to my calves. Breathing in, breathing out. I'm about to make my way up to my knobby knees when I hear a noise overhead.

Something whirling.

I sit up and toss the covers away. "What the...?"

The ground shakes like the house is about to be ripped from its foundation Wizard of Oz style. Isn't it enough that I'm already *not* in Kansas any longer? Now what?

I pad into the Great Room, squeezing my bare toes in the thick rug as I stop and listen.

Something choppy in the air.

Something rumbling.

Something predatory.

I run to the front of the house and look out over the yard. There are massive white light from above. They're hovering. Circling. It looks like they're searching, seeking... for...

Oh Holy God!

Please don't tell me all those years of watching science fiction movies and TV shows has warped me to the point that I actually think aliens are about to land at Hardwick Poultry and whisk me away.

But the whirling and rumbling grows louder, more distinguishable. The house shakes further, moaning and groaning from the motion above.

This is complete and total bullshit.

I am so not going to be abducted by aliens.

Nausea. Panic. Heart attack.

I twirl around in my third freak out of the day. More choral chaos joins the mixture of sounds from above. Oh, wait, that's me screaming bloody murder.

"Help! Help! Oh, God! What's going on?"

Puddy Tat bolts past me. I follow and watch her dash under the Barcalounger. Oh sure, like I can hide under there.

"Someone help! Hellllllllllllp!"

Lights from overhead inch over the house. The whirling and chopping becomes more distinct.

Out of the corner of my eye, I see Jake bust out of his trailer and fly up the steps of the farmhouse. I hadn't even bothered to lock the back door, so he roars into the adjoining dining room like a conquering hero in an action movie.

Only, he's got a weapon drawn. *Whoa.* That's a big gun.

"Isabella?" he calls out. "Where are you?"

The noise outside is immense and damn near painful. I cower next to the chair and do my best "duck and cover."

"I'm over here," I say weakly.

The rumbling overhead is fierce; the rattling intensifies. Jake pulls me up by the elbows and I collapse in his arms.

"I don't want to go," I plea. "Don't let them take me. I know we're out in the country and they can probably take us, test us, and return us in the morning without anyone knowing, but I can't deal with this. Not after everything I've gone through!"

He tucks the gun into the waistband of his jeans. His eyes are fiery, trying to decipher what I'm ranting about.

I shake my head and lay my forehead on his warm shoulder. My God, he doesn't have a shirt on. Again. But I can't think of that. All I can focus on is the horrid noise from above that seems to be hovering over the house.

I can't stop from babbling. This is that proverbial last straw that breaks *this* camel's back. "I can't take anymore. I inherit a God-awful, failing business, my boyfriend dumped me, and I haven't had sex in half a year... now this! Freaking aliens! I can't handle it, Jake!"

He cradles me against him and I feel the hammering of his heart under my fingers. "Shhh, it'll be over in a second," he says gently as his arm protects me.

"I don't want an anal probe. I'm not strong enough to handle that." Like a fool, I let the floodgate of tears open. I need an alien hunter, a ghost hunter, any of those people from TV who hunt the paranormal. Hell, an exorcist for that matter to cleanse my life from this shit storm.

A deep laugh rumbles through Jake's chest and his arms tighten around me. "They're almost done."

The horrific noise is dissipating, pulling off, roaring away like a jet plane on a runway.

I look up at him through the hair that's fallen into my face. "They? You know them?"

"Yeah, it's okay." I swear, it feels like his lips brush my hair. We're about to die together and he thinks to do something so comforting. This guy really is the calm before the storm. So, he's experienced this before. They've taken him, tested him, and returned him. That's why he's so unruffled.

The whirling fades away into the distance, into the night, as quickly as it came, and the tranquil serenity of the country air returns to normal. Whatever it was—whoever it was—the house survived. I survived. We survived.

I push away from the safety of Jake's warm chest and try to regain my composure. "Was that a close encounter?"

His smile is devilishly handsome. "Well, it was for me."

He looks as if he's going to kiss me. After that horrendous incident, I'm going to let him.

I close my eyes and let my head fall back, ready for what's to come.

CHAPTER THIRTEEN

I feel his breath on my skin and I shiver a bit.

Then his hand brushes across my cheek in an oh-so protective way.

Take me. Take me.

Then I hear him chuckle.

My eyes fly open. "What's so damn funny? We almost died."

He tips his head back and laughs even harder. "Not hardly. I guess I should have warned you."

"That there are extraterrestrials visiting us after all?"

"Damn, you're adorable," he says to me. "That wasn't E.T. That was the Army."

I need a Q-Tip, because I don't think I heard him correctly. "The Army? Like Uncle Sam? Like 'Be All that You Can Be?' They're supposed to be on *our* side?"

Jake's smile cocks to one side and he steps away, breaking the contact with me. "I should have mentioned it to you. Fort Rucker is a couple hundred miles from here. Those were Apaches."

God, I feel like a complete idiot. "Indians?"

"No, silly. Helicopters. Fort Rucker is the home training base for the Apache helicopters. A couple of times a month, they practice maneuvers around here. They wait until it's really dark so they can use their night vision."

All right. Now I'm pissed off. "You mean, I was scared shitless by a bunch of flying leathernecks cowboying around and buzzing the house?" My heartbeat threatens to pound out of my tank top. Either that or I'll drop dead from a myocardial infarction.

Jake snorts. "Flying leathernecks are marine pilots."

"Whatever!" I shriek.

"It's okay. Like I said, it happens every now and then," he says, trying to reassure. "I should have warned you."

I blow out a breath and unfurl my fists. "I'm going to write a letter to the local congressman. That's bullshit. I bet it was that freaking noise that killed Stella in her sleep."

"No, she had a stroke at the chicken house."

"Oh. God. That's horrible." I don't want to think of Aunt Stella lying dead amongst the chickens. Since I only know what she looked like at age thirty, all I can picture is myself. Face down in the pine shillings. It's bad enough that my pulse is still rapidly reacting to the near miss with the United States Army. And with Jake's... *gun?*

"What are you doing with a fucking gun?" I wince at my harsh words. He doesn't seem taken aback with my colorful language, though. "Is this an it's-my-right-to-tote-a-gun thing or are you a cop or something?"

He sighs hard.

"I don't really want to talk about it." He removes the large gray gun from his pants and sets it on the table next to the Barcalounger. "Sorry. You screamed. I reacted. Reflexes, you know?"

"I'm not taking that as an answer this time, Jake." When I screw up my mouth into a flat line and glare at him, he seems to figure out I need more than his brush-off response.

Running his fingers through his thick hair, he says, "I used to be a cop, okay? Can we drop it? I thought you were hurt. I was coming to help."

Conscious of my lack of clothes—and his, too—I cross my arms across my chest. I've got to lighten this. "Well, you told me to yell out if I needed anything."

The lightness returns to his dark blue eyes. "I did take an oath to protect and serve. But you were never in danger."

"I know that *now*." Then, I suddenly remember everything I spewed out in my moment of terror. The fear that consumed my thoughts. I'd just relayed everything to Jake about the state of my life.

Maybe he wasn't listening.

"You know," he says, breaking the moment of silence. "I think we could both use a drink. What do you say?"

"I thought you said you were out of beer."

His grin turns into a smirk. "I am. But I know where Stella stashed her wine."

I nod and smile. A man after my heart. Well, figuratively speaking. "I like the sound of that plan."

Stealthily, he goes to the china cabinet and opens the bottom cupboard. Inside is a wine rack with at least ten bottles.

"Aunt Stella, you wino," I say.

Jake pulls out a bottle of red and brushes the dust off it. "This is probably as old as we are," he says with a laugh.

I want to know more about this guy. This loner. This cop. "Which is?"

"I'm thirty-two. And you?"

Feeling flirty, I say, "You're not supposed to ask a lady her age."

A laugh catches in his throat. "I think after what we've been through today, I deserve a little of the '411,' don't you?"

My pulse accelerates again, only this time in a good way. In a way I haven't felt in a while. "I'm thirty, thank you."

Walking into the kitchen, he mutters, "You don't look your age."

"Neither do you," I add.

He shrugs. "It's only a number. Age is in your mind. Stella knew that. She was headed toward seventy, but she was twenty-five at heart." He paws through the utility drawer for a minute and then stops. "Weird, I can't find a cork screw."

"No worries. Hold on." I run to my bedroom, rummage through my makeup bag, and head back to the kitchen. I hold up the black and silver item I'd retrieved and say, "I always travel with my own personal bar tool."

Jake's smile lights the dimly lit room. "My kind of gal."

I try not to let his words go to my head. Alcohol consumption. That's the main goal here. Not tickling my libido.

In the kitchen, Jake selects two jelly jar glasses from the cabinet and I pop the cork on an impressive bottle of Beaujolais. I'm not usually a red wine drinker, but I'll make an exception in this case. I don't even bother with the classy act of tasting the wine or sniffing the cork. I simply gulp the first sip in a frat-boy-during-rush-week manner.

"I needed that," I say with a sigh.

He clinks his glass to mine. "Apparently so." He salutes me before drinking down the wine. The one small light over the stove casts a shadow over his face. His eyes look far off, as though they're focusing on something else. Then I realize that "something else" is my bra-less, tank top-covered chest. Or my erect nipples, to be exact, standing at attention for all to see. My body is betraying me over the close quarters with Jake and his shirtless self.

"I'll... umm... be right back."

When I return from my room with an Old Navy pullover on, I see Jake's opened the bag of Doritos I'd bought earlier. I look over his shoulder at the red rooster clock on the wall.

"You know, it's after midnight, which technically means it's tomorrow."

He drinks more wine; his eyes smile over the rim of his glass. "Your point?"

I can't believe how at ease he is standing in front of me with no shirt on and the top button of his jeans opened to reveal—I gulp hard—a Calvin Klein waistband.

"So... you, umm, said you'd tell me your life story 'tomorrow.'"

His eyes zero in on mine. "Ah, the things we say in the heat of the moment."

My face heats knowing he's referring to all I belched out to him when I thought I was going to be abducted. "Yeah, about that..."

"I'm sorry your boyfriend dumped you and you haven't had sex in a long time," he says. "That has to be really hard. I know what it's like to have a relationship go south."

"You do?" What idiotic woman tossed this man aside?

He shrugs and I take that as yet another topic we're not supposed to touch upon. That's what I get for spilling my guts when I'm scared shitless. Then again, he'd admitted he was a cop without adding the details of what he's doing here in Dilligus Flats. In either case, one of us needs to speak. Soon. The tension in the air is a palpable sizzle.

We finish the first bottle of Beaujolais in complete silence, both of us seeming to need that soothing affect the warm wine provides. He slips into the dining room and returns with a second bottle. Swiftly, he peels off the foil wrapper, pops the cork and refills my glass.

I down my wine and then pour more for both of us. The aroma of flowers and fruits are complex, exuding scents of roses, violets, and raspberries. Okay, maybe I shouldn't have taken that wine-tasting class with William last month.

I'm starting to feel a warm buzz. "Where were... I mean, are you a cop?" I ask Jake.

His Adam's apple bobs up and down as he swallows. "Manhattan."

"New York City? Doing what in particular?"

"Undercover unit for two years."

"Before that?"

"Beat cop. Well, after college, that is."

I nod. Impressive. Cops are always in tip-top shape. It certainly explains his powerful build and nurturing personality.

"I can't see you in a cop's uniform, though." The only image of this man that's burned into my corneas is that of his broad, muscular chest.

His eyebrow lifts. "What *can* you see me in?"

I drain my glass one more time and fill it again. "I guess the wine's gone to my head."

His smirk is apparent in the low-lit room. "So, you're from Boston."

I lift the container to my lips as I peer over the rim at him. I thought it might be fun to stand here in the near dark and drink with Jake, but suddenly I'm sweating like some sort of farm animal. My pulse is trilling in my head and I'm sure he can see my heart beat through the fabric of my clothes.

"I live in Boston now, but I grew up in the Chicago area."

But, he nods and continues to drink. "Best St. Patty's Day parade anywhere."

"Better than New York or Boston?"

"I haven't been to Boston's. Maybe I'll check it out after I leave here."

The thought of him going away makes my chest ache. Something made him flee New York and his job as a cop. I wonder what that *something* was.

I fan my hand in front of my face and place the nearly empty glass on the butcher-block counter. I really shouldn't be drinking red wine. It always gives me the sweats.

My heart is fluttering away underneath my clothes and I can't tell if it's from the tannins in the wine or the mischievous look on Jake's face. "I suppose I should go to bed."

Jake moves in and points to the side of my nose and squints. "I didn't notice earlier that you had a hole in your nose."

I layer my fingers on the left side of my nose and cringe that he saw this. "Oh, I pierced it a few years ago. Trying to be a rebel. I haven't worn a stud for a while hoping it'll grow over."

"Wild child, huh?" Jake stretches out his hand and is about to touch my face.

Oh God, he can't do that. I can't let him. Or else, next thing I know, those loose jeans of his will be off and I'll be splayed on that butcher block with my legs wrapped around his waist. Talk about breaking into a sweat!

In a dead panic, I step back hurriedly and whack the heel of my foot against the dry sink.

"Watch it!" he warns, too late.

"Dammit all!"

I hop up and down, holding onto the counter. "Crap! That hurts!" I try to limp away, but the twinge is white-hot. "I really should go to bed now."

Jake follows me as I hobble three steps.

"Hold on," he orders. "Where are you going? Let me." Next thing I know, he sweeps into his arms and carries me toward my room. "This one, right?"

I gnaw on my lip and nod.

He deposits me onto the bed and tucks my feet under the covers. "Enough adventure for one day. Get some rest, Isabella."

Embarrassed beyond words for like the twelfth time—and biting back the tingling pain in my foot—I feign a smile and say, "Thanks for taking care of me today, Jake."

He sits on the edge of the bed and studies my face. I don't dare blink for fear that he'll disappear. Every fiber of my being is on Orange Alert with this man in such close proximity. I want him, plain and simple. I want to feel the weight of his body pressing me into the mattress as we work up a sweat together. And it's more than something physical. I feel this connection to Jake. Like he's a piece of magnet that's drawing me to him and I have no control over it. Unconsciously, I lick my lips as he stares at me.

"I can't," he whispers, reading my mind.

"Can't what?" I ask coyly.

"I can't get involved with you, Isabella."

As my soul caves in for the second time in three days, I put on a brave face. "Who said I wanted to get involved with you?"

Jake snickers. He's a sexy guy. He knows when women are interested. It doesn't have to be spelled out for him.

"I'm no good for you. For anyone."

I sigh. "I don't believe that for a—"

He stops me. "It doesn't matter if you believe it. Because I do. I've hurt too many people."

With that, he stands up, his weight leaving the bed.

"Jake—"

"Get some sleep."

I curl up under the quilt and watch him leave the room. At the door, he turns back and calls out to me. "Hey Isabella?"

"Yeah?"

"Don't worry... I won't tell Jimmie or anyone that you thought we were being abducted. You're safe from the little green men."

The heated rush returns to my cheeks. Only this time he can't see my embarrassment. I listen as Jake walks through the house, out the door and returns to his trailer.

I may be safe from aliens, but am I safe from Jake?

CHAPTER FOURTEEN

The musical interlude on my Android sounds out—loudly—wiping away the delicious dream of Jake, naked and towering over me.

"What?" I moan.

It's six in the morning, yet I feel as though I just fell asleep. Who's rude enough to call at this hour?

I glance at the display and see, "Coldren, Claudia."

Of course. The Boss from Hell.

I slide the green bar to the right to answer. "Hey, Claudia."

"Tell me this is some sick joke, Isabella," my boss snaps into the phone.

"No, I'm sorry. My aunt died and I'm the executor of her estate. Just like I said in my voice mail."

Claudia clicks her tongue. "You didn't have my permission to take time off work."

Jesus, lady! "I'm sorry, Claudia, you can't exactly plan ahead for someone's death."

"Don't get smart with me, Isabella. You know how much I rely on you. We've got the product launch in two weeks and there's a hell of a lot of work to get done."

"I know. But this is family. Our company president always says, 'family first,' so that's what I'm taking care of," I say, pleading my case.

"Well, that's true," she says. "Maybe you can work while you're there. Do you have your laptop?"

I lie. "No, I don't. Besides, I have a lot of responsibilities to oversee here as my aunt's executor. I wouldn't have time for anything other than these matters this week." I don't know how I've suddenly grown a backbone with this woman who scares hell and four dollars out of me. Perhaps it's the eighteen-hundred mile difference that's helping.

There's a significant silence and then Claudia speaks. "I don't like this, Isabella. I don't like it one bit."

"Neither do I, Claudia. Let me take care of my family business and I'll be back at work next."

She sighs noticeably into the phone. "What choice do I have? I'll expect you here at seven a.m. Monday. No excuses."

The phone clicks dead and I stare at the blank screen.

Oh, and thanks for the condolences there, Claudia. "Bitch." I don't understand how someone like her rose to management with an attitude like that and a total disregard for anyone else. Wait, sure I do! If I were on a rotating sex schedule with the Vice President of Sales, the head of Client Services, and the Executive Vice President of Finance, I'd have job security like her. Did I go there? You bet I did.

I roll back over, close my eyes, and desperately try to pick up where Dream Jake and I left off.

The real Jake must have had enough of me that first day because I don't see him for the next two. Jimmie tells me that Jake's working on the back fence, clearing brush, and repairing the planks. I hope that's the case and it isn't a reflection on the plethora of idiosyncrasies I displayed in my debut on the farm.

What a dumb ass, thinking aliens were coming to get me. I blame it on William downloading the "Ancient Aliens" series and putting ideas in my head of rural alien abductions.

I look at my watch. Ten of seven. P.M. The eighteen-wheeler full of chickens should be here any minute. Well, that's what Dwayne from Double C Farms told me.

"Why are we doing this at night?" I ask Jimmie, who's relaxing in the cab of his Dodge, gnawing on a Slim Jim. He must not realize how many grams of fat are in those. Not to mention it's like made of cow guts. Gross.

This farm is going to turn me into a vegan. Jimmie offers the beef jerky to me, but I shake my head. I ate a bowl of cottage cheese and peach slices earlier. Besides, I don't want to even consider what other byproducts make up his snack.

In the distance, I hear the rumbling of a large vehicle chugging along the small country road. Guess that means the chickens have arrived. *My* chickens. Suddenly, the thought of a tractor-trailer full of fifteen thousand chickens seems a bit daunting.

Headlights click to the bright setting and pull into my front driveway.

The chickens have landed.

Paint me a weirdo, but I'm slightly excited. And my hands are a little shaky in anticipation. Jimmie closes the door to his truck and leads me by the elbow into the closest chicken house. The smell of fresh pine shavings—that I'd spent the last two days tossing around—fills the air.

At the far end of the house is a door into the front room where the eggs will be gathered off the conveyer belt that runs underneath each set of metal nests. I've had a full orientation on Egg Gathering 101. Jimmie shuts the door and makes sure the rubber flap is covering the cut out holes surrounding the conveyer path. This room will be my home for the foreseeable future as I learn all about the egg operation.

"They're bringing them chickens in one crate at a time."

"In a crate?" I ask. "What do we do? Let them out?"

Jimmie reaches into his pocket, pulls out tobacco and places a hunk of it in his front lip. "Nah, they dump them out and the chickens go flying everywhere."

"That sounds incredibly inhumane?"

"We ain't here to entertain them. Think of them as your employees. You done given them good working conditions, food, water, and somewhere to sleep. Now it's time for them to get the job done."

I cringe at the horrid analogy, yet I stay silent.

I get up my courage and try to calm the ridiculous pounding of my heart. "Is Jake coming to help?"

Jimmie spits into the pine shillings. "I don't reckon so. I saw him drive off on his motor bike earlier. Must have a big night planned."

On a Wednesday. In Dilligus Flats.

He probably headed to The Twin Twigs for some of that "soul action" they advertise.

Five minutes later, the red Massey Ferguson tractor turns in with a large steel cage held high in the air on the end of the forklift. The machine bounds in over the floor litter with Dwayne behind the wheel. The doors of the individual cages are bouncing and banging. Dwayne pulls up almost directly in front of where Jimmie and I are standing. Suddenly, he adjusts the forklift and the cages go from vertical to horizontal. The crates fly open and out dump tens of chickens, wings flapping, beaks squawking and feathers flying.

"Oh, my God!" I yell, cringing and backing up.

The birds land on the soft ground in a riot of *bwawk-ing*, clucking, and scurrying over each other. I gasp at the mayhem surrounding me, almost gagging on the dusty air.

Dwayne backs out, retrieves another cage and proceeds to dump them only a few feet from the first batch.

"That has to hurt them," I note.

Jimmie laughs. "They's chickens. They don't care."

Three hours later, both houses are completely packed. It's a sea of white birds, milling around in a farm version of a cocktail party, getting to know each other, claiming the best nest, and bellying up to the trough of corn and soybeans that has calcium added to make the egg shells stronger. At least, that's what the marketing blurb on the feedbag read.

Jimmie sidles up to me, lifts his hat, wipes his forehead, and snorts a bit. "Them's all of them. Now we let them get settled and tomorrow we're back in business."

I can do this. All these months of working late hours stuck in a cube tells me that I need a break. Besides, a little physical labor never hurt anyone. It'll help rebuild my tattered heart muscle, too.

It'll be a new me: *Isabella Perry, Entrepreneur.*

I'll start a new trend. Farming will be the new black. Others will follow in my footsteps. Hardwick Poultry will be the company that everyone will pattern their businesses from. A success story for this still-new millennium.

I'll be on the cover of *Business Week* and *Forbes*. I can see it now: "Chicken Heiress Conquers All."

I smile over at Jimmie. "Damn right we're in business."

I'm nearing the end of my week in Dilligus Flats, yet I'm no closer to having things together than when I got here.

I've seen Jake precisely three times, mostly in passing as he leaves in the morning to go work on this alleged fence. I don't know if he's avoiding me or just uninterested in hanging out. Not that I have time to just laze about with a hot hunk of a handyman.

Yet, I can't get him out of my mind.

Or rid myself of the image of his sexy body wrapped in that small white towel.

I snap out of my reverie. I'm here to run the chicken houses. Not open a cathouse starring me as the Madame and Jake as my one and only client.

And in my few days working the chicken houses, I have gathered twenty-seven—count them... *twenty-seven*—eggs. It's like some insane Easter egg hunt only without the candy prizes. I root around the pine shilling for surprises the hens might have left for me. Jimmie says it's perfectly natural for the chickens to be nervous at first, as they're getting used to their surroundings.

This isn't camp. They're chickens. They lay eggs. They get fertilized. I make money. End of story.

Start producing!

So far, this blue-skied Friday morning, I have discovered only eight eggs. Perhaps the chickens are Jewish and preparing for the Shabbat at sunset. For good measure, I sit in the plastic chair at the end of the steel encased conveyer belt and flip the switch on. There's a big, black magic-marker "X" on the belt to show me my starting place. I run the belt that transports the eggs from the nests, until I reach the other end, four hundred feet away, marked by yet another large, black "X." Jimmie tells me I'm to do this three times a day. It is the most boring thing I've ever done in my life. There's no TV, no radio, and it's impossible to surf the web or do anything on my Android since my hands are tending to the eggs.

That leaves me time for one thing.

Thinking. And over-thinking.

The belt continues to slide along, gears moaning. I bend down and peer into the depths of it at a shadow creeping slowly toward me.

"I see you, you little bastard!" I say excitedly to the silhouette of an egg a few feet away. I nab the oblong, white item and set it tip down—as taught—into the plastic egg crate.

This isn't so bad, sitting here in the quiet, with nothing but my thoughts, although that's not my favorite thing to do. However, I won't hash on everything that's gone wrong for me. I'll be positive. It's time to reflect. Relax. I don't see how this is stressful work. Course, I don't see how I can make money off it either with these obstinate chickens refusing to lay eggs. Guess they're still getting to know each other. I can't assume all of the hens are big old skanky 'hos who'll hook up with just *any* rooster. I'm sure the chicken world is as picky as the human world. As I conjure up a bizarre image of a rooster surfing Match.com for that perfect Rhode Island Red—the curse of a creative mind—I'm thrown back by reality.

"Ewww... gross!"

The belt churns and out comes the biggest pile of nauseating goo I've seen yet. It resembles something one might find in the back alleyways of Chinatown, following close of business and dumping out of vulgar leftovers. A certain queasiness bubbles up my chest, burning at the back of my throat.

"Jimmie!" I flick the conveyer switch off and flee the utility room. He's probably in the other house filling the bins with food. "Jimmie! I need help. I've got a wicked nasty situation going here."

Instead of finding him, I run nose to chest into Jake.

He steadies me with his hands. "Whoa! Everything okay, Isabella?"

My heart does that stupid flippity-flop motion at the sight of Jake Hansen. He's wearing dark sunglasses and a backwards Yankees cap. His faded jeans are scuffed with red dirt and the sleeves of his chambray shirt are rolled up high to his massive biceps.

I wipe my hands down the sides of my hips, not caring if any chicken ick gets on my well-worn 501's. "Well, look what the cat dragged in."

Jake pulls off his sunglasses and tucks them into the front pocket of his shirt. "Missed me?"

I shrug non-committal. His on-again off-again flirtiness totally discombobulates me. It's like one minute I think he's interested, but then something shuts him off. The man definitely has demons; I can see the pain in the depths of his eyes.

His smile is gut wrenching and touches a place deep inside of me that reacts with a hitch in my pulse. "Sorry, I've been busy. Working on that back fence," he says, stepping under the awning between the two chicken houses. "It's a hell of a mess. I've put it off as long as I could, but I had to make some headway with it. I promised Stella."

From the serious look on his face, he must have been spending time thinking things over in his life, as well.

I smile up at him and try to act nonchalant. "So what's up?"

"Had to tell Jimmie something. Nothing urgent."

"Yeah, I was looking for him, too."

Jake stretches his arms over his head and hooks them on the edge of the awning, showing me just how tall he is; an ominous hunky hulk standing spread out before me. "His truck's out front, but that could mean he's anywhere."

"Oh " I say, dropping my eyes. I don't need to be staring at Jake with such intensity when I don't know what might be smeared on my clothes, or worse, my face. Besides, he's made it clear that he's not interested in me.

"Do you need help?" His question hints concern, like he's feeling guilty for avoiding me since our "alien" encounter.

I screw up my nose, wondering if I should show him the yuck on the belt that I honestly don't know what to do with.

"I sort of have a mess in there." I point into the room.

Jake steps in front of me. He walks in towards the halted belt and coughs as he laughs. "Damn, baby. That's *nasss-tay!*"

I can't help but laugh, too. "No shit, Sherlock." I look up at him and notice my guffaw. "No pun intended."

"Can't you clean it up?" he asks.

I wince, gritting my teeth together. "I could, but I have this horrible gag reflex."

Jake takes off his hat and rakes his hands through his hair. Setting the cap back on his head, he walks past me into the small bathroom in the corner. He comes out with a wad of paper towels. "I think getting rid of it would be ideal."

I stop him, though. "I have these production charts to fill out. Am I supposed to count the mutilated one?"

"Trash it." He sweeps the messy disgust into the towel and wipes at the belt.

My natural reflex is to retch. I try to think of something pleasant. *Puppies and kitten scampering, waves crashing on the beach, Jake and me frolicking together....*

"Thanks for doing that," I manage to get out.

"I helped Stella on occasion."

"I thought you said you didn't 'do' the chicken houses."

He cranes his neck and smiles at me. "Stella was a lot older than you. She needed a hand every now and then."

I put my hands on my hips. "Hey, I need the help, too. I've got to get this operating into some semblance of a successful entity so I can get back to Boston."

"You're that eager to get out of here?"

I screw up my face. "Well, yeah... I mean, sort of."

He shakes his head. "This is a good place to be to sort things out."

He says it like that's exactly what he's been doing.

"Seriously, I could turn this business over to you," I tell him.

"Right," he says, rolling his eyes.

I swat at him playfully. Jake dumps the used towels in the large trashcan and advances on me. "You wanna start a fight?"

I giggle nervously and retreat into the corner, the plywood wall against my back. Jake takes both of my wrists in his large hand and holds them over my head. His eyes shine with mischievousness and a low laugh burbles from him as he tickles my ribs with his free hand. I squirm and semifight, but I have to admit I'm terribly turned on. My legs turn liquid, as does my womanly center. I swear, I'm going to orgasm just from his touch and tickling. I'm one big ball of hormones that's about to explode like a dormant volcano.

"Jake! Stop!"

He keeps tickling me, though. God, he's enjoying this. Just like a guy needing to be in control. I'm loving it too, squirming away, yet still somehow managing to brush my breasts against his chest.

A low groan escapes his throat and I know I'm getting to him. He doesn't stop, though, Mr. Can't Get Involved. Oh, he's involved right now.

"You're killing me, Jake," I say through uncontrollable laughter.

His face is close; his eyes are alive. "You started this, Miss Thing."

If I don't get away soon, I'm going to literally jump on him. I break my hands out of his grip and run toward the open door, screaming and laughing. Jake's right on my heels like a sixth grade boy trying to pop my bra. I bolt in the direction of the other house for refuge.

"What's going on here?" Jimmie's voice barks out.

Jake and I stumble to a halt like two cartoon characters, crashing together with him slamming into my back. He steadies himself by grabbing my arms and then drops all contact.

"I was just trying to help Isabella out, Jimmie."

I twist around and see that Jake is actually embarrassed. Look at that blush! He takes his cap off and turns it around, the white-stitched NY logo now in the front.

"Stupid Yank-mes fan," I tease.

Jake rolls his eyes. "Don't tell me you're a Red Sox fan."

I couldn't care less, (I'm a football fan, quite frankly) but the fact that it keeps the banter going is all that matters. For the first time in a long time, I'm actually enjoying being me. Flirting and having fun and acting carefree. I've been so tense lately with my hours and the pressures from Claudia and always having to be Ms. Professional that I've almost forgotten what it's like to let loose. Jake brings this out in me, and dammit, I like it.

Jimmie spits to the ground. "Y'all act like you're in heat. There's too much work do."

Oh. My. God.

My cheeks burst into flames.

I can't believe Jimmie just said that.

I need to get serious. Getting reprimanded by Jimmie isn't on my agenda of "things to do." Although Jake is quickly inching up on the list.

Jake scuffs his foot in the dirt path. "I probably need to get back to work. You all set here, Isabella?"

"Yeah, thanks for cleaning up that nastiness, Jake."

"Whoa there, Jake." Jimmie stops him with a hand on his shoulder. "I need you to take Isabella up yonder to the house."

"Why's that?" I ask.

"Floreen Potter done told me she's coming over to see you in a little bit."

I put my hands on my hips and I know I've got a scowl on my face. "What the hell is a Floreen Potter?"

Jimmie screws up his nose and his eyes drill into mine like I've said something really awful. "Floreen's the head of the Pie Ministry at First Baptist. She's coming out to welcome you to Dilligus Flats."

"Oh," I say, feeling like an ass. "What's the Pie Ministry?"

Jimmie scratches at his graying curls. "The church members get together and bake pies for people in need. The sickly. The needy. And they do it as a gesture of friendship, too. They know you're here 'cause of Stella's death and they's just reaching out to you."

I wring my hands. "That's... umm... sweet."

"So Jake here'll take you back up to the house. Right Jake?"

He lifts his head and says, "Sure. Whatever you need, Jimmie."

"Much obliged." Jimmie steps aside and heads into the first house. Then, he sticks his head back out. "I'll walk the houses and weed out any dead birds I find."

I cringe. "Why would we have dead birds?"

"Lots of fighting and cannibalism, you know. Survival of the fittest in these here houses. We take the carcasses and throw them back in the incinerator."

"Oh, that big black thing out back." I was wondering what that was. Looks like a gas tank.

"World's largest barbecue," Jimmie says with a laugh.

Trying not to think of bird cremation, I follow Jake to his bike that's parked at the end of the long row of chicken houses and wonder what in the world he's even doing here. I thought he'd come looking for Jimmie. He certainly didn't act like he needed him for anything urgent. My skin tingles at the thought that he actually came out here to check on me.

"Hop on," he instructs.

There aren't any helmets, but it's not like we're going out on the highway, throttling down, and running the chance of spilling our brains.

"Where should I hold on?" I ask tentatively, knowing damn well where I'm *supposed* to hold on.

He tosses a look at me over his shoulder and smiles. "Anywhere you'd like."

CHAPTER FIFTEEN

O*kay, Mr. Beefcake.*
Make me an offer like that; I'm not going to be shy. I may be stale in the sex department, but I still know how everything works. I slide my hands around Jake's sides and across his rock-hard stomach. I hear a sharp intake of air from him. He leans into me, his back brushing against my nipples. They've perked to attention at the mere encounter of his body. I haven't been out of circulation so long that I don't get that there's major flirtation going on here.

So much for not getting involved. I'd say we're about to dive into the deep end. And me with no life jacket.

Of course, it could simply be the fact that I'm the only person near his age who he can hang and have fun with. I'll quit over-analyzing and hold onto him for dear life. Pressing my hips against his legs, I'm snug against his ass as he cranks the bike and takes off.

"Hold on!"

As we bump along the weaving groove in the pecan orchard that was etched out by former herds of cows, I luxuriate in the feel of Jake's warm back pressed into my chest. I feel a little dirty straddled behind him, pressing my you-know-what into his butt, but hey, it's a bike and these are close quarters. Might as well entertain my raging hormones while I've got the opportunity.

My fingers grip his sturdy and turgid muscles around his waist. I try not to let my hands explore the sensation of his skin just underneath his thin shirt. My thighs ache at the intense contact with his firm legs. My womb screams out to be touched with each bump of the bike.

My libido hasn't been this heightened in… a long time.

That has to be what this is. I can't honestly be interested in someone I've only known a week, especially coming out of a serious two-year relationship. My friend, Marina Baye, texted me that the rule for mourning a breakup is exactly half the time of the total liaison. I don't have a year to grieve Rick, though. I refuse to suffer through a period of silence and chastity. That was the last five months with Rick.

In any event, I press my breasts into Jake's back again—due more to the mound of dirt he just hit than a come on—and I swear I hear him groan. If he keeps this up, we're either going to end up in the barn, rolling in the hay, or I'm going to need another cold shower. I'm almost ashamed at how sexually on I am right now. I blame those damn tight jeans of his.

But my farm fantasy ends when we pull up in front of the house and a stick-figure old woman with fresh from the beauty salon hair-helmet and thick black glasses steps out of a Lincoln Town Car.

Well, hello Miss Daisy.

"You must be Isabella," the woman sings out to me.

I swing my leg off of the bike and walk over toward the woman with the obvious display of Southern hospitality. She extends a gloved hand to me while simultaneously throwing a dirty look Jake's way. He doesn't seem to notice it as he pulls his bike around the back to his trailer.

I smile and take Floreen's hand. "Yes, I'm Isabella. Nice to meet you, Mrs. Potter. Jimmie told me to expect you."

"Poor James," she says with a sigh. "I don't know how he copes with all of this tragedy in his life."

I squint at her, not understanding what she means.

Mrs. Potter stares at me mouth agape. "You're the spitting image of her."

"Excuse me?"

She clears her throat in a tiny, pay-no-attention-to-me manner. "Stella. The resemblance is uncanny. Then again, it seems you have more things in common than your looks." She cranes her neck around to look to the back of the house in obvious reference to Jake.

I furrow my brow. "What do you mean?"

Floreen clutches the Reynolds Wrapped pie closer to her person and lowers her voice, looking around like someone's going to catch her gossiping. "Everyone knew Stella and that biker had something illicit going on here. A woman her age consorting with a younger man. It's just not right."

And now she assumes I've picked up where Stella left off.

Honestly. Is this what people in this tiny town think? I bite my lip, trying not to imagine this. Trying not to let the idle gossip be true. "Why don't we go into the house?" I say more than ask, pointing the way.

Floreen follows me into the first room on the right—the parlor—and takes a seat on the burgundy Victorian couch. Good, because it's hard as a rock and it will be a pain to sit on. Therefore, hopefully cutting Floreen Potter's visit short.

I take the pie from her and tug at the foil to check it out. I'll admit it smells heavenly with sugary goodness, tangy nuts, and swirling spices. The buttery aroma from the crust makes my mouth water in a Pavlovian response.

She picks off her old lady white gloves and crosses them in her lap. "It's the Pie Ministry's duty to make sure everyone in the community feels welcomed."

"I appreciate it. This looks amazing." I really don't need to eat it all myself. "Would you like a piece?"

"No, dear," she says. "You save it and have it with your... *friend* back there." She says the word as if it's a curse.

I ignore the comment about Jake. It's not any of this old biddy's business what is or isn't going on with Jake and me. Or for that matter, Jake and Aunt Stella. Still, the thought of them together makes my pulse pound. It doesn't help matters that the entire town thinks they were banging each other. People need to get their own life and leave others alone.

I place the pie on the marble coffee table and take the gold brocade lady's chair in the corner. I wonder how long I have to entertain this woman to make the Pie Ministry visit long enough to be sociable, but short enough so I can get back to my day.

"So... were you and Aunt Stella close?"

Floreen's thin lips flatten out even further. "We were in the same church congregation, although I rarely saw her. Stella wasn't as... *godly* as some people in Dilligus Flats."

"Oh." Judgmental old crow. I bet Stella could have kicked this stick figure's ass with one hand tied behind her back. I grind my teeth, but sit here politely, smiling at her words.

Floreen rises and walks across the parlor to the door. She peers across the front hall into Stella's bedroom. "I see you haven't attended to her things yet."

"Well, no. There hasn't been time with the new chickens and taking care of the farm." Not that I need to explain myself to this stranger so she can report back to the rest of First Baptist.

Turning back, Floreen says, "I could help, if you'd like. There are several charities the church works with. We'd be happy to take donated items."

I stand and nab the pie. "I'm sure I can do it on my own. In fact, I was planning on working on it tomorrow before I have to leave."

Her brow lifts. "Oh? You're not staying?"

"Well, no. I have a life and a job back in Boston."

Floreen nods and treats me to a slight grin.

I want her out of here. I don't like the way her eyes are shifting around, sizing up Stella's belongings like she has a right to them. Judgment is oozing from her pores. Not only of me and what I have or haven't done, but also of Aunt Stella, her way of life. And Jake, too. I don't want to think that this rumor is true even though I'd foolishly suspected it myself. I'd initially ruled it out, but it would certainly explain the carefree way Jake moves around Stella's house. Like he's part of it, too.

I can't fathom this. I want to be away from this woman who smells of dime store pressed powder.

"Thanks so much for the pie, Mrs. Potter. But you know, I really have to get back to work at the chicken houses. Those eggs don't pick themselves up." I laugh nervously.

"Not exactly the type of work for a refined young lady."

I shrug. "We do what we have to do."

Floreen returns to the couch for her wicker pocket book and gloves. "I understand, dear. You call me if there's anything I can help with." We're almost to the front door when she turns back. "You know, we have a singles social every Thursday after Bible study. There are several eligible young men that might tickle your fancy. Unlike that man who lives here."

I hustle her out the door. "Thanks for your concern. I assure you, I'm not interested in men. Thanks though."

Her mouth drops open. "Oh dear, you're not a—" She looks around as if to see if anyone is listening or watching and then she whispers, "—a lesbian?"

"God no," I blurt out. I don't understand why I have to indulge this busy-body. "I just got out of a serious relationship. I appreciate the invitation all the same. So nice to meet you."

Floreen's mouth is open to say something, but I shut the door between us.

I listen for a moment until I hear her car crank, and slump in relief against the door.

"Thank God that's over."

I trod into the kitchen and set the pie on the counter. The sweet aroma wafts over to me and my hunger gets the best of me. I slip to the sink to wash my hands. Then, I grab a knife from the drawer. Dessert is always a good diversion for troublesome thoughts. I slice into the gooey pecan pie and plop a healthy serving onto a plate. I have never actually had pecan pie. My mother was never big on feeding us sweets other than Jell-O. If this pie tastes anything like it smells... As I rummage for a fork, I hear the back door open and slam shut.

"What did The Mouth of the South have to say?" Jake asks, bursting into the room. He goes to the fridge and pulls out a bottle of cold water like it's his kitchen.

I watch him move around the space in comfortable familiarity. Could what Floreen suggested be true? Aunt Stella had a boy toy in Jake Hansen. Now everyone in Dilligus Flats thinks the great niece that looks like her is taking her place.

I don't take an old woman's sloppy seconds.

I stab the pie with my fork, pecan pieces breaking apart as I cram the sugary treat into my mouth.

Jake stares at me. "Are you mad? What's wrong?"

I've never been good at playing games or hiding my emotions. I'm sure my irritation shows.

I chew and swallow. "Floreen had plenty to say. Mostly about you."

He reaches for the pie knife. "Oh yeah?"

"You... and Stella."

He throws his head back, tossing his hair in the process. "Not that? Unbelievable!"

"So, it's not true?" I prod and take another bite to shove aside my unjustified irritation. Or maybe that tickling sensation in my throat is coming from something else.

Jake places both hands on the counter and leans forward. "You don't honestly believe the gossip of that crazy old woman, do you?"

My eyes must give away my doubts.

"Come on, Isabella. Not you, too?"

I step back, unsure how to proceed. My throat is killing me all of a sudden and my lips feel like they're swelling up, as though I've had a collagen injection gone bad. Swallowing hard, I muster up the words. "What am I supposed to think, Jake? Look at you. You shower here, you walk around the kitchen like it's yours and you..." The dryness in my throat cripples me and I break into racking coughs. My lips hurt like hell.

"Are you okay?" he asks in a gentleness I don't deserve.

"I... I... I can't breathe..." I eke out. My voice is squashed. It sounds like it's in the next county. My hands tremble terribly and I want to douse the fire in my throat with at least six gallons of water.

"Jesus, Isabella, your lips are huge. And your voice—"

"Jake, help," I squeak and gasp for a breath. "Something's wrong."

He looks at my plate. "It's the pie. You must be allergic to something in it."

I reach up and feel my lips; they're huge. Tears stream from my eyes as I try to get a good breath. It's not coming. I grip my hands to my throat as I gag on nothing.

No air seems to be getting in.

My throat is swollen shut.

"I... I..."

Without hesitation, Jake grabs the truck keys and pulls me along behind him. "The hell with this! We're going to the hospital."

CHAPTER SIXTEEN

"This is the *most embarrassing* thing ever," I whine as I sit in the emergency room with my head in my hands. My voice is almost non-existent and my breathing is labored.

Jake rubs the back of my neck with his strong hand. "Just don't talk, Isabella. They'll get you back in just a bit."

I struggle to get a good breath and don't know whether it's from the allergic attack on my body or having Jake's touch against my skin. In either case, my heart palpitations threaten to overtake me.

"Stupid Pie Ministry and their poisonous desserts," I say barely above a whisper.

Jake fusses at me. "Don't. Talk."

"Isabella Perry?" a nurse calls out.

Finally. If my throat closes up anymore, they're going to have to administer CPR on me. Jake curls his palm around my elbow and guides me back through the double doors into the examining room. Thank God Dilligus Flats was in driving distance—a fifteen mile radius that Jake made in about eight minutes flat—of a hospital. Edgeland Regional Medical Center.

"Have a seat right there, sweetie. The doctor'll be back to take a look at you in just a sec," the nurse says to me. She's wearing "Hello Kitty" scrubs, so it's hard to take anything she says seriously.

Lying back on the hospital bed, I flail my head against the pillow. If Vanessa or William could see me now, they'd shake their heads and laugh. "That Griz. She's the poster child for 'Shit Happens.'"

Yeah, well… whatever.

Part of me thinks Floreen Potter purposely poisoned me to get me out of the picture so she could abscond away with all of Stella's personal treasures. Over my dead—a possibility—body.

Jake hitches his hip up onto the edge of my bed. "Breathe slowly," he instructs.

"You act like you've done this before," I eke out.

He puts his index finger to his lips. "Shhh. I had to handle a lot of situations as a cop. Believe me, I've seen everything.

I have ten-thousand questions I want to ask him about his days in uniform, as well as being undercover. Why would someone as young as him walk away from the police force? I can't coordinate the thoughts of my interrogation right now. Not as long as it seems as though I might choke on the size of my tongue.

The curtain slides aside and in walks the doctor. "So, what do we have here?"

"I had a—" I try to get out.

Jake stops me with his hand on my thigh. I freeze and stop talking, not because he'll do a better job at explaining. Rather, the feel of his warm touch on my leg lights all sorts of fires in my loins. Does he have any idea how crazy he makes my body?

"She ate some pecan pie and immediately began experiencing a swollen throat, protruding lips, and difficulty in breathing."

The doctor clicks the end of his pen. Once. Twice. Fifteen times.

Please stop!

"Sounds like you've got a nut allergy," the doctor says. "You're experiencing anaphylactic shock."

"Anna who?" I ask.

Jake rolls his eyes at me. "They haven't given her anything since we've been here."

"I'll be right back," the doctor says and then disappears through the curtain.

"What's going on?" I beg.

Jake's eyes are soft, a more vivid blue than ever before as he explains. "You're allergic to nuts. The pecans had an adverse effect on you, so he's going to get you an adrenalin shot."

"But I eat peanuts all the time," I say through my cracked voice and thin breathing.

"Peanuts are legumes," Jake tells me. When my brows furrow, he continues. "They're beans. They grow on a vine underground. You're obviously allergic to tree nuts."

I close my eyes and rub my head. Fighting for a good breath, I say, "That's the most ridiculous allergy I've ever heard of."

Certainly it would afflict *me*. Why the hell not? The gods must be saying, "Look at Griz down there. She hasn't had enough shit happen to her lately. Let's give her some jackass allergy and embarrass her in front of a cute guy."

The doctor comes back into the examining room with the nurse in tow and a large needle in his hand. "I'm going to give you a prescription for an Epi-pen. You should have one on you at all times now moving forward so this doesn't happen again. It's not something to mess with our take lightly."

I nod in agreement.

"Belinda will take care of you and get you a shot. Just lie there for a little bit while the medicine works its way into you."

The doctor turns to leave and Jake thanks him, shaking his hand.

"Okay, now sugar," Belinda says to me. "Let's get those jeans off of you."

"What? I… umm…" I stutter as my eyes shift to Jake.

"Oh, he's your boyfriend, honey. He won't care."

Jake snickers and doesn't do anything to correct the nurse. Instead, he crosses his arms over his chest and stands at the end of my bed while Belinda tugs at my jeans. I feel too horrible, repertorily challenged, and swollen to fight, so I let the nurse slide my pants down around my knees.

"Stand up, hon."

I do as she tells me, leaning next to the bed.

Immediately, Jake's eyes are on me, checking me out in my undressed state. A smirk covers his face, making his eyes sparkle naughtily. Then he starts laughing when he takes in my choice of underwear. I glance down, not remembering what I had put on this morning before setting out to the chicken houses. Now, I feel my face turn ten shades of red as both Jake and the nurse snicker at my boyshort panties.

"Well aren't those cute," the nurse sings out.

"They sure are," Jake says with an evil grin.

My hot pink underwear is not only an obnoxious color, but across the butt it reads "Party With Me" in black shimmery lettering.

When my eyes sync with Jake's, he smiles and says, "I'll party with you any day, baby," and winks.

This is so not the time to tease me.

"Okay, sugar. This'll be a little prick."

That comment cracks my resolve and I giggle a bit before Belinda jabs the Epi-pen into the top of my thigh.

"Oww "

"Give it a sec, hon," she says. "You can lie back."

I tug my jeans back up, covering up my fuchsia undies and scoot back up on the bed. Immediately, I feel the adrenalin coursing through my veins, fighting off the stupid pecan pie that tried to stop me.

Nothing will stop me, though. Not a manipulated business contract, not a whole flock-load of chickens, not Claudia and her terse texts I've been ignoring. And certainly not Rick.

I'm not mourning the loss of that relationship anymore.

Maybe that's it. As I lay here on the table with the medicine twisting through my veins, I rewind my relationship with Rick and realize that although we claimed to love each other and had gotten used to being together, I barely knew him. Sure, I was psyching myself up for a marriage proposal that never came because I wanted to get on to the next natural stage in my life. It's apparent now that Rick didn't get me since he broke up with me so easily, so swiftly in a rip off the Band-Aid way.

Well, screw him.

My pulse trills away underneath my skin. My heartbeat picks up as the adrenalin begins to course through me. I'm psyched. I'm jazzed. I'm encouraged. "You know, Jake, I'm tired of all the stupidity. I'm going to get on with my life. I'm still young. I have the future ahead of me. I don't have to live by anyone's rules but my own."

"Good for you," he says, obviously appeasing me.

I reach out for his hand and lace my fingers into his, squeezing a bit. He smiles down at me and lets me play with his hand. I sense hesitation from him. I know he's interested in me. I mean, I haven't been out of the game so long that I don't get when a guy is attracted. Jake oozes sexuality from every fiber of his being. Yet, he also has a "Do Not Disturb" sign hung dead center on his chest. He has to understand how dead-sexy he is. How hot he can make a woman. How hot he can make me. I'm not a damn nun. I have every right to have sexual wants and desires. I don't need permission from anyone. Not Vanessa, not William, and not Claudia Coldren, the Boss from Hell.

My flight leaves in the morning. Back to Boston. Returning to the rat race. The commute on the T smashed against people I don't know and may never see again. The long hours in my cube with little to no sunlight, nary a potty break, or nutritional recharging. Once more into the breach of corporate wage slave world, not marching to my own drum, but serving a thankless ladder climber who's sleeping her way to the top.

Maybe it's the adrenalin shot doing the thinking for me, but I know what I have to do. The responsibilities I must see through. The man I need to get to know better whether he wants me to or not.

I look over at said man and try to find the words through the pounding of my heart. "I can't leave yet, Jake. Things are still up in the air. There's no one to do the everyday work but me. Stella entrusted me with her farm, her business, her legacy. I can't let her down."

He bobs his head. "None of us should."

His thumb moves up and down the outside of my hand, stroking my pinkie ever so slightly. Just enough to make me squirm in my "Party With Me" panties.

"My boss is going to go ape shit," I say.

"You have to do what you have to do, Isabella."

He's right. I need to focus on getting the farm up to speed, selling it off, contract and all. I have the vacation time and this is, technically, family leave. Claudia will have to deal. It's what I have to do. Then, I'll head home and stand witness for Vanessa and Kyle as they get on with their lives. Everything will work itself out.

Jake and I sit in silence for about fifteen minutes as my body races high, high, high on the adrenalin, and then I begin to crash, hard. Exhausted from internal roller coaster ride, I let my eyes flutter shut and let out a long breath.

"You won't leave me, will you, Jake?"

He answers with a sigh of his own. The man has an internal war that's raging that he won't let me in on. Yet, I ask for nothing other than his help, his support, and his presence. When the time is right, he'll let me in and tell me everything there is to know about Jake Hansen.

"I'll do what I can, Isabella."

As the adrenalin rush subsides, I let myself drift off to sleep. I've got everything covered. My new motto is to 'take care of number one.'" That would be me.

And if that means lusting after a certain hunky handyman, then so be it.

CHAPTER SEVENTEEN

"You're *what?* Absolutely not. I won't allow it!" my boss screams into my cell phone Sunday afternoon when I called to ask to take my additional week of vacation. "While you lollygag about doing *whatever* it is you're doing in Alabama, I have to triage the mess of unfinished web pages and graphic files you left behind."

My hand shakes as I hold the cell phone to my ear, but I muster up some backbone. "Claudia, I wouldn't exactly call what I'm doing 'lollygagging.' I'm having to run the operation of the chicken houses and—"

"Give me a break, Isabella! How long does it take to mourn a dead relative and then get back to your responsibilities?" Claudia snaps at me.

I've always known Claudia Coldren was a cold-hearted bitch. She just proved it, though.

"Look, Claudia, there are things I have to take care of and I just need a little more time. I have the vacation time coming to me, so I'm not asking for anything out of the ordinary."

"Like hell you're not! Two weeks out of the office right before a product launch is tantamount to career suicide. I'm warning you, Isabella. Get back here," she says in no uncertain terms. Then, I hear her pull the phone down to talk to her daughter. "You're mighty precious, Hayden.

Mommy loves you so much, my perfect little princess. No…
no… don't put Mommy's Rolex in the sink. No! Hayden!"

Inwardly I praise the seven year spoiled Beacon Hill brat
who I have to hear about ad nauseum every day at work.
Right now, the kid is my hero.

"Claudia, I have to go," I say, trying to get the woman's
attention again.

She turns her ire back to me. "Listen, you get this personal bullshit taken care of and get back here. You're not
the only graphic designer in Boston. Don't make me take a
rash course of action."

I stand tall in the kitchen and thump my hand on the
counter. "Are you threatening me, Claudia? Because our
CEO, Don Pyler has said time and time again that 'family
comes first.' I'm trying to do just that while working within
my vacation time allotment." A sharp pain dives from my
stomach down to my intestines ending up in a twisted knot
of stress. I'm not trying to be a rebel. I'm just trying to be
responsible.

"Hayden! No! Not Mommy's new Kate Spade clutch!
Bring it to me," she growls. Then to me, says, "Keep me
posted."

With a singular click, the phone call is over.

My breathing is labored and I think my left eye is twitch-
ing over Claudia's every worrying word. She's never been
particularly nice to me, but just now, she was downright
asshole-ish. Monday, I'll call the HR lady and let her know
what's going on and head off Claudia's tirade.

Stella entrusted her world to me and I see it through.

I owe it to her.

And to myself.

⚜ ⚜ ⚜

I pour all my energies into the egg operation, soaking up as much information from Jimmie as possible. Things are going well and the chickens are producing according to schedule. By Tuesday, we're up to over eight hundred eggs a day per house. And considering we get paid like twenty-five cents a dozen, the more the merrier.

On Wednesday afternoon, after I run the belts twice, clean a multitude of shit off the eggs, and store the full trays on the metal push cart in the cooler, I decide to start tackling the chore of cleaning out Stella's house. Jimmie offers to help, but there seems to be a distant pain behind his eyes.

"Everything okay, Jimmie?" I ask when I see him dab his eyes with his handkerchief.

"Just some dust making my eyes water," he says, obviously lying.

What *is* it with these new men in my life who won't just come clean with what's churning and boiling inside of them? Geesh!

We start in the den and work through stacks of *Life* magazines that are damn near collectibles. Stella also had a large supply of Vogue patterns stored in a wicker basket. Tres chic The designs date back to the 50s and 60s. I decide to save these and send them home to myself. I can definitely do something with them, like sell them on eBay for a healthy profit.

"Jimmie, I'm going to hit the bedroom next."

He screws up his face as he takes his John Deere cap off his head and scratches his scalp.

"What?" I ask with my hands on my hips.

"I probably shouldn't go in there. That was her... private space."

"Oh, Jimmie, come on. You and Stella were friends for years."

"I don't know if I should," he says, suddenly shy and I wonder if this man has ever been in a woman's bedroom.

He hangs his head low, but follows me to the front of the house. He sits carefully in the rocking chair in the corner and watches as I attack Aunt Stella's drawers. Literally. Talk about granny panties. There are a ton of them. Definitely boxing those up for the charity Floreen Potter mentioned.

Jimmie rocks stoically, like his mind has gone to another place. I don't bother him, but go straight to the expansive armoire against the back wall.

"Look at all of this!"

I can't believe what I see when I open the doors. Stylish, fashionable, damn near couture clothes hanging in the cedar closet. "Aunt Stella was a fashionista."

"She liked to sew," Jimmie tells me.

My eyes widen. "*She* made all of these?"

"Yeah," he says wistfully. "She sold her old Singer sewing machine a couple of years back when the bills started piling up. Got a good chunk of change for it."

I pull out this one dress that is a breath away from amazing. There's a hand-stitched label in it. *Pierre Cardin for Vogue* with the pattern number written in. Classic, sleeveless mod A-line dress with jewel neckline, gray with black trim. I hold it up against me, the thick fabric coming just above my knees.

"This is amazing. I have to try this on."

Jimmie acts like he's going to get up, but I disappear behind a dressing screen in the corner by the armoire. Besides, I need an audience for my vintage fashion show. Oh, I wish I had my knee-high black boots that are back in Boston.

I twirl around like a go-go dancer, loving the look of this get-up and feeling like it so matches my personality.

"Don't you look all fancy," Jimmie says with a slight smile. I can see that I'm entertaining him.

Plunging back into the closet, I pull out a light, black dress with a tag "Couturier Design Jean Muir Capped Sleeve Evening Dress Vogue Pattern #2883" on it.

As I pull the A-line off and toss it over the screen, I call out to Jimmie. "Did Stella get paid to make these?"

He signs heavily. "No, it was her true love. Her life."

"How so?" The capped sleeve dress fits perfectly on my size eight body. It's like Stella made this dress especially for me.

Jimmie gazes out the sheer curtained window. "Stella had a whole other life away from Dilligus Flats."

I stop admiring my fashion finds and sit on the trunk at the edge of her bed. With all the madness surrounding me, the farm and the chickens, I've barely had time to learn anything about my benefactor. "Tell me about her, Jimmie."

He pauses for a moment, as if conjuring up the memories of his good friend. "She grew up here in Dilligus Flats. I remember her in grade school. Skinny, long legs. Lots of freckles," he says almost wistfully.

Hmmm, sounds like he's describing me at age twelve.

He continues. "She always longed to get away from here. Dreamed of New York City. Fashion. It consumed her. She'd sew anything she could get her hands on. Staked out at the Five and Dime and bought all them there patterns she could. Made this whole fancy wardrobe from designers you've probably heard of. Back then, they put them labels in the pattern packages so you could sew them into your clothes and make it seem like you done bought it at a fancy store."

Apparently so. I stand and thumb through the assortment of pantsuits, party dresses, church attire, and casual wear. Calvin Klein, Pierre Cardin, Christian Dior, Sybil Connolly, Jean Muir, Oscar de la Renta. Sure, I've heard of most of them. These finished products hanging in front of me could have been fashioned by the original designers themselves.

I turn back to Jimmie, fingering the ribbon trailing from the black dress I'm wearing. "So, she worked in fashion. I think that's so cool."

"She was only in New York City 'bout three years. Couldn't really get her designs bought. She worked on Broadway as a seamstress, making other people's designs. She said it was great, but I know she wanted to break out on her own."

"How old was she when she did this?"

He lifts his hat and rubs at the thick curls on his head. "Oh, I don't know. I reckon she was twenty or so at the time. I remember the day she left. July 28, 1965."

I wonder if he remembers the hour and minute, too.

Suddenly Aunt Stella seems very cool. A young and ambitious woman setting off to take Manhattan by storm. It's brave to leave everything you'd ever known to pursue your dream.

Of course, I did that when I left Chicago. Maybe Aunt Stella and I are two affiliated souls, after all.

Jimmie seems lost in memories. His eyes shift about the room and I see a soft smile paint his face.

"You liked her, didn't you," I say more than ask.

He chuckles. "Oh hell, you couldn't help but like Stella. She was so full of life. Never sat still."

I select a Bill Blass pink jacket and skirt set and return to the dressing area. "So, she came back to Dilligus Flats in 1968?" A very tumultuous year in American history. Probably for Stella, too, having to walk away from her dream.

"Yep," he says. "Cost of living in New York was too much for her even back then. Money was tight and her career wasn't taking off like she'd planned. So she come home." His voice mutters the last sentence as though it's a curse.

I button the jacket and step out to show Jimmie. He applauds approvingly.

"What happened then?" I ask.

"Well, as you can imagine folks didn't take too kindly to her coming back. Most of her family done moved by that time—up yonder towards the Carolinas and some even venturing up north. Town folk, they saw Stella as some sort of deserter. A traitor."

"Dear God, that's so stupid." I whip the jacket off and toss it to the bed.

"Funny, she had a saying for this town. For the name." He laughs as he remembers.

"What's that?"

"She said Dilligus stood for 'Do I Look Like I Give Uh Shit?'"

I bust out laughing. Aunt Stella sure was a tart. "People here obviously didn't get her. Or appreciate her."

"Aww, Stella didn't mind none. She wasn't trying to prove nothing to no one except herself. She'd saved some money from her job and got enough of a loan to buy this here farm. She figured living out of the city limits would give her distance from the people judging her."

"Which I'm sure they did," I interject. I pull out a yellow and orange flowery Oscar sundress that flutters to my knee. This would be the perfect dress to wear in Kyle and Vanessa's wedding, if they weren't doing the all-white thing. I take the dress and try it on anyway.

"Well, Old Hardwick showed them all. For a long time, this farm was quite the success. She had beef cattle for years, then Brahman bulls that people done fell over themselves buying."

"What's a Brahman bull?"

Jimmie hunches over in the rocker to demonstrate. "Big old suckers. Grey and white with humps on their backs. Ugly things. She used to show them in the county fair. I bet you'll find the ribbons around here somewheres."

I shake my head. Aunt Stella keeps getting more and more interesting. A pang in my chest tells me that I missed out on meeting a very special relative. I bet she and I would have had a lot of fun going drinking together.

Jimmie keeps talking. "Anyways, she done had pigs and cows and peanuts growing across the road. She rented the back field out for corn and people used to pay her to fish catfish out of the lake. She done good."

"Until?" I can't help but ask.

"Until them durn chicken houses. She got suckered into the contract and it drained her capital." He scratches his face, pulling his hands up and down. Then he moves to his ear and twirls his pinkie around inside like a Q-Tip.

"Well, it sounds like Stella stood her ground. Made a life for herself and did what she wanted to do. That's to be admired," I say. Then I wonder more about Stella and her path in life. "Why didn't she ever get married? Surely a husband could have helped with the load here on the farm?"

Jimmie coughs to cover up an emotional blip. "Y'all excuse me. Nature calls." He stands and moves past me. Something I said? I hear the bathroom door close and the water begin to run. Oh, okay. Maybe he had to go.

I look over on the wall to a portrait of Aunt Stella as a young woman. The resemblance to me is eerie, but it's also comforting. She was a strong woman, bold, and courageous. She didn't care what people thought. She did what was best for Stella. My eyes sync up with the ones in the black and white photo and I feel her smile radiating out at me. She cared enough to leave me all of her worldly belongings. My heart lurches in my chest and I feel a bit—*what's the Yiddish term?*—verklempt. I wave my hands in front of my eyes to dissipate the mist and then turn back to the armoire. I'm supposed to be going through this stuff to give to charity, but damn if I'm not keeping half of these clothes for myself.

That's when I see it.

In the back.

In a tattered clear bag from the dry cleaners.

It's a delicious, creamy, white satin gown. I push the other clothing aside and reach far behind to nab this jewel. I hang it on the door of the cabinet so I can admire the workmanship. Or Stella-ship.

My pulse tap-dances away as I peel back the covering. Then I gasp.

CHAPTER EIGHTEEN

I t's a work of art. A masterpiece. A vintage gem.

I trail my fingers along the soft fabric, shaking ever so slightly at the marvel before me. The plunging neck, the sleeveless curves, the slim waist, the V dip in the back. The straight skirt hangs to a tea length and there's a smart overskirt with a tie-waist. Simply breathtaking! There's no designer tag on this one. No Simplicity, Butterick, or Vogue claim on the design. It has to be a Stella Hardwick original.

I strip the gown away from the lovely padded satin hanger and nearly fly to the dressing screen. I shuck off the current outfit and drape this stunning garb over my body.

Please let it fit.

It does.

Like the proverbial glove.

I tie the overskirt around my waist, setting it just right on my hips. Speaking of gloves, I need them. They are, of course, in the top drawer of Stella's bureau, along with her hand-embroidered handkerchiefs. She was a lady after all.

Ah yes. Perfect. Classy.

I stand in front of the mirror, unblinking.

I am a vision in vintage satin.

This is totally the dress I'm going to wear in Kyle and Vanessa's wedding. It's unique, stylish, and so damn beautiful that I want to cry. I feel like a queen. I just need a tiara. I giggle at myself, wondering if Stella has one of them stashed anywhere in her room. I turn back to the mirror though and sip in air for fortification. Damn if I don't look absolutely, without a doubt, completely—

"Gorgeous," I hear from behind me.

I whirl around and meet his intense blue gaze. "Jake. I didn't hear you come in."

He swallows noticeably as he stares at me. "I was, umm, looking for Jimmie. I saw his, err, truck out front." He stops, takes a deep breath and presses into the room. "God, Isabella. You look amazing."

My face heats and I feel the blush all the way down to my bare feet. The rapid pounding of my pulse ticks away underneath the soft evening gloves, threatening to reveal the emotions I'm trying so hard to hide. Jake's face reads an immense emotional level that I've never seen before from him. Appreciation. Hunger. Wanting. The wall he's built between us crash lands in a pile of rubble at his feet as he moves into the room.

"You're… breathtaking," he says in a whisper. "And you do take my breath away."

Which is no easy feat, I realize after the short time we've spent together. Jake Hansen has been a hard nut to crack, but his tough-guy resolve is crumbling fast. At this moment, the tension is gone from his face. His stern jaw is more relaxed and his eyes have somehow softened. Under the badge of the cop lies a very real man. One that I want to know more. One I want to know me. In every way. When Jake lets out a long sigh, it has nothing to do with his usual frustration—or even Satan leaving him. It's one of a man who's content. Right now. In this moment, there's a fissure of the man he must have been before rolling into the country haven from whatever he's running from. There's a raw honest in his words and the way he's looking at me. Like he's peering into my soul. He's shown me his humor, his stubbornness, is protective nature, but finally, he's showing me his heart.

I'm at a loss of words. Rick complimented me this way. Hell, Rick never *looked* at me this way. I simply respond, "Thanks, Jake. Stella made this."

He walks toward me, slowly, meticulously. He's got this crazed look in his eyes, like a man who's gone without food too long. Or maybe without love. He's a mystery wrapped up in and enigma encased in denim and leather. I want to peel back those layers and get to the real man underneath. Not just the flesh and bone, but what's in his soul and what makes him tick.

The man who swore to protect and serve, yet he walked away from it. The man who says he can't do a relationship, yet something tells me he's been stung. The man who looks like liquid sex, yet has pushed away from me up until this very moment.

His blue eyes connect with mine and he reaches his hand out to touch my cheek. I tense up at first in a defensive manner, then relax at his gentle caress. Much like a whisper. Similar to a prayer. Perhaps one we've both sent up.

Unconsciously, I wet my lips, only to draw his attention to my mouth. Profound tension surrounds the two of us, pulling us toward each other in a tractor-beam of need. My body sings out for his and he seems to be listening. This dress is some sort of aphrodisiac. It has to be because I'm having a hard time breathing myself and if Jake touches me again, I'm going to completely lose it.

"Beautiful," he whispers a mere inch away from me.

Oh my God, he's going to kiss me.

My eyes flutter closed and I have to say what I'm thinking. "You've been so distant from me since I got here."

"I know. I'm sorry. It was best."

"Why?"

"I'm damaged, Isabella."

Eyes wide open now, I say, "We all are. It's called being human."

He trails his knuckles softly down my cheek and onto my neck, igniting a fiery path of heat.

"My damage runs deep," he says.

I want to know more. I want to heal him, help him. Later, perhaps. Right now, I want to feel and live. I had no idea that I'd merely been walking through the motions of life with Rick back in Boston. Get up, get dressed, go to work, meet up for dinner and time together, go our separate ways to our apartments. Day in. Day out. The proverbial rat on a wheel. It's not living. Not when your heart is withering away from the lack of touching, feeling, living, and loving. How did I not see this?

Rick actually did me a favor breaking up with me the way he did. Had he not, we may have gone on and on for years. We may have married, had kids, and then realized we were totally wrong for each other only to have a long, drawn-out, expensive divorce of who gets the kids for what holiday and who get the good China and wide-screen TV.

I realize, at this moment, with Jake Hansen in all of his manly glory, sexiness, and—finally—crack in his façade, that I am totally over Rick. Over.

And I want this man standing before me like nothing I've ever wanted before.

"Life is full of hurt, Jake. It's how you overcome it that makes you strong," I say, concentrating on his lips.

"It only sounds good when you say it," he says with a slight smile. "I'm no damn good for anyone. You should run away while you can."

Now it's my turn to chuckle. "I don't have my sneakers on."

Jake's smile grows larger. "Good, 'cause I'll be damned, I can't get you out of my every thought."

His words are like gut-punch of desire, nearly knocking me to my knees. Rick—nor any other guy—ever talked to me this way. I can't blink or breathe for fear of somehow waking up from this delicious dream.

Jake takes my hand; his head is down and his hair falls into his eyes. He raises my gloved fingers high and actually twirls me around. I laugh and do a little strutty-strutty for him.

"You look like a princess."

I tip my head back and toss my hair. "I feel like one."

He drops my hand and takes me by the shoulders—oh, the feel of his fingers on my skin—to have me face the mirror. In the reflection, I see the intensity in his eyes as they sweep over my body. I feel appreciated. Worshipped.

I'm afraid of what might happen next. What might *not* happen next. I'm riveted in place. Must think. Must react. What would William or Vanessa tell me to do?

Semper Fi... no, wait, that's not what I'm trying to think of, that's the Marines motto...

Carpe diem. Yeah, that's it. Seize the day.

I pivot around and face Jake. The crooked smile on his face makes my toes curl and my stomach do that turbulent, yet exhilarating, riding on a roller coaster sensation.

Speak. Think of something clever.

"I-I-I think I'll keep the dress," I say hoarsely.

"I think you should. It looks like it was made for you."

Our faces are so close that I can feel the wisps of breath from his words. Jesus, Mary, and St. Joseph, I want to kiss him. But I want him to kiss me first. I want him to want it more. I don't want to appear as starved for affection as I am.

Jake lifts his hand and sifts his fingers through my loose hair. A chill skittles up my back in a thousand zaps of electricity. I tilt my head to the left; he goes to the right. The angle. The move. The—

The bathroom door closes down the hallway and Jimmie starts to trod back to the front of the house.

I jump away from Jake when I hear the noise. I'd almost forgotten that Jimmie was still here, what with everything Jake filling my five senses.

"Jimmie might see us," I say in a pathetic whisper, like I've been caught doing something wrong.

Jake retreats from me. "Isabella, we should—"

I smooth my hands over the front of the dress and fiddle with the tie at my waist. "So, I wonder what Stella used this dress for." I comment, trying to gain my composure and settle my whacked out pulse. "Not like there are many cocktail parties in Dilligus Flats."

Jimmie gasps when he enters the room. "You shouldn't have that on, Isabella."

"Why not?" I ask, stroking the dress.

Emotion crackles around his every word. "It was her wedding dress."

I look down at the frock and back to Jimmie. "But you told me Stella never got married."

Jake pipes in. "Yeah, Stella told me she was an Old Maid her whole life."

Jimmie's jowls quiver slightly and he wrings his hands. He opens his mouth to speak, although nothing comes out at first. Then, his voice breaks slightly as he says, "She never did get married 'cause the day she left for New York, she left *me* at the altar."

With that, Jimmie bolts from the room, from the house.

I stand there in utter confuzzlement at this change of events.

Holy. Shit.

CHAPTER NINETEEN

"How the hell did I not know she almost married Jimmie?" I scream to Jake as he calmly baits the hook on his fishing pole. He'd thought it was best to whisk me away from Jimmie following the Great Wedding Dress Incident, so we came to the lake.

The moment between us not only passed, it was obliterated by Jimmie's reaction.

"That old dog. He never let on," Jake says with a cross between a scowl and a grin.

I mess with the strap of my overalls that I'd shoved back on after I abandoned Stella's wedding dress. I'd gone from total fashion chic to total farm geek. As I changed, I heard Jimmie making tracks in full retreat toward the chicken houses to be alone with the thoughts and emotions stirred up by the unintentional walk down memory lane. I hate thinking I upset him or that he's mad at me. It was never my plan to hurt him. I had no freakin' clue what that dress meant.

I can't help but feel like I did something horrible that has terribly scarred Jimmie.

"How *would* I have known? He never said a thing. Never let on," I rant on, ashamed of myself.

Jake passes over the baited fishing pole. "Hell, Stella never said anything to me all those times Jimmie was around. I can't believe I didn't pick up on things."

I cock my head sideways and roll the fishing pole in my hand. "What do you expect me to do with this?"

A soft laugh rumbles out of Jake. "Well, you're not going to joust with it." He takes a seat at the end of the rackety wooden pier and begins baiting another hook.

"Jake, you don't actually think I can fish, do you? I *order* fish; I don't catch it."

He shakes his head at me. "It'll calm you down."

"I'm not *un*calm," I scream out.

"Obviously not," Jake says with a smirk.

Okay, so maybe I'm more unsettled by Jimmie's proclamation than I think.

Jake squints up into the sun and pats the deck next to him. "Come on. Sit."

"It's too cold and windy to stay out here. Looks like rain, too."

"We're near the Gulf Coast. It always looks like rain. Come on."

I glance up at the ominous black cloud rolling in from the distance. It's been days since I've looked at a television or a weather report. We could be in for torrential rains for all I know. It's probably still hurricane season. But Jake seems determined to fish right now.

Fine. Whatever.

I kick off my worn Keds—that used to be white before I tracked through the red dirt of Southwest Alabama—and sit crissy-cross and barefooted next to him. I watch as he meticulously picks through the tackle box filled with a selection of hooks and lures with feathery flies attached to them. He chooses a bright yellow one and ties it to the end of the clear twine. So much concentration. So much effort. Just to catch a fish? I'm sure there's a seafood counter at the Piggly Wiggly in 'downtown' Dilligus Flats.

I blow out a breath, lifting my hair out of my eyes. I stare out over the shimmery blue green lake that somehow twinkles in what's left of the afternoon sunlight that's beaming through the gray clouds. The lake seems so full of life and nature's glory.

Then it hits me.

This belongs to me.

It shouldn't, though. It should belong to Jimmie. Jimmie... Stella's love. At least at some point in her life.

I face Jake. "Why do you think she left him at the altar?" I twist my fingers around a lock of hair. "You don't plan a wedding, make a gorgeous dress, invite friends and family, and not go through with it."

The tension in Jake's jaw is back and the vein pops out signaling his frustration or perhaps anger.

"Okay, you're not playing the brooding guy anymore. What's pissing you off?"

Jake shrugs. "I had this...friend in the force who got stood up at the last minute."

"That's terrible."

"It is what it is." Jake looks out over the lake and holds his finger up, as though he's testing the whirling wind. Then he returns his attention back to the pole across his lap.

"Weddings cost a fortune and there's so much pressure. I mean, back in Stella and Jimmie's day it wasn't like that, but still. There's the dress, the bridesmaids, the cake, the minister, a reception, presents to return, a honeymoon to cancel, refunds on—"

Jake snaps. "Yeah, I know!" This anger is more than a friend done wrong. It seems more... *personal.* "You know, I went through it with my buddy."

"Jake, are you talking about yourself? Is that why you ended up on your bike... her in Dilligus Flats, Alabama? Where God lost his shoes?"

He tugs on the fishing line and stares out into the distance. I'm right. I know I'm right. Whenever someone starts a story with "it happened to my friend," it's more than likely a cover-up for the real happenstance. I place my hand on Jake's arm and try to get him to open up.

"What happened? Why did she do it?" I ask.

He shakes his head again, probably to dislodge the raw memories. "It was what she wanted. She wanted to get married. Insisted on it. Told me all her friends were getting married and she was tired of waiting. That I needed to 'fish or cut bait.'" He casts off that moment for emphasis.

I, on the other hand, cringe all over hearing the nicer version of "shit or get off the pot."

"So you didn't want to get married?" I ask, hoping to prod him.

"I didn't know what I wanted. I was confused. Things happened. My plans on the force had changed. Melinda's an insistent woman. She wanted what other people wanted. A thirty-thousand dollar diamond, a wedding reception at The Plaza, and bragging rights with her girlfriends over who nabbed the best man."

"How did you fall in love with *that* kind of woman?" I cover my mouth with my hand, horrified that I asked this out loud.

"It's okay," Jake says. "I've asked myself the same question a million times. We met in college and both moved to New York. Climbing the corporate ladder in her financial firm hardened her. She wasn't the fun sorority girl I'd met sophomore year. We went through the motions for six years of dating. I can't blame her for wanting to know where it was going."

"So you proposed." I fiddle with the fishing pole next to me.

"We sort of proposed to each other," he says with a hitched laugh. "Things happened for me—at work—and I had to take administrative leave from my job. Melinda said I was distant and uninterested in the wedding. Maybe I was."

I want to ask what happened at work, but he'll tell me in his own due time. Instead, I provide the comforting shoulder and a listening ear since he's finally opened up to me.

He rocks back on lets out a long breath. "I showed up at the church, she didn't. I got to tell two hundred guests that the ceremony was off and they wouldn't be getting their steak and lobster dinner. After that, I just got on my bike and started riding."

Even though he laughs, I can still see the fresh pain in his eyes. What a bitch.

I flinch at the image of a tuxedoed Jake standing there waiting for a bride who never came. It must have been awkward as ass for the guests, as well. I've always wondered what it would be like to go to a wedding where something *happens*. Where chaos ensues. Or shit hits the fan. One of my sorority sisters from Clemson passed out cold from stress and nerves in the middle of her vows. I missed it because Claudia wouldn't give me the time off work.

Typical.

"Where's Melinda now?" I press Jake.

"Still in New York. Still being the social queen of Park Avenue, I'm sure."

"I can't believe she did that to you," I say sadly.

Jake levels his blue gaze on me. "If someone is getting married for the wrong reasons, it's best that it doesn't happen at all."

Taken aback, I ask, "Are you defending Melinda's actions?"

He nods. "I guess I am. Sure, I was pissed at her, but what's done is done. I can't change it now. Melinda had to make the best choice for her future."

Maybe Stella had too. My great aunt struck out on her own, to make a name for herself, and to take a crack at making it in the fashion world. For some reason, Aunt Stella had chosen herself over love.

I wonder if she was ever happy. I mean, *truly* happy.

I drop my head forward and stare at my bare toes. I can so relate to what Jake is sharing considering the near miss I had with Rick. And of course, Stella isn't here to defend her actions or why she left Jimmie. I have to assume she had important reasons. Just like how I have to eventually find myself, my place in life, and not rely on someone else to make me happy.

Damn, that seems like a heaping plate of self-realism.

Jake reaches over and moves my hair back behind my ear. I shiver in a good way. In a goose bumps all over my arms and legs sort of way. Suddenly I remember the intensity of his touch earlier and the uncontrollable urge I'd had in the bedroom to attack him. That was, before Jimmie came in and pandemonium ensued. Now, Jake's looking at me again with those clear eyes and touching me in a warm, familiar way.

"All that wigged you out, huh?" He asks so sweetly that I feel my heart will melt right here on the unbalanced old pier.

I toss my hair back and forth. "No. Not at all. I kind of hate that Melinda person." I level my gaze right on his. "Then again, I kind of like her."

Because Jake's here. With me. In those fitted jeans and a t-shirt stretched across a muscular chest so much that it practically molds to him. And he's real.

I chew on my bottom lip with my top teeth and wonder exactly what I should tell him. He's been so open and honest with me and dammit, I'm developing a terrible crush on him. I'm sure it's purely a rebound thing and the fact that I'm so sex-starved.

Maybe it's more. Jake makes me feel special by the way he looks at me and the tone of his words. He's still here at the farm, living up to his promises even though Stella's no longer with us. Something's keeping Jake here. My heart skitters a few beats with the hope that I'm that something. It's time to fess up about what happened before I came here. I want to be forthright and honest with Jake.

"Where'd you go just then?"

"I was back in Boston," I finally say, answering his question. "In a bathroom. Getting dumped."

He furrows his brows. "I don't follow you, sorry."

I shake my head. "At my friends' engagement party, my boyfriend and I went into the bathroom for some... err... private time. And he dumped me."

"What an asshole." Jake moves his hand away and sets it behind him, putting his weight on it. "You want to talk about it?"

I gnaw on my lip a little more and adjust myself to face Jake. "I think I do." I feel like I need to tell him about my past, no matter how damaged it might sound.

Jake sits back up, grips his rod and flings the lure out into the middle of the lake. He secures the pole in the crook under his knee and smiles. "I'm listening."

"It's just..." I stop and think for a sec. "How do you know when you're in the moment with someone—no matter if that moment lasts two years or six or twenty—whether it's the real thing and if it's going to be a happily ever after?"

"That's just it. No one knows. It's all a matter of trust and love," he says calmly, like a cop talking to a witness.

I sigh deeply. "But how do you *know*? How can you be sure you won't get left at the altar or broken up with in a ladies room?"

"You don't, Isabella. You can't not live your life under the assumption that any situation will end bably." Jake looks like he wants to say something. His jaw is tight and the light has left his eyes. He seems a bit more on the brooding side all of a sudden.

"Says the guy who drove his motorcycle from Manhattan to Alabama," I say jokingly.

Jake smirks. "I didn't say I was a model of how to do things. So, why did your ex do it?"

I press on. "Rick was getting pressure from our engaged friends to propose to me. So when I was trying to be intimate with him—which I've admitted to you has been a long time since—he said to me, and I quote, 'I'm getting off the pot.'"

I lift my head and stare at Jake. The vein on the side of his neck pulsates and it seems as though he's angry. I'm not sure, since he's always displayed utter calm around me. Besides, it doesn't make sense for him to get pissed off. I'm the one who had the sad story actually happen.

After a moment, he says, "That's the lousiest fucking thing I've ever heard. As in 'shit or get off the pot?'"

I shrug. "That's the saying he quoted. Although, personally, I prefer the more charming phrase 'fish or cut bait' that you mentioned."

Apropos of our current activity, I suppose.

Jake mutters a curse under his breath and then nabs the fishing pole that seems like some sort of weird metaphor of my life. Quickly, he reels in the line and then tosses it out again.

Punching him lightly on his thigh—the rock-solid thigh—I ask, "Are you mad?"

He grits his teeth. Then, he looks over at me. His strong, handsome features soften momentarily. "I know we've only known each other a short while and I have no business judging someone I don't know, but that guy," he says, through clenched teeth, "is a total asshole for treating you like that. You're better off without him."

Yeah, I sure am.

"Thanks Jake." I nod and smile. It feels good to get this off of my chest. A bit of a ritualistic cleansing.

Jake is no priest or psychologist, but I do get the sense he's a friend.

A drop-dead gorgeous friend.

A friend with the firmest ass I've ever seen.

A friend with eyes I'd like to drown in.

A friend with lips that could cover mine and kiss away the pain.

Arms that could wrap around me, pressing into my flesh.

Fingers that could dance over my skin, bringing me orgasm with a single touch.

Yeah, he's just a friend.

A friend that I totally want to have hot and dirty sex with.

CHAPTER TWENTY

I've got to stop making everything into sex or my lack thereof.

Jake clears his throat as though recognizing my carnal thoughts. "So is that why you came here?" he asks.

I stretch my legs out and dangle them over the dock, not touching the water. I'm afraid to dip them in as I'm not exactly sure what lies beneath. "I came here because Esterhazy told me I *had* to." I try to toss out the lure, though it lands about a foot in front of me. "I feel like I've fallen off the planet in a lot of ways."

Slowly winding the clickety reel, Jake sighs. "I know what you mean. I've been out of commission, shall we say, for almost five months."

"From police work."

Rubbing his chin with his left hand, he nods his head in the affirmative.

"Administrative leave," I say, repeating his earlier words.

"More like, 'Take some time and get your head on straight, Hansen,' my captain said."

I decide to see if he'll reciprocate in the sharing of personal information department. "How did you decide to become a cop?" I ask, taking another shot at pitching the lure into the water.

Jake fingers the end of his t-shirt and adjusts one jean-clad leg to hang off the wharf. "I don't know. How do any of us choose our careers?"

"That's a cop out, Jake." Then I laugh hysterically. "Get it... cop... cop out!"

He chortles another one of those laughs that indicate he shouldn't be enjoying my warped sense of humor. "Ah, the pun. The lowest form of humor," he says.

I spread my arm out and take a mock half bow. "I aim to please." I straighten my face. "Seriously though."

"I don't know. I played cops and robbers as a kid, learned how to shoot a gun, stuff like that."

Hand on hip, I glower at him. "Jake, I admitted my boyfriend dumped me while I was trying to give him a blow job in the bathroom. You can give me more than that."

His eyebrow lifts curiously. "You didn't tell me about the blow job."

My face heats to the temperature of molten lava. "Oh. I didn't? That's not the point. I shared, now you share."

"Yeah, but the blow job adds just a whole other level to the—"

I slam my fist to the pier. "Dammit, Jake!"

"Okay, okay." He stops for a moment, thinks, then speaks again. "It's one of the reasons I'm here."

I stop acting all cheeky and reach over to put my hand on his knee. I don't mean it in an "I want you, baby" way, rather a soothing "tell me your troubles" manner. I echo the comforting words he'd said earlier. "Something other than Melinda walking out on you?"

He hangs his head. "Yeah."

"I'm listening."

His eyes connect with mine and hold for a moment. A lifetime.

Breathing deeply, I say, "I won't judge."

I feel his tense muscles relax.

"My big brother, Grant, was a cop," he says in an exhausted stream of air. "I was the type of kid brother who always tagged along, trying to do what he did. He got a bike, so did I. He played football, so did I. He became a cop, I did, too."

"Makes sense. Perfectly natural." I think of my three sisters, two of whom are happily married. I wonder if I deserve the same good fortune they found.

I shake the thought. I need to pay attention to the luscious guy sitting next to me, telling me his past and admitting his hurt. In my years with Rick, he never confessed kind of any failure or fault, although I could list them all in a five-subject notebook.

I have to remind myself that this is about Jake and not me. "Sounds great to have a brother that close to do things with all the time."

Jake seems to think he's gotten a bite on the line, but when he jerks at the pole, nothing happens. "False alarm." He tosses the line out again. "Grant's a year older than me. We've always been the clichéd two peas in a pod. Same university. Same fraternity."

"Oh yeah? Which one?" I interrupt, trying to keep things light and keep Jake talking.

"Sigma Chi."

"No way! I was Sigma Chi sweetheart my senior year at Clemson."

His smile is heartbreaking. "Of course you were."

I lay my hand on his arm and he flinches as if to acknowledge the immediate sizzle of skin on skin. I press ahead. "I'm sorry. I got off track. You were talking about Grant."

Jake regards me for a minute as though he's savoring the electricity that passes between us, similar to what almost happened in Stella's room. Then he sits back a bit and presses ahead, the cloud of anguish returning to his eyes.

"When Grant moved to New York, I followed. Went to the police academy together, were in the same unit. We worked together, got commendations, moved up through the ranks."

Impressive. Jake's a good cop. I can totally see that. "Were you partners?"

He swallows noticeably before he speaks and I can tell this particular question might have hit too close to home. Like I've touched a panic button with him. That something that was so bad that Jake had to run away from his brother, and his job Does it have something to do with that scar on his shoulder?

He clams up. I can see he doesn't want to "go there," but he's already started and the curiosity inside me wants to know the end of this story. If it'll provide a deeper insight into this complex, gorgeous man, I'm all for it.

"Come on, Jake..."

"We weren't partners, but we worked in the same unit," he snaps a bit as he says this. "Sorry. It's hurts to remember."

Oh God, something bad happen.

Jake jerks the reel and flips it another time, this time with gusto that damn near sends it across the small lake.

Blowing out a gust of air, Jake says, "Grant and I did a lot of undercover work. Trying to smoke out drug dealers selling crack, pot, and ecstasy to kids. We were pretty good at it. Neither of us look our age, so we could get in with the dealers and gain their trust before busting up their operations."

"That's a noble thing, Jake."

He slams his fist to the quay and it shakes in reverberated anger. "Not so noble when you die."

"Grant?"

Jake nods, his gaze lost out in the middle of the lake somewhere.

I gasp noticeably and cover my mouth with my hand. A sharp stab punches my insides and I actually hurt for Jake. I wasn't prepared for this. I'd imagined his big bro got shot in the ass and retired to Hoboken. I didn't think he actually *died*.

"What happened?" I ask softly.

"I don't really want to talk about it anymore. Not right now. It's still too fresh," he tells me.

Jake drops his head forward, the golden hair tumbling into his face. Agony is written all over his skin in self-accusatory words. The vein in his throat throbs double-time and I can almost swear he's biting back his emotions. I feel like a shit for pressing him to open up. Just like Jimmie earlier. I had no way of knowing.

Setting the pole next to me, I pull myself to my knees and lean toward Jake in a sideways hug, draping my arms around his chest with my head on his back. He trembles slightly and I can't make out whether it's a laugh or a sob. Either way, he moves his hands up to encircle my right arm.

We sit there for a moment. Locked together. Not in any kind of sexual way. In an understanding, supportive way.

After a while, he pats my arm and releases me. "I sure know how to bring the room down, huh?"

"It's okay," I say. "Sounds like you needed to talk about it."

He smiles crookedly. "I haven't talked to anyone since the police psychologist suggested I take some time off."

"Not even Aunt Stella?"

He squints at me. "She knew not to ask. But I'm glad you did."

My stomach lurches in that crazy way again and I feel honored. "I'm here to listen if you want to tell me more."

A lazy smile crosses his face. He reaches out, but doesn't touch me as his hand drops. "Not here. I come to the lake for the distraction. To get away from my thoughts and enjoy the peace and quiet of nature."

"And there I go making you get all deep and emotional," I say. "I certainly don't want to ruin this spot for you."

"You didn't, Isabella. You made it better."

Awww...

Pang in chest.

Tingle in toes.

I let go of him, return to my place, and snag the stupid pole that I don't know the first thing about. We sit in silence for what seems an eternity while I watch him fish. This is a good segue to lighten the conversation. I waggle the pole at him. "Why don't you show me how to use this?"

He chuckles and swats at the pole. "I thought you were trying to be an independent woman and figure it out yourself."

Waving my hand at him, I say, "Independent-schmindependent. If my dinner depends on me catching something, I best get to it."

He scootches back on the planks and pats the open spot in front of him. "Only way I can show you how is by doing. Come sit in front of me."

My eyes widen. This could be interesting.

Chapter Twenty-One

I step between his legs and crouch down, careful not to bump my bum up against his crotch. Before I can catch a breath, his hands are on my hips and he slides me toward him. My back touches his chest and his arms snake around to grip my wrists.

The mood changes instantly. The lake seems steamy around us; the afternoon sun wraps us in its warm embrace. My heartbeat accelerates and my insides itch.

Is this some sort of foreplay?

"Um, so what am I supposed to do?" I ask with a hitch in my voice. Good Lord, he's going to think a man has never touched me before.

"Are you right or left handed?"

"Right."

He moves the pole to my left, which seems to defeat the purpose. But then he takes the pinkie finger of my right hand and hooks it around the nylon thread. He places the rod in my right hand.

"Now, hold it just like that. Tight."

His breath tickles my ear and as much as I want to squirm like a five year old, I sit still and listen to his instructions. He pulls my arm up in the air and back and says, "When I say 'now,' let your finger loose so the line can fly. Don't let go of the pole."

With ample power, he heaves my arm forward and shouts, "Now!"

I release my little finger and watch the shimmery line sail out to the middle of the lake. "Holy crap! I did it."

He laughs softly and I can feel it against my back. "Well, sort of. Let's do it again."

Hmmm... yes, let's.

I can't help but luxuriate in the comfort of his arms around me. Not to mention the fact that I'm nestled against him as I continue to learn from an obvious fishing master.

"Good," he says. "You've almost got it."

He rubs his hand up and down my left arm in encouragement, or flirtation, I don't know which. All I know is I'm alive. Like never before. As though someone breathed new life into me. All this talk of death and disappointment is somehow on the back burner, simmering for another conversation. Living each day to the fullest is what I want to focus on now. I'm on fire. And boy, oh boy, is fishing the *last* thing on my mind. I don't see what is remotely relaxing about this activity. Not when every cell in my body is on Orange Alert with the need to notify Homeland Security.

Whispering against my skin, Jake says, "Now reel it in slowly."

I turn the crank deliberately and excruciatingly slow. Each twist of the line brings me closer to Jake. His hands are now resting on my thighs and his breath is warm on the side of my neck. His hands feel so good. A welcomed invasion. A liberation of sorts.

I spin the reel a bit faster in anticipation of what might happen next. Jake's left hand circles my waist and tugs me tighter against him.

"Keep going," he instructs.

I want this over and done with. I want the line back in and the rod out of my hand. I want to lay Jake out on the dock, draping myself on top of him and feeling the warm life surging through both of us.

From the way his fingers are kneading me through my overalls, he wants that, too. "Almost there," I say in barely a whisper.

"You can do it."

Just as I'm about to wrap this exercise up, my line snags. Something's on the end. I bolt up and grab the fishing pole with both hands, sliding forward a bit on the dock.

"Jake! I've got one!"

"Seriously?" he asks, shocked.

"This is a big sucker." I reel hard, tugging back until the pole shape resembles a "U." This two-ton bastard fish fights me by swimming under the dock and pulling my line along with him. Jake hangs over the side and tries to snag the line, but the fish is on an escape route.

"Reel him in!" Jake shouts at me. "Hold tight!"

With all my might, I roll the lure back into its housing on the fishing pole, the murky wetness of the lake skitters down the nylon thread onto my hands as I wind tighter. My biceps and triceps sing out in solid protest. I hold my breath as I struggle to pull this stubborn fish on to land.

Jake grabs a net sitting next to his fishing tackle and leans out to where my lure dips under the water.

"Damn, Isabella," he says, "What do you have on the end of that hook? Jimmie's truck?"

Just then, a huge splash wets us when the gigantic fish flops out of the water and up into the air.

"Jesus! Did you see that?" I scream.

"He's enormous!" Jake yells with excitement in his voice. "We've got to land him. Don't give up."

My arms are throbbing with this massive workout. "Jake, I can't do this alone." And no, I'm not looking for some more warm bodies pressed against each other action. I need some frickin' help with this underwater beast.

Jake's eyes connect with mine in a playful dance and he positions himself behind me once again. He leans around and places his feet on either side of me on the deck for leverage. Taking hold of my wrists, he pulls back and we both thrash about trying to reel in this granddaddy of a fish.

The slimy bugger peeks out of the water again. "I swear, he just winked at me," I say.

"And we'll wink at him when he's fileted and cooking on the grill," Jake says with a laugh.

I lean back into his chest.

"Pull!"

"I'm trying!" I say in my defense. I'm not a professional fisher-person, so he's going to have to give me some slack.

"Harder!"

"I'm doing as much as I can," I say.

God, this sounds like dialogue from a bad porn movie. Now we just need the wack-a-cha-wah music in the background.

"One more good yank. You can do it," he says. He tugs me with him, the two of us heaving with all our might. Anyone listening in around the corner will think we're going at each other for the sex-capade of a lifetime.

Suddenly, the fish flies out of the water. Jake grabs the end of the line and scoops the fish into the net, capturing the flailing creature. "Caught!"

"We did it!" I fall back on Jake's chest, exhausted. I'm spent, panting, and gasping for breath.

The magnificent blue-green bass wiggles around inside the net, his eyes resigned to the fact that he *is* dinner tonight.

Jake hugs me to him with his forearm over my chest. Surely he can feel my chaotic heartbeat.

He sets the fish aside and laughs deep in his throat. "Was it good for you, too, baby?"

"Oh you know it," I say, almost blushing at the unveiled sexual reference. I wonder if I'll ever really know how good it can be with Jake.

Right then I realize: I'd like to.

CHAPTER TWENTY-TWO

After we feasted on my catch of the day, Jake got a series of voice mails that had him scowling, and then he disappeared to the trailer. That was two days ago. Something is bothering him and he's closed back up. We'd made such strides to chip away at his tough veneer, but apparently it's going to take more than one round of hot and heavy fishing to get him to open up more.

As much as I hate to admit it, I want to see him. There's a connection with Jake that I've never experienced before with another guy and I thought he might sense it, too. Yes, it's mainly physical, but there's something... *more.* Like we were both destined to be at this farm at the same time. Two unaffiliated souls. However, him keeping distance from me isn't going to further this flirtation we've got going.

Add to it that Jimmie's been feeling under the weather. Told me he got a bad batch of pimento cheese sandwiches that have knocked him for a loop. Poor guy.

Then Vanessa calls before I make it out to the chicken houses for my early morning walk-through.

"Griz, what on earth is going on?"

"What do you mean, Double V?"

"I'm getting married in four weeks and you're still in East Podunk?" she says with a bit of fanaticism in her voice.

"It's West Podunk, actually," I joke, trying to lighten things.

She's so not amused. "This is my *wedding*, Griz. You know, 'I do' and forever and ever, friends standing by to witness."

I wipe my mouth to get any remnants of my leftover self-made breakfast sandwich. "Things are hectic here, Vanessa. It's bad enough I've got Claudia on my back constantly. I don't need pressure from you, too."

"Rick's been asking about you," my friend says quietly.

I'm tempted to ask, "Rick who," but I bite my tongue instead. I let the comment slip by unanswered. Vanessa isn't having any of it, though.

"He's worried about you, Griz."

I harrumph and try not to choke on the irony. "Really? Could have fooled me."

Vanessa interrupts my thoughts. "So, I don't know if I should tell you this, but he's miserable."

Good. "Sorry to hear that," I say, keeping my voice light.

"Bullshit."

"Okay, so I grinned a little. What's got him so down?"

"Kyle says things are bad at work for him. That he's under a lot of pressure and that's probably why he did what he did to you."

Of course. The reason for his misery can't be that he's missing me or regretting how he left things. I don't care, though. Rick's not part of my life anymore. He had his chance. Two years' worth of chances. I don't owe him anything and I'm certainly not pining for him. I've moved on. My libido is on full alert for one handsome, bike-riding, ex-cop, current handy man who seems to get me more than Rick ever did.

"Well, he made his bed," I say. "Now he has to sleep in it."

Vanessa snorts at my stupid cliché. "He'll be at the wedding, you know. He's Kyle's best man."

"I know. It doesn't mean he's *my* best man anymore."

"I don't blame you, hon," Vanessa says. Then she takes a moment before saying, "Are you okay with being around him?"

I shrug, like she can see me. "It's not about me, Double V. It's your day. I can be civil."

"I know it'll be hard."

"Nah," I say with a soft laugh. "It'll be fine. I'm really okay with the whole situation. I've been so busy here that I haven't hashed on it further." I've had other distractions. Like a six foot three, blue-eyed diversion. "I will be there. I'd never let you down."

I can't let my life down. I have to get back to my regular routine in Boston. I can't miss more work and risk pissing off Claudia any further, even though HR says it's okay for me to be here dealing with things. Things being Stella's business, the contract with Double C, and the day-to-day operations. Yet, I find myself worrying more about the Jake situation and where we're going.

With him conspicuously absent, I can't help but wonder if he's tired of our flirtation or if the secrets surrounding his exodus from New York have finally caught up with him.

I'm bored out of my mind. I'm tired of watching crappy network TV at night. I'm sick of waiting for the Army helicopters to come back and buzz the house. The phone line is as old as Methuselah and it can barely hold my Internet connection for more than a few minutes. God, I need a break! I hear the clucking of the chickens in my sleep. I see red beaks and white feathers whenever I close my eyes. I feel like there's chicken shit permanently housed under my fingernails. The pungent tang of bird poop and pee is downloaded forever into my sensory bank. I seriously doubt I'll ever be able to erase it.

I've got to strike some sort of deal with that shyster Esterhazy, who conveniently dodges my calls and refuses to return them. The man is hiding something, but I'll be damned if I know what it is. No one can be as country bumpkin as him and yet have passed the bar exam. The man's got a hidden agenda.

My stomach aches as the tossed salad-like escapades of the last week play out in my mind. Rick. The inheritance. The chickens. Jake. Jimmie. Claudia. All of it. It's a conglomerated mess wrapped inside confusion and the unknown. I'm lonely and alone. Yes, I still hurt from the sting of Rick's inappropriate breakup. I crave what I can't seem to have from Jake. I'm a tight ball of emotions; a maelstrom ready to erupt.

I sink down onto the floor next to the bed, choke back the tears that are building, and swallow hard. The last thing I need is for Vanessa to pick up on my doubt. "Listen, I'm up to four belt runs a day to keep up with the egg production, so I really need to go get started. Don't worry, I'll be at the wedding. Don't think twice about it."

"I miss you, Griz! Come home."

Here come the tears. Hot and salty leaving tracks on my cheeks.

I wipe them away with my hands. "I miss you, too." Then I click the call off before I turn into a gushy mess. While I miss William and my apartment and my Vox martinis, I suddenly realize if I left here, I'd miss Jake more. A man I barely know yet one I'm inexplicitly drawn to like the proverbial moth to a flame. Those moths usually get burned, though, and I'm still healing from the last scorching. With the continued secretive machinations buzzing around Jake,

I have to wonder where things could possibly go for us. It's obvious we've both been without the pleasures of a physical relationship. However, it's more than a deep sexual desire for him that's churning inside me.

I swallow hard at the abrupt awareness that I'm starting to fall for this guy.

I pull myself up, run into the bathroom, and splash water on my face. As I towel off, soft fur rubs against my calf. I look down to see Puddy Tat smiling up to me. Yes, she's smiling. She's purring like someone switched on a button inside her. I scoop her up in my arms and hug her to me. She swats playfully at my nose in her cute little kitty manner. Dammit all. I'm starting to fall for her, too.

Puddy Tat jumps out of my arms and runs to the back of the house to do whatever she does during the course of her kitty day. I shake out of my reverie, strap on my Boone Dockers, as Jake and Jimmie call my work boots, and head out the door. I breathe in deeply, inhaling the scent of morning and nature. It's a beautiful day, crisp and dry—not cold—yet promising an afternoon's warmth, even for November.

Instead of getting into Stella's truck and driving it through the pecan orchard to the chicken houses, I decide to walk. God knows, I need the exercise from all the comfort food indulgences Jimmie's been serving to me.

But just as I make my way down the front steps and cross the lawn, a large brown truck pulls into the dirt driveway.

Wow, who knew UPS delivered way the hell out here?

The man in his short brown uniform adjusts his cap and steps out of the driver's side. He nods at me and disappears around to the back of the truck. Two seconds later, he emerges with a large envelope in one hand and his UPS scanner in the other.

"Isabella Perry?" he asks lazily.

"*C'est moi*," I say, smiling at him.

He shoves the stylus at me, saying nothing, so I take the hint. I sign my name the best I can on the electronic pad and pass the machine back to him. I'm not expecting anything from anyone. Not that I'm aware of. Rick and I weren't married, so these can't be formal divorce papers. The envelope's too small to be a present from a friend like Vanessa or Marina which would no doubt be something fashionable like shoes, a purse, or clothing.

"Have a nice day," the UPS man says as he thrusts the thick packet to me.

I glance down and see the return address on Boylston Street from my employer. A sigh escapes me as I figure Claudia sent me work to do while I'm here, even though I told her I didn't have my laptop or the time. Honestly, she's a graphic designer too. Can't she just finish up the project while I'm dealing with family matters? It's not exactly like I'm lying on a beach in Antigua having cut pineapple fed to me by a cabana boy.

The truck cranks, reverses, and speeds off out of the driveway, stirring up a cloud of red dirt in its wake.

Leave it to Claudia to find me in the middle of nowhere.

I shrug and pull at the tab to open the envelope. Then I withdraw a thick stack of papers. My hands begin to shake and I feel as though I'll be revisiting my breakfast cereal any moment when I read the words that sting my eyes:

Dear Ms. Perry:

This is to inform you that you have been relieved of your position at Tactris Global Associates due to failure to execute a crucial work assignment in the proper time. Enclosed, please find a check to cover the last period worked, as well as your remaining vacation time and...

The rest of the words before me blend into a psychotic alphabet soup that I can't stomach. My ears begin to ring and my heartbeat triples to the point where I think it might stop all together. I try to make sense of this. I try to comprehend what's happened. I blink hard, trying to focus on the letter. Something about transferring my 401(k), signing up for COBRA, and mailing back my ID card.

I don't fucking believe this.

First Rick, then Stella's inheritance, then the unbreakable contract... now this?

"That bitch!" I scream out to the trees. "She's *fired* me?"

My entire body trembles in both anger and disbelief. This can't be happening. I can't be standing here holding a UPS package with a not-so-fond farewell from my employer. What about that raise I just got? And the "exceeds expectations" performance review. Doesn't that matter at all? So much for the company's bullshit mantra of "family first." It's all just talk. I don't matter. I never did.

I shake my head and raise my fist in defiance. But there's nothing to defy. What's done is done.

Claudia Coldren has spoken and I am the one who's totally screwed.

CHAPTER TWENTY-THREE

My phone call to Claudia goes straight to her voice mail. "Coward!"

What? She couldn't have called me? Talked to me? Treated me like a human being? No, that would have been the decent thing to do. Talk about chicken shit!

I scoff at the bad pun that is my life.

The next phone call is to the HR woman at Tactris. When that call, too, goes to voice mail, I know I'm being ignored. My gander is not only up, it's pissed off. I snort out my sigh, flaring my nostrils as I hold the cell phone in a death grip. "Yes, this is Isabella Perry. I just received the notification of my employment termination. This is totally unjustified and uncalled for. You should know that I will not go away quietly. I will be consulting with an attorney and filing suit against Tactris Global Associates." I steady myself, hoping my voice isn't quivering. One more punch to the corporate beast. "It would be a real shame to have to go in front of a judge and testify to all the shenanigans and 'extra-curricular activities' of the officers of the company that I know about." Then I click end.

I sure know how to talk a good game. Exactly where I'm going to find this lawyer I speak of, well, that remains to be seen. Mainly, I just want to scare the shit out of the company since they had no concern about kicking me to the curb.

I sink down at the base of the tree in the front yard, trying to gather my thoughts, my breath, my life.

My fingers rub at my temples and then plunge into my hair. I try to knead at the career-halting blow I've just taken to the temporal lobe. I shake my head at the utter insensitivity of an employer to boot me out the door when I'm trying to handle a personal, family matter. God knows Claudia takes unexcused time off whenever she pleases to attend her daughter's dance recitals or karate matches, or even the two-hour lunches where she and whichever Tactris male executive slip away for the fish and chips with a side order of extramarital sex in the corporate-discount suite at The Lenox Hotel.

"It's not fair!" I scream out to the cosmos.

What a clusterfuck my life has turned into in the course of two weeks. I don't understand what I did to deserve this. What universal god did I piss off?

In downright defeat, I cross my arms over my knees and lay my head on them. Off in the distance, the rev of a motorcycle engine touches my ear. Jake. Who else in Dilligus Flats has the sexy purr of a classic Triumph bike like his? I hope beyond hope that he somehow senses my disappointment and distress and comes to me. That sixth sense that cops seem to possess. And right now, I need comfort.

But the roar of the engine grows further and further away from me, taking Jake out of the equation right now to ease my pain. He has his own that he's dealing with and sussing out in his own head. He doesn't need the burden of my mucked up problems.

Instead, I just sit here. Breathing in. Breathing out.

Because that's the only thing I have control over right now.

Not Claudia Coldren.

Not my firing.

Not the chickens.

Not this business.

And certainly not Jake.

Ten minutes later I gather my wits about me. It's asinine to sit here crying as if that will change my circumstances. I have to make things happen for me. I must stop being a victim to other people's scheming. So, I wipe my eyes with the back of my hand and stand up tall. I have to deal. I have to move forward.

The gently dancing breeze blows across the lawn and tickles my arms, painting me with vibrant optimism and a remarkable buoyancy. In the air, I feel it. The changing of nature. The changing of the seasons.

The changing of Isabella Perry.

Then it hits me. Maybe the universe isn't angry at me; rather it s trying to teach me a lesson. Sort of like rebooting a computer when it freezes up from being on too long. I'm in reboot mode. That's the message. I read it loud and clear. I gulp at this newfound confidence suddenly boosting me up. There's a tingling around me of freshness and life regenerating itself through the fall harvest, through the dormant winter, and into the blooming spring and summer.

I can do this.

I can succeed.

I can make this work for me.

I can be all that I can be and all of those other catch phrases advertisers throw at me.

Weaving my way through the orchard, I press ahead to get to my morning task, buoyed by my determination to make Stella's farm a success. I round the last bend toward the two chicken houses; my goldmines waiting to be excavated. They're the much-needed opportunity that's knocking. I'm going to answer. I'm actually looking forward to walking the houses and running the belts today. I'm convinced there will be even more eggs than ever before. Our production is going to kick into high gear. Double C Farms will give us the plaque for "Egg Producer of the Year." I can see it now... the ceremony... the chicken dinner—

Gag, maybe not a *chicken* dinner...

As I walk between the long stretches of the houses, however, there's a strange niggling in the back of my mind. One I didn't sense before when the UPS truck drove up and presented a packet that pulled the rug out from under my feet. Now, the hairs on my neck are suddenly sensitive and itching.

Something's not right.

"What's that hissing sound?" I ask to no one.

It's as if a water hose has sprung a leak. I have no clue where it's coming from.

I notice that the plastic curtains that are supposed to automatically lift to vent the houses are closed. That's strange, considering the warm night we had last night. The curtains should be all the way up, allowing air to flow freely through the space.

Walking towards the house on the left, I click open the padlock and step into the front room. I dig out my yellow rubber gloves from the drawer and slip my hands into them. First things first, I have to walk the houses and pick up any dead chickens I find. Not my favorite part of the day.

But the hissing sound keeps getting louder as I reach to enter the inner sanctum of chickendom.

I open the door and stand back to take in the horror before my eyes.

What the hell?

Water is everywhere, springing from the ceiling sprinklers. The stench of musty, wet chicken feathers and clotted corn feed fills the air and burns my nostrils.

My hand flies to my throat and the bile forms immediately. I fear I'll be revisiting that pimento cheese sandwich at any moment. For, in front of my eyes, amongst the drenched flock are tens... no... *hundreds* of dead chickens piled on top of each other in an Evian-esque Jonestown incident.

"Oh holy God. What happened?" I gasp for fresh air, but there's none to be had. With all my might, I muster up the best breath I can gather and scream bloody murder. "Jimmmmmmmmmie!"

The black curtains surround me. Like static from Aunt Stella's old television, spilling out over my eyes in a conglomerated mess, blurring my vision.

Whoa.

Dizzy.

Head rush.

Then nothing.

CHAPTER TWENTY-FOUR

When I come to there's a frickin' rooster pecking at my ankle.

It's the one I'd admired only yesterday as a Chanticleer-looking fellow with his broad red comb and green tail feathers scattered amongst the white. He's managed to nick away at the skin right above my boot and there's a fresh trickle of blood soaking my sock.

"Beat off, you freaking chicken!" I shoo him away and scramble to my feet.

However, Chanticleer, with the crazed crack eyes, comes after me; poised like Ralph Macchio on the wooden post in "Karate Kid," ready to strike. The evil rooster flies toward me, wings flapping, and his pointy beak pierces the back of my left calf.

"Get away from me!" I wave my hands, but he's got fire in his eyes. Revenge for the death of all of his friends and lovers here. He advances on me and squawks ferociously like he's mad with the Bird Flu. The wild expression in his eyes tells me he's not screwing around.

He wants blood. *My* blood.

I turn tail and run at the open door. The rooster is hot on my heels and I can feel him nip at the back of my boot. It's like some sort of demented Stephen King novel, only Chanticleer has turned into the rabid Cujo. I kick my feet with all my might and manage to get out and slam the door behind me.

Breathing hard, I try to figure out what happened. There are so many dead birds. I thought I saw some of the survivors dining on the bodies of the deceased. I sequester the gag that rises in my throat and try to get a hold of the situation the best I can.

I have no fucking clue what I'm going to do.

Yes I do. I'm calling Jimmie.

I'm outside leaning against the cooler shed when he pulls up in his truck. "D'ain't I told you not to leave them misters on," he says, chewing on the end of a twig of hay. He peers through a crack in the curtain to survey the damage within the house.

What misters? "I don't remember turning them on."

He points toward the ceiling of the house. "They're usually manually operated, but they do kick on sometimes themselves."

I pull off my gloves and tuck them in my back pocket. "Jimmie, I don't know what you're talking about. When I finished last night, I shut off the lights, turned on the switch for the curtains, and then I left." The curtains are on a temperature/time control that allows them to rise and fall depending on the heat or cold. "They should have been up full force this morning to let air into the houses, but they weren't."

"Maybe the timer done gone out," Jimmie says, matter-of-fact. "See, what happened, I'd say, is the mister turned on to try and eat up some of that humidity and it never shut off."

The mister, as I now remember learning from Dwayne, is this tiny stream of fine vapor that kicks in from time to time to drop small molecules of water in the air to help eat up the hot air. Then, the fans swirling throughout the houses literally suck up the moisture and filter it out of the house, thus cooling the operation and the chickens.

Jimmie tosses the hay twig to the ground. "Those chickens' lungs get full up with water and they die immediately of respiratory problems."

"This is a bloody nightmare!" I shove my hands into my hair and massage my suddenly throbbing temples. This is all my fault. I screwed something up. I look through the wire-encased windows at the piles of dead bodies. I've unknowingly sent these poor creatures to their death like some sort of mass murdering fuck-head like Hitler or Pol Pot.

"I need to check the other house," Jimmie announces.

I follow on his heels and am relieved to see that the second house has been spared the mister disaster. Still, I've got to deal with the carcasses in the other house. I don't know if my constitution is going to hold up. "Jimmie, what do we do?"

He stands by me and rubs my arm in a calming manner. "First off, we need to get them dead birds out of the houses. Those chickens are gonna start turning on each other soon since all their feed is wet."

My stomach roils, but I breathe deeply and listen. Jimmie's in charge here. I don't understand why—the man won't even let me pay him—yet he's here helping, directing, and correcting this tragedy.

I wish Jake were here.

I could use one of those awesome hugs like we shared at the lake.

Maybe later.

Jimmie rubs his palm up and down over his bulbous nose. "You drag out the dead chickens and then thrown them in the back of my truck. I'll get Dwayne on the horn to come out here and take a look at them misters. Then, I'll dig a hole where we can bury the chickens."

My brows furrow together. "We incinerated the dead ones." I paid attention when he showed me that step. One big outdoor barbeque. Although, no one would ever want to eat these chickens. Come to think of it, I don't want to eat *any* chicken. Ever again. Goodbye beloved chicken finger dinner with the yummy honey mustard sauce.

He shakes his head at me. "We done got too many dead ones in there. We have to bury them. Deep too, so the coyotes don't get them."

I expel the breath I've been holding. Horrifying disgust seeps from my pores.

Jimmie pulls a freshly laundered red bandana with the words "Roll Tide" printed repeatedly all over it from the pocket of his pants and hands it to me.

I take it from him. "What's this for?"

"I suggest you wrap it around your face to drown out the smell." He lifts his cap and scratches his nest of curls. "It'll take a while to clear this place out. When the sun gets hotter, it's gonna stink to high heaven."

I will not freak out again. I will not flake. I can handle this.

This is no time to go all delicate. There's work to be done. A mess to clean. And I've still got to run the belts and gather the eggs. This is going to be a long-ass day. So maybe the sun wasn't shining hope down on me. Maybe the gods were spotlighting my failure for all to see.

I have to get through this test. I *have* to.

I secure the bandana around my face, sniffing the Ivory freshness of the fabric. Hopefully the clean scent will linger long enough to get me through this.

As Jimmie turns to call Dwayne before going off to dig the hole, I turn to survey the death trap. I shut my eyes tightly and count to ten. I can do this.

"Lord, give me strength."

Two hours later, all of the muscles in my arms are protesting against this morbid workout. Forget the Cybex machine at the gym. Wet, dead chickens weigh a lot. And since I've been hauling them out four at a time, my biceps are becoming as sculpted as a Hollywood stuntwoman's.

Jimmie's doing all he can. He called Dwayne, who quickly showed up with all sorts of tools to fix the misters. Something about a malfunctioning timer, but he refuses to admit it's Double C's fault for installing it improperly. Jimmie scoops out the wet—*wasted money*—feed and replaces it with dry kernels. The chickens pound away angrily at the food, scrambling over each other to get to the small troughs. What a crappy way to live.

I steer clear of Chanticleer, who's still leering at me as I make my way around picking up his dearly departed friends. I continue to pile the chickens up in the bed of Jimmie's truck, but I can't stand looking at them, flopped over on each other, lifeless and morbid.

I try not to think about it. About the extent of the death and, moreover, the effect it will have on the egg production's bottom line. A lot of the dead are roosters, which means fewer males to knock up the hens. If the eggs don't get fertilized, then I don't get paid as much. It's one big, fat domino. No eggs, no money. Bad flock, bad reputation. Bad rep, no sale.

Just after noon, Jimmie shows up with bottled water and bologna sandwiches, which he and Dwayne immediately begin gnawing on. The thought of food nauseates me, so I grab a bottle of water and take this opportunity to run the belts. Despite the tragedy, the hens have been laying like gangbusters. The eggs are piled tightly together on the belt and there's a lot of breakage.

Around two p.m., my nostrils are filled with the stench of death and my eyes sting from the heat of the day. I've pretty much dragged all of the dead chickens out into Jimmie's truck. He's already made two runs to the funereal ditch to deposit the remains.

"We're almost there, Isabella. Hang in there like a hair in a biscuit," he says to me.

I laugh in spite of myself as this is a Southernism my Clemson sorority sister, Emily, used to say and I'd been known to use in my less sophisticated college days. The days before I moved to Boston; a city designed for an ambitious woman trying to find herself. A gal who appreciated the fast pace of thousands of people, five-o'clock artery traffic jams, and major sports franchises. A woman poised for the corporate world, ready to face challenges head on with style, grace, and professionalism.

I catch a glance at my reflection in the windowpane of the door.

I don't think that girl exists anymore.

Not after what Rick did to me. Not after my weeks on the farm. Not after the UPS package arrived.

My eyes are hollow and my face looks drawn and tired.

I'm losing myself. My identity.

I lower my chin to my chest and let my hair fall into my face, shielding me from the stupidity that surrounds me.

A loud squawk—which sounds more like a woman screaming—shatters the air inside the house. I jerk open the door to investigate. A melee of feathers and pine shavings fly through the air about halfway down in the middle of the building. I slalom through the chickens who scurry out of my way as I rush to the ruckus. There are two dead chickens I'd missed earlier and it's apparent my feathered employees have turned cannibalistic. And leading the pack is Chanticleer, standing proud and defiant in front of me.

"You again, huh? Well, bring it on."

I've obviously gone mad; talking to a chicken and challenging it in some sort of farm version of the Jets and the Sharks.

Chanticleer cocks his head to one side to get a good look at me, daring me to cross into his territory. Other chickens gather behind him, obviously aware that he is the boss. He lifts one clawed talon and rapidly digs it in the pine shillings.

Like he's marking his territory.

Or telling me to cluck off.

"This is my farm, you dumb ass chicken. Now hand over the dead bodies."

That's got to be the most ridiculous thing I've ever said in my life.

The rooster sneers at me. Okay, so he has a beak and no lips, but I know a sneer when I see one. Turning back to his fallen comrade, he reaches over and pecks the *eyeball* right out of the poor, unfortunate chicken.

"Oh *hell* no! Stop that!" I advance, stomping my booted foot to get him and his lackeys to back off. "Please! For the sake of all that's holy! That's disgusting!"

He makes another pecking move and I lunge forward, grabbing the foot of his victim. He doesn't take too kindly to that and surges forward, feathers flying, crowing at the top of his lungs. Since I'm bent down, he's got a perfect angle on my head and completely takes advantage. I raise my arm to protect my face and his stinger claws connect with the flesh of my forearm. Blood hisses from the cut and the skin swells immediately.

Sort of a—

I. Am. Pissed.

"Who the fuck do you think you are?"

I realize I'm yelling at a rooster, but the hell with him. I'm not dealing with this abuse any longer. I am at the crossroads of rationality and insanity. Lunacy overcomes me. Psychosis from the heat, the smell, the life that I'm living. I scream at the top of my lungs, then shriek at the crazed bird in front of me. A wrenching, guttural battle cry of agony and confusion.

Suddenly it's silent and I gasp in horror. The rooster's eyes widen. His proud comb flops over in defeat. He freezes in place, then huffs one final desperate, yet defiant, *bwaaaaaak* and falls over dead.

My mouth drops open and a scream chokes in the back of my throat. Nausea covers me in a blanket of shame. Breathing is a chore.

"Mother of God! Did I give him heart attack?"

The answer trilling in my head is straight from *Gone With the Wind*. I hear Scarlett's words, accusatory and aimed at me this time. "I done committed murder."

That's what I've done.

Gallus domesticus-icide.

CHAPTER TWENTY-FIVE

In sheer horror, I make my escape from the chicken house, stopping only to bolt the door so none of Chanti's peeps can seek revenge on me.

I pushed their comrade to the brink.

I killed him with my words. With my tirade.

He probably keeled over from the respiratory problem, as well; still, the madness consumes me.

I don't know what came over me.

Yes, hell, I do!

No inheritance is worth this.

This is no way to live.

Dead chickens, gathering eggs, battling gangsta roosters, and watching cannibalism. No sane person can do this day in and day out and not bend toward the lunacy. Perhaps this is what pushed Aunt Stella too far. What caused her own heart attack? No one should exist in this manner.

I need people. Friends. The city. Pavement and sidewalks. Cabs and T buses. Complex cocktails and happytizers. I need sex, affection, a good roll in the sack sweating and panting and gasping from the pleasure.

I need the life I used to have.

I have to get back. I have to file for unemployment. I have to update my resume. I have to register on Monster.

com and with a good headhunter. I have to find an employment attorney. I have to... find myself.

Tears blur my field of vision and I must flee. I hear Dwayne coming and I don't want him to see me in this state. I don't want *anyone* to see me in like this. I'm a freak of nature who's got chicken shit under her nails and death in her nostrils. I've lost everything... my boyfriend... my job...

I've lost my soul.

I don't know who I am anymore.

I snag the large rolling cart full of trayed eggs and steer it out of the house, hiding behind it with my unsteady hands and wobbly legs. I scoot along the cement path toward the cooler that sits in the middle of the walkway. Wrenching open the door, I wheel in the bounty of the afternoon into the cooling air of the large refrigerated room. I push the cart next to the other full ones and then I slump over on the high pile of feedbags stacked up against the wall in the corner.

Wracking sobs consume me as I relive the horrors of this day. The hurricane-force gale of torrential shit storms battering me from every angle. Nothing but death, destruction, disappointment, betrayal, waste, and most of all, regret.

Regret for ever taking Esterhazy's call.

Regret for ever getting on that plane.

Regret for not breaking the contract with Double C and daring them to sue me.

Regret for not saying screw it and getting back to my world... *ASAP.*

My arms break out in goose bumps from the refrigerated surroundings, yet I'm too weak to rub them away. I'm spent. Defeated. I've had it. I'm thirty years old and dare I say I want my mommy. I at least covet one of her comforting hugs. She knows just how to do it, too. She gathers me to her and wraps me securely in her love, shushing me, and telling me everything will be all right.

God, do I need that now.

I hear a voice outside of the cooler room. "Isabella? You in there?"

Jake.

No!

Not now. Not when I'm at my worst.

At least I don't regret getting to know him. He's the one comfort in this insipid situation.

I brace myself on the bulky feedbags and lean back, hoping the egg crates hide me. Jake's already seen me at my most spasmodic best time and time again. I don't need him to be here for rock bottom.

The door cracks open and he pops his head in. "Isabella? Didn't you hear me calling to you? I just saw Jimmie and he told me what happened. I thought I'd—"

Our eyes sync and time stands still for me.

His words halt when we visually connect.

I swipe away the tears streaming down my face and try to get my composure. Jake doesn't say a word, yet his hulking presence lets me know that he's in charge. He's going to take care of what's hurting me. He steps inside the cooler and closes the door in a whoosh behind him. In three long strides, he advances on me. His face has concern written all over it.

I hold my hands up to stave him off and to hide my face. I don't want him to see me like this, but it's too late.

"No, Jake... don't..."

"Isabella, are you okay?" he asks, stopping directly in front of me and looks at my blood-covered arm.

He turns and goes to the paper towel dispenser on the wall, whacks off a length, and then comes back to press it firmly into my flesh wound. I wince and he apologizes with his eyes.

"What the hell happened to you?" he ask as though he's trying to keep me from going into shock. Ahh, the cop training comes through once again. Tend to the victim. Keep them tasked and focused.

"I was attacked," I say flatly.

"Apparently," he mutters. "By what?"

"A rooster."

Jake shakes his head in disbelief. His blue eyes are soothing as he gently wipes away the caked-on blood. I want to dive into the depths of those orbs and surface to a new reality.

I so want to be a strong woman and not a neurotic flake. I want to show Jake that I'm resilient and can handle any adversity.

That ain't gonna happen, though.

I let my head fall forward onto his chest and I heave a sigh. That woman in the Pensacola was right: Satan rules my life. "Everything totally sucks, Jake. I can't do this anymore. I'm sick of death and failure and chicken crap and—"

My words are swallowed in the expanse of his T-shirted chest as he pulls me by the elbows and gathers me into his arms. He folds me against him, warm and protective. This man reads my needs with no request or directions. He's offering what I require now: strength and caring. He cradles me gently, weaving his hands around my back and pulling me closer, closer, closer into his muscular chest. I let go of my fears and luxuriate in the comfort of his embrace.

"Shhh..." he whispers close to my ear. His hand strokes my messy hair away from my face. "It's going to be okay, I promise."

Although he really doesn't know if it'll be okay or not, I do appreciate the sentiment all the same, wanting to wallow in his confident assurance.

His soothing words puncture my heart and the floodgate opens. I can't hold back anymore. The emotional turmoil of so much piled on overtakes me and I can't think.

Don't want to.

All I want is to *feel.*

Experience life and living.

I pull away from Jake's hold and flatten my hands on his chest. I feel his heart beating underneath my fingertips. Warmth from his skin emanates through his soft T-shirt. My hands wander across the expanse of his pecs, appreciating the hours he must have spent in a gym to keep in top physical condition for his job. A job he doesn't do anymore, yet the police training is ever apparent in how he's caring for me.

It's so much more than that, though. It's a meshing of our souls. A reaching out to a kindred spirit. I may not know the details of what made him flee New York, yet I'm glad that it's brought him to this moment with me.

A whispered, "Isabella," escapes from his lips. Lips that I can't take my eyes away from. Ones that I want to feel pressed against me, consuming me, and satiating the hunger of my deprived body.

I lift my lashes up, taking in the scruff of his day-old beard and the chiseled angle of his nose. His blue eyes blaze into mine when I dare to look directly into them. Tidal waves of emotion churn like the sea in his irises as though he wants to tell me everything, yet words don't belong right now.

His right hand appears next to my face and he pivots it to allow the back of his hand to caress my cheek. Involuntarily, my eyes close at his touch, soaking in the contact and the electrical charge it causes that ignites my passion and stokes a fire down below. My womb clenches in liquid desire at the mere stroke of his hand.

I shuffle my feet forward, closing the miniscule distance between us.

He smiles slightly, telepathing what he wants to happen next.

We're two minds on the same track, colliding toward each other, yet not caring about the consequences.

I pull my hands up from their exploration of his chest and let them wander into the thick recesses of his hair. So soft. So silky. So sexy.

The smell of him fills my senses and I want to drink in all that he is. An elixir to cure my wounded life. A salve for what ills me.

Although I'm not at my best, I don't care.

I want Jake and all he represents. And he's longing for me, too.

I read it in his eyes. I feel it in his touch.

Now s not the time to question. It's not even the moment to analyze or decipher.

It's time to act.

I can't remember ever making the first move on a guy before in my life. But as I've noted, my life has changed. So, with every bit of intestinal fortitude I can muster up, I lean forward and pull Jake's face toward mine.

He tilts his head to the right.

I do the same.

And in one fiery explosive moment, our lips meet.

CHAPTER TWENTY-SIX

At first the kiss is soft, tender, healing. A blending of our injured souls. Sweet nips that join our lips together. Our noses bump. We quietly laugh, kissing and curing and exploring one another.

But everything quickly turns. The pent up frustration from month of hardly any touching r kissing or petting or necking. No one should go that long without contact from the one they love. It's wrong to deny what comes so naturally to men and women. I eat up all that Jake is offering. Heat and passion replace all rational thoughts or doubts. Instead, I open my mouth and accept his plundering tongue that seeks to mate with mine.

If Jake ever had any hesitation when it comes to me, it all melts away as he goes from good cop to *baaaaaad* cop. His hands encircle me and explore across me. They find their way south to my bottom and cup each cheek in his palms. A moan of pleasure escapes me, drowned in the cavern of his kiss. Without thinking twice, my fingers plunge into his thick hair again, tugging his head closer. Our tongues fuse together, battling for position. Then, his hands glide up my bare arms and hook around the straps of my tank top. He groans. Or maybe it's me. I don't know.

Does it even matter?

If I have any doubt that Jake might be attracted to me, it's totally out the window now. His fingers move across my skin leaving a heated trail in their path. In return, I slide my hands around to hold his face, cupping his jaw while I pour every bit of myself into this kiss. Jake's mouth moves over mine in a bit of a feeding frenzy. We're obviously both starving for each other's.

This masculine touch that I've gone without for way too long.

I deserve this.

As does Jake, apparently.

I've been kissed plenty of times in my life; not like this. Not so... thoroughly and thoughtfully. Of course, I've been kissing the same person for the last two years, so I've probably forgotten what this newness is like. That spark. That stomach dip. That first-time excitement. Sorry Rick, you can't hold a candle to this man.

I've got to stop thinking about Rick when I'm completely surrounded by Jake.

Jake.

"Jake."

The thought of him. The reality of him.

"'Bella...'" he whispers.

It's my name, it also means beautiful.

All thoughts of the chickens, death, destruction, and corporate failure fade into oblivion. Even though I'm a farm-hand mess, Jake Hansen thinks I'm beautiful, and that's all that matters.

I angle my body toward him more, bracing my feet on the concrete floor. There's an exhilarating energy field sparking between us as his tongue continues to probe my mouth. Moist. Moving. Wanting. Taking.

I give as good as I receive, nipping at his tongue with my teeth. The silkiness of his mouth continues to rove over mine, fusing our lips together in a semi-permanent position.

Our fingers fumble around reaching for straps, hems, and seams. I run my hands up under his T-shirt with the overwhelmingly desperate need to feel his skin. Skin that I've seen plenty of and now want to taste for myself. He moves to cup my neck and tip my head back. This allows him deeper access to my mouth, which I'm more than happy to grant. Then, his other hand skims across my stomach since my tank top is somehow bunched up underneath my breasts.

My hands fan out over his torso, massaging the vast muscles under my fingertips. His skin is smooth, yet taut, and his nipples are tight buds that react to my touch. I move to his waist and slip my fingers into the band of his loose jeans. I don't care how cliché it sounds in my head, the man is chiseled perfection. Created by an artful master from another time and sent to me when I needed him the most. In an act of near madness, I flick away at Jake's button fly and move my hand in for the kill.

That moan is definitely him.

"Oh, baby," he says. "Yesssss."

Through the cotton of his boxer brief, the man's thickness fills my hand, pulsating in anticipation. My exploration only accelerates the depth of Jake's kiss, as well as the advancement of his hands. He moves up my stomach and takes my breasts in a caress like a true pro. My nipples now respond to his invasion, pebbling into his rolling fingers. It's been so long. Too long. My breasts ache with a need that shoots to the core of my womanhood. I tense up as I try to breathe, feeling the passion and desire slither through me. The tension in my bra slackens and I realize Jake's made short work of the front clasp of the garment.

I gasp in his mouth. I feel him smile.

The sensations flowing through me are phenomenal beyond words. God, I *soooooo* need this. Not so much because

I've been without sex for such a long time, but more like I've been without Jake my whole life. He flips a switch in me that I never knew had been installed. A purr that generates from between my legs to wrap around my heart in a fervent pounding of need. Jake is breathing life into me. He's pumping me with the kind of adrenalin that makes me want to throw caution to the wind. To lay back and wrap my legs around him. To open the windows of my soul and let him march right in and set up residence. Hell, the need he's stroking deep within me makes me want to have sex with him right here, right now in this cooler.

My eyes fly open.

Egg crates and feed bags surrounding us breaks the bewitching spell.

Reality crashes in like a five-car pile-up.

Whoa up!

We can't do this in here.

Not on top of bags of chicken feed.

A roaring truck engine helps bring me back to my sense. Like a slap in the face.

Jake freezes up for a second and holds me away slightly as he listens to outside. Then smiles down at me. Wickedly. Like a teen who's been caught watching low rate porn on pay-per-view.

A key rattles in the outer lock and I realize with cold understanding that it's the Double C Farms truck here to pick up our supply of eggs.

And here Jake and I are going at it like rabbits in heat.

My face must show my astonishment and embarrassment because Jake laughs softly and says, "Don't worry. It's okay, Isabella."

No. It's. Not.

It's *so* not.

Trying to get control of the situation as expeditiously as possible, I push Jake away from me—a bit too hard. His brows furrow and he looks confused as I scramble away and tug my tank top back into place. Having no idea what to do with my unhooked bra, I cross my arms in front of me.

I lift my hand up to cover my mouth in horror over my actions. My lips tingle from Jake's kiss and his unshaven whiskers that he used to brand me. My body shakes from his energetic touch. I take a step back, away from him, away from the feedbags that had nearly acted as a convenient bed.

"Jake... I'm sorry. I never should have—"

The door jerks open and sunlight floods the dimly lit room. Jimmie pokes his head in and looks around.

"What are y'all doing? Get locked in?"

With his back turned, Jake stealthily tucks Little Jakey back into his pants. He tugs his T-shirt down to cover his obvious erection as I sense my face turning a thousand shades of crimson.

Jake clears his throat. "I was, umm, seeing how I could help."

Jimmie looks at Jake, then me, then Jake again in an exaggerated manner. Sure, he's a good old country boy, but I'm sure even *he* can figure out what he interrupted.

I need to make distance.

I need an escape from this closed space.

I need air that doesn't smell of Jake.

"Jimmie," I say, feigning weakness. "I don't feel very well. Can you drive me up to the house?"

I can't meet Jake's blue stare, although I feel it on my skin.

Jimmie's smarter than I give him credit for. Without saying a word—or casting judgment—he steps over and takes my arm.

Jake moves towards me. "Look, I can—"

Jimmie stops him. "Why don't you help Dwayne out there load up these here eggs onto the truck?" he asks with a knowing nod. "I'll take Isabella on up to the house and get her cleaned up." He takes a look at my battered arm and continues. "That's some nasty cut. We should get some Mercurochrome on that. Heal you right up."

I lift my eyes to watch Jake go off obediently to help with the eggs. Poor guy. Ms. Vulnerable literally attacked him. Course, he wasn't fighting me off. Even though I apologized, deep down, I'm not sorry at all.

I needed that.

And I want more.

CHAPTER TWENTY-SEVEN

J immie and I ride in silence in the musty heat of his
pickup. Thank God I have the brief time to catch my
breath and reel in my enflamed libido.

Once at the house, Jimmie follows me in and steers me
to the bathroom. His gentle touch is almost more than I can
stand. More than I deserve.

When he wipes the wet, worn washcloth over my scabbed
forearm, tears start to drip down my cheeks. I really have
no control over my emotions. I need some strong drugs.
Something that will ease my pain and turn my thoughts
from frantic and impulsive to calm and soothing. One of
those drugs like they advertise on television that have people running through fields of flowers or scampering on the
beach. Yeah, I need a pill like that.

Jimmie opens the medicine cabinet and nabs the rust-
colored bottle of Mercurochrome. He blows on my skin
before applying the stinging agent. I cringe at the first
touch, then realize this is for my own good.

Stupid Chanticleer. I'm glad the evil bastard is dead.

"You ain't having a good day," Jimmie says, not asks.

"No, I ain't."

"Got some bad news?"

"Yep."

"Anything I can help with?"

Let's see, get me a new job, a buyer for this damn farm, and a man who won't abandon me. A tall order. "I wished, Jimmie."

He thinks for a moment. "You know, Isabella, I think you need to get away for a couple of days."

My head snaps up. "What do you mean?"

Jimmie keeps his attention on the cut on my arm, never meeting my eyes. "You need a break. Away from the chickens. Away from the farm. Away from—" He pauses. "Well, away from other things that upset you."

Bless his soul. Jimmie Hemi cares.

I can see where he's going with this, although I don't dare tell him Jake's not upsetting me. It's my uncontrollable, animalistic reaction to Jake—considering the bizarre circumstances of the day—that has me completely discombobulated.

"I can't leave, Jimmie. Who'll take care of the chickens?"

"I'll do it for you." He stands, caps the bottle and returns it to the cabinet.

A snorted laugh escapes me. "And I'll pay you how?" I still don't exactly understand why he's helping me to begin with. Probably some displaced loyalty to Stella and what they once meant to each other. "Besides," I say as I place my hair behind my ears. "I can't afford to go anywhere."

"Sure you can. Don't you have credit cards?"

I reach over and get the brush to pull it through my hair. It catches a tangle at the end that requires me to tug a few strands out. I think about that never-been-used Clemson alumni Visa card tucked in the secret compartment of my Kate Space wallet just sitting there waiting until the proverbial rainy day.

It's pouring buckets now.

I don't want Jake to think I'm running away. He's liable to believe it's him and something he's done when in reality it's me. Me, me, me. Griz the Flake.

Jimmie straps two large Band-Aids across my cut and then tosses the washcloth in the hamper. "Look here, I know this ain't your scene. You're a city gal—just like Stella—and you need to refresh yourself. I don't reckon you can go back to Boston yet, but you can get away. You've worked hard and you deserve a break. Take a nice long weekend pampering yourself."

"Just like Stella, huh? And I suppose she up and left the farm whenever she felt like it?" No wonder the place was in such dire financial circumstances and total disrepair.

He laughs to himself. "She had places she loved going. I'm sure you could find something to make you happy."

"Where will I go?" I ask, hearing the lilt of my voice.

"Anywhere you want."

It sounds so tempting, though. A few days in luxury to get my thoughts together and figure out what to do next. I can't keep going on like this. I'm not cut out for this business. I know Esterhazy said no one would buy this property with the debt attached to it, but maybe with some time away, I can creatively come up with an answer.

There are no easy answers, yet this one seems obvious.

"It would be irresponsible of me to run away," I say.

"Not if you have permission," Jimmie says with a laugh.

I rub the bandage and then look Jimmie straight in his eyes. Everything seems so clear suddenly. "I need a city."

He scratches his graying mop. "Well, you've got Montgomery up I-65, about three hours."

I screw up my nose. "Not big enough."

"Birmingham is about five hours. Atlanta's about six."

"Tempting. Keep trying." I'm actually getting excited. Noise. People. Really complicated cocktails.

Jimmie's eyes light up. "Well, you could always try out one of Stella's favorite haunts. 'Bout two and half hours west, if you drive like she did."

Hope surges through my veins, pumping with the will to accept his offer. *Yes. Yes. Yes.* "I think you've talked me into this, Jimmie."

He pats me on the back. "Tell you what. You go get your things together and I'll make a phone call to arrange everything. All you have to do is show up."

I smile; the first genuine one in a while. "Does this mystery place have alcohol?" I definitely need a strong drink of anything.

He snort-laughs. "Little lady, where I'm sending you, you can drink all night long, if that's what you want."

I nod approvingly. "Go make that call."

Chapter Twenty-Eight

Two hours and forty-five minutes later, I'm in paradise. I'm sitting on a wrought-iron balcony overlooking the liveliest street in all of America, taking in the sights and smells surrounding me. Jasmine fills the air. Music spills out everywhere, blending together into a harmonious city buzz.

Okay, I'm not in paradise, per se, but heaven to me is a crowded city street, people everywhere, clubs and restaurants to choose from and life sparkling all around.

I pull out my cell phone—which now works—and dial the familiar number at Harvard University.

"Alumni Relations, William McEwan speaking."

"Working late, I see," I say with a laugh. It's just past six Eastern Time, yet it's happy hour here.

"Griz?"

"In the flesh." The waiter sets a plate of food in front of me as I say to William, "Guess where I am?"

"I haven't the first foggiest clue."

I lean forward and sniff the bountiful aroma curling up from the spicy jambalaya, the tang of the sausage, the sweetness of the rice, and the zest of the tomato sauce. I take a heaping spoonful and close my eyes as I savor the taste. "Guess."

William's annoyance at me is clear on this 4G network. "Guess what? That you're talking with your mouth full? That's apparent, Griz."

"No, guess where I am, silly."

"Since I don't hear chickens fornicating in the background,' he starts, "I'd say you're not in Dilligus Flats anymore."

"I'm in New Orleans," I say triumphantly.

I hear him switch the telephone from one ear to the other. "What the hell are you doing in Louisiana?"

I take another bite of the piquant local dish. "Jimmie ordered me off the farm. Too much crapola happening to me." I'd already texted William about the fired-by-UPS package.

William chuckles. "Griz, you take 'shit happens' to a whole new level."

I shrug. I don't care. Sure, he's right, but it doesn't matter right now. I'm in New Orleans. I'm in the French Quarter. I'm on Bourbon Street.

There are people everywhere, laughing it up and living life to the fullest. The street is decorated for the coming Christmas season and everyone is tossing beads and bouncing along to the Zydeco music pouring out from the many open storefronts as though it's full-out Mardi Gras season.

A police siren sounds out in the distance and the raucous laughter of college students below rings out. Civilization. People. Action.

"I don't get why you're in Nawlin's," William notes. "If things are that bad, just come home, Griz. I miss you. And Vanessa is starting to obsess with the wedding planning. I need a buffer."

"It's not that simple. Besides, I could drive here."

"Whatever," he mutters.

"Look, this is the most relaxed I've been in almost a month, William. I needed this break. Oh, my God, you should see my hotel room. Garden view, double French doors, Jacuzzi tub and a deep, inviting bed."

I looked like the poor country cousin when I pulled Stella's Chevy Shit truck into the hotel garage and handed over the keys to the valet. He winced when he saw what he had to park, but I tipped him five bucks to ease the pain.

"How are you affording a luxury hotel?" William asks.

"Breaking in that Clemson alumni card." I honestly don't care. "Jimmie got me this room at the Dauphine Orleans Hotel. Get this, it used to be a whorehouse and it's allegedly haunted."

"That should make for an interesting night's sleep," William quips.

I wipe my mouth with the paper napkin and take a swig of the yummy local beer, Abita. "When I checked in, they handed me this brochure and gift basket. Looks like I came here during their Kama Sutra weekend."

William hoots long and loud. "What does that entail?"

"It's hilarious," I continue. "There's a copy of the Kama Sutra book, love oil, massage cream, bath gel, edible honey dust with a feather applicator—"

"—Ooo, snag me one of those."

"—a coupon to attend a one hour tantric sex class." I feel dirty even telling him this. I wonder if Jimmie realized he was sending me to a hotel with such kinky promotions. Maybe he and Stella ever came here together. In which case, I don't want to know.

"Too bad you're there alone," William says, giving me a swift kick in the ass back to reality.

I slump in my chair. Funny, I didn't feel lonely until William mentioned it. Now, I'm overwhelmed with a pressing pain in my chest. Only a few hours ago, I was far from alone in Jake's arms. Memories of his ardent kiss still coat me. His scent remains on my skin.

Maybe I shouldn't have run. Or, perhaps, I should have invited him along. But he wasn't even around when I tossed my bag into the truck and headed out.

I heave a sigh. Certainly a satanic one, considering I am in the city where their motto is "*Laissez les bontemps rouler.*" Let the good times roll.

I shake my head. Surely the feelings I have for Jake— and the incredible attraction—are only rebound pangs. Is it simply the need to reach out to another person and know that I'm still desirable? I can't do that to Jake. He's not the kind of man to use and then forget.

"Thanks for the reminder, Wills," I say. "And here I was starting to feel good about things."

"I'm sorry, Griz. You know what I mean. I'm only thinking about you. I want you to be happy. You deserve it."

"I know. I want that, too."

William snaps his fingers. "You know what Dr. McEwan is ordering for you? A nice, long, hot bath with those kinky oils you've got, then a spoil-you-rotten dinner, and then head over to Pat O'Brien's, down a few Hurricanes, and pick up the first cute guy you see. You need a one-night stand."

I almost choke on a piece of sausage. "Right, because that's so like me."

"You need to get laid, Griz. Trust me."

"This from the former slut, now Mr. Relationship."

"Honey, I get laid plenty," he says with great confidence.

"TMI alert, Wills."

William groans. "Well, if you won't look a gift horse in the mouth, then you're a hopeless cause."

I smirk into the phone. "I appreciate the suggestions, just the same. Okay, I'm going now. There's a lot for me to do. Places to go, people to see."

"That's my girl. Of course, I expect a full report."

"You got it," I say.

I click off the phone, signal for my tab, and decide maybe William's idea isn't so off beat after all.

First stop? Where else? I'm in Nawlin's ain't I?

Pat O's.

Halfway through my third Hurricane, I decide to get a "to-go" cup and head back to my hotel. The delicious fruit and rum concoction is just what I needed to sooth my frazzled nerves, but I'm afraid my time on the farm—early to bed and early to rise—has affected my party girl chromosome. Sure, there are a lot of cute guys hanging near the fiery fountain and standing around the iron tables, however, none of them float my boat.

They're not Jake.

No one is.

William would be so disappointed in me. I think I will heed his advice, though, and take a long, hot bath. Besides, I have all of those oils and gels from the Kama Sutra basket. Might as well use them.

The bartender transfers the red liquid and fruit into a large paper cup for me. I weave—not in a drunken stupor—my way through the foot traffic of Bourbon Street that's closed off to cars. From higher up on the balconies overlooking the walkway, partiers toss beads down to people walking buy, just because. I catch strings of green and blue and wrap them around my wrist for fun. The air smells earthy, rich and full, almost sweet. I'll have to get out tomorrow and see more of the city to find out what kind of flowers paint the air with such a fragrance.

Back at the hotel, I slip through the iron fence that leads into the garden. The trees are decorated with white Christmas lights, outlining the trunks against the dark sky. I insert my keycard into the slot of room 140, open the double French doors, and relax in the comfort of my room. The large mahogany bed is covered in a fluffy lemon yellow comforter and I can't wait to dive in and wrap myself in the huge pillows.

First, I'll take that relaxing bath in the Jacuzzi tub, rest up a little, and then head back out to dinner somewhere. I'm in the Big Easy, surely I can get a meal after nine o'clock. Something that's not made of cheese, mayonnaise, or potted meats.

I kick off my shoes, peel off my khakis and black top and reach for the Kama Sutra basket. "Might as well not let this go to waste." I giggle at myself as I choose a bottle of the love oil to go in my bath.

I get the water going in the tub and strip out of my underwear. A big, thick, white terrycloth robe hangs on the back of the bathroom door. I drape it around me and go sit on the edge of the tub that's starting to bubble with the warm water. I can almost feel my pent up frustrations begin to wither away as the steam rises around me and the Jacuzzi jets kick into action. I drop two capfuls of the oil, as per the directions, and shuck off the bathrobe.

I dangle my feet in, then slide my calves in, getting used to the heat. The massaging energy of the water burbles around me, reaching out and stroking my cares away. I reach for my paper cup still filled with an ample supply of Pat O's famous concoction. Right before I immerse in the steaming water, my legs start feeling itchy. I look down and nearly choke on my gasp.

"What the...?"

I withdraw my left leg and notice that from my ankle to my kneecap are tiny bumps everywhere. Hard, white bumps. Itchy, too. They've sprouted out viciously, like acne on a fifteen-year-old boy's face.

"Oh my God," I yell out, like anyone can hear me. "Now what?" I rub hard at my legs, trying to dissipate the bumps. But they continue to pop up in a leper-like rash all over my legs. What could have—

The love oil.

I snap up the bottle and read the ingredients. "Almond oil!" Are those tree nuts? They come from California, so I guess they grow on a tree. Lovely. There goes my relaxing evening in the Jacuzzi. Thank heavens I didn't get all the way in the tub. I'd look like some sort of pimply freak.

I pull the robe back around me and secure the tie at my waist. I probably should have looked at the ingredients before I used the product. This is the most retarded and stupid allergy ever. I try not to scratch the living daylights out of the itchy mounds, but instead I plow through my cosmetic kit for the extra Epipen I got at the hospital. I settle on the bed, count to ten, take a deep breath, and jab the pen to my thigh. The spring needle pops out into my skin and I wait patiently as the epinephrine takes charge.

Falling back on the bed, I start laughing hysterically. "Only you, Griz. Only you."

The shrill buzz of the phone interrupts my self-flagellation.

"Ms. Perry, this is the front desk. We have a delivery for you."

"Are you sure?" I haven't ordered a cab or a pizza. Besides Jimmie, William's the only one who knows I'm here. "Umm, do I need to come to the front desk or something?"

"No," the woman responds. "As long as I have your permission, I can send the delivery to your room."

"Yeah, sure, that's fine. Can you tell me what it is?"

"Flowers."

"Oh, okay. Cool, send them over."

They're probably a nice cheer-me-up from Jimmie. I wouldn't put it past him to be this thoughtful, considering how he helped me earlier today.

Earlier today...

I can't believe it was only this morning that I was knee-deep in dead chickens. Just this afternoon that I had my arms wrapped around Jake and had his tongue down my throat. Merely a few hours ago I fled Dilligus Flats for the much-needed refreshment of a real city.

Peeking down at my legs, I notice the bumps are starting to subside. Not like I need to show my legs off any time soon, but I would like to wear my cute little black and red flowery skirt out to dinner if the allergy abates.

When the light rap on the door draws my attention, I dive to my purse to get a couple of bucks out for a tip. I make sure my complimentary robe is properly covering me and I cross to the door. I pull back the heavy gold drape that blacks out the light from outside and unlock the French door.

In front of me is a huge bouquet of tulips: yellow, purple, and pink. The sweetness of the spray tickles my nose.

However, my eyes grow wide and my body reacts when the flowers lower and I get a good look at the hunk of a delivery guy with the familiar blue eyes.

"Well, Isabella, looks like I found you."

Chapter Twenty-Nine

My heart almost stops beating. "What are you doing here, Jake?"

He furrows his brows. "Why did you run away from me?"

I didn't. "Why did you follow me?"

He waves the flowers at me. "Come on, you're a smart girl. I think it's pretty obvious, don't you?"

Well, duh, last time I'd seen him I had my hands in his pants, headed for The Promised Land. I honestly had no idea he'd show up here. The realization of what this means hits me hard and I think my heart's going to pound through my ribcage.

He drove over two hours to see *me*.

I step back and tug my robe closer, even as I take the offered spring bouquet. "You're a good cop, finding out where I came."

Jake enters the room and closes the door behind him. "Not really. Jimmie told me." He runs his hand through his hair, causing the golden thickness to fall into his eyes. My insides do a little loop-dee-loop and I will myself to breathe like a normal person.

Jake's here.

In New Orleans.

And he came for me.

Stalling for time, I turn and place the flowers on the bathroom counter. "I'm surprised he told you where I was."

Jake moves towards me. "I had to make a convincing argument."

"Oh yeah? Like what?" He looks so damn good, I could eat him in one spoonful. Those jeans mold to his muscular thighs and his black T-shirt certainly does a body good. He smells of a light citrus freshness mixed with the aged leather from his jacket. The combination of scents almost does me in, so I take another step backwards.

Jake gives me that crooked, heartbreaking smile that makes my knees go weak like some sort of swooning woman. Okay, that's me. I admit it. This guy has been in my thoughts and dreams and suddenly he's standing before me here in New Orleans... in this hotel... alone together. There can be only one outcome to this.

He reaches out and brushes my hair behind my ear. "I promised Jimmie I wouldn't hurt you."

I swallow hard at the lump in my throat that threatens to end my life right here and now. I don't know what I've done to deserve such tenderness, such kindness, from a guy. But I'm apt to roll around in it.

"I know you wouldn't hurt me, Jake," I manage to say. "Not intentionally."

"You ran away, though." His voice almost cracks with the emotions that must have propelled him to come after me. It makes my chest ache just thinking about it.

I shake my head. "Not from you. From everything. From things I couldn't control. I don't know what I'm doing anymore."

"You know exactly what you're doing." His hand moves to cup my face. "There are very few things in life we can control. Take you, for instance."

"Me?" I'm intrigued.

"Yeah, you," he says, a smile lighting his face. "I certainly didn't plan on you when I ran away from my life in New

York. And I certainly can't control how you make me feel. I didn't expect to meet someone like you, someone so head-strong and determined, yet someone who... needs me."

As a bit of a feminist, I should be offended, but I'm not. I *have* needed him. I've depended on him unlike anyone else before. I've needed a lot of things, but what I want most of all is now standing in front of me.

I deserve this. I'm not using Jake as a replacement for all the stupidity in my life because he's available. He's been hurt, too, being left at the altar. We need to heal each other's wounds.

His hand continues to caress my chin and I fear I may be lost forever in him. I reach up and still his hand, looking into his eyes. "I've been through a lot, Jake. My heart's been trampled." I don't want to think about Rick right now, or the time we shared—those wasted years—however, I need to be fair to Jake. He needs to know where I stand. "I don't want you to be my rebound guy."

He places his other hand on my face and leans his body into mine. "I don't want to be your rebound guy either, Isabella."

"And I don't want to be your rebound from Melinda."

He shakes me off. "Melinda's out of my life."

If Jake kisses me now, that's it. I'm done for. I have no sane decision-making power as long as he's touching me. I turn my head to the side to try and gain some rational control. Still, what I truly want to do is give in, live it up, enjoy Jake and everything he's offering. The guy did *follow* me here.

I look into his eyes again.

This can happen. I can allow it.

He must pick up on my thoughts because he gathers me into his arms and holds me tightly. With his lips hovering a mere breath away from mine, he says, "Let it happen, Isabella."

"You told me you weren't looking for a relationship," I say, reminding him of one of our first conversations.

"I wasn't."

"But you said—"

I feel his body chuckle. "Let it go. Let *us* happen."

That's all I need.

I kiss him for all I'm worth, opening up and wrapping myself around him. Around his support. His mouth is warm, covering mine and breathing life back into me. I grip onto him as the realization of what I'm succumbing to hits me like a kick in the gut. Dear God, I'm nuts about this guy. Plain and simple. I can't fight this.

I make short work of his leather jacket, black T-shirt, and jeans. At some point, he kicks his shoes off, but damn if I heard or saw it because I'm concentrating on his amazing physique, clothed only in Calvin Klein boxer briefs. They're not exactly hiding what's underneath either and I can't wait for an introduction. He pins me to the bed in the yummiest way, tracing kisses down my neck and into the open collar of the hotel robe. His fingers deftly loosen the knot at my waist and I gasp when I realize I'm naked as the day I was born. He seems surprised, too, but I was in the bathtub for heaven's sake.

His smile hitches up. "Were you expecting me?"

I smack at his arm and laugh. "Cocky bastard."

Snickering, he buries his head in my neck and continues his journey over my body. I'm hoping that the time imbibing on Jimmie's cock-eyed culinary concoctions haven't ruined my figure. Jake doesn't seem to care as he pushes the terry cloth aside and begins his exploration south.

Whoa...

I pull my left leg up so he can run his fingers down the length of me; so glad I'd shaved my legs last night. I love feeling Jake's hands on me. There's this amazing energy pulsating through me that I realize has been dormant for too long. I'm not simply talking about not having sex with Rick since like forever. I'm talking about feeling that someone else can't get enough of me, that I'm sexy and wanted, and important.

Jake looks at the leg he's caressing. "What in the world have you done to yourself now?" he asks with a slight laugh.

Oh geez, he's examining the allergy bumps. What a complete turnoff!

I roll to my side, cowering against his body. "Nut allergy struck again."

Jake cradles me to his chest and rotates to his back, pulling me along on top of him. Taking a nip at my lips, he asks, "What did you eat this time?"

"Would you believe I put almond oil in my bath?"

"Sure I would. Where did you get something like that?"

I lift up on his chest and motion my head to the complimentary Kama Sutra basket. "Came with the room," I say with an evil laugh. "A special package they have this weekend. Meant to attract couples."

He stops pushing the robe off my shoulders and reaches behind him for the basket. Of course, he snags a long strip of condoms. Flavored ones according to the packaging.

He raises an eyebrow. "I think we can make use of these."

"I don't see why not." Considering his underwear-clad manhood is pressing hard into my thigh, I get the feeling we'll be at this for a while. We both have a lot of catching up to do for lost time. "I'm game if you are," I say.

The teasing stops and Jake's face grows ever so serious. He flips us around so that he's on top again, pressing me into the fluffy mattress with the welcomed burden of his weight.

"I'm serious about this. I'm not playing games."

Oh. My.

I lace my fingers through his hair and pull him close. "Neither am I. I want you, Jake," I whisper. "So much."

He sighs against my skin. "You've got me," he says before he captures my lips again.

A deep understanding passes through us and the fire ignites.

There's no long, drawn out foreplay. Not at first. Not now. It's replaced by a need to be as one. His fingers dance across my skin and mine to the same with him. He's a work of human art with his tanned, muscular body. I spread my legs to welcome his invasion. One that's built to an all-consuming need. He positions himself over me; his strong arms flexing as he moves into place. Then he swiftly enters me in a quick heartbeat. I sigh in ecstasy and wrap my legs around his waist, accepting the onslaught of powerful emotions. I resist the urge to cry. Not tears of pain—although it's quite apparent to both of us that I haven't been practicing this carnal act for a while—but tears of relief.

Our hearts beat together, a rhythm to match the pace of our love making. I run my hands over his smooth rear, gripping tightly to the glutes as he sends me soaring to heights I'm not sure I've ever experienced. We move together in a syncopated rhythm, a musical interlude all our own to match the frenzied heat and pleasure of Bourbon Street outside. Sweat from both of us mingles together where our chests meet, sliding against each other in a flurried passion. His eyes squint at me as he rises over me with such concentration on his face. I pull my hands up to grasp the amazing pumped arms that hold him above me.

I'm alive. Like never before. My body sizzles. My insides beg for more.

And Jake's only too happy to assuage my sexual hunger.

The moment comes. Everything tenses. My breathing stops and then escalates, like I've just had the workout of a lifetime. I'm hit with a powerful wave of energy and delight that tingles from my head to my toe to the very heart of my womanhood.

Jake cries out. I do, too.

We clasp onto each other, riding out this satisfying union.

In our mutual climax, I am filled with his essence. He has given me the strength to face my life and the challenges before me, head on.

With inspiration like this, how can I go wrong?

CHAPTER THIRTY

I listen to the silence surrounding us. The stillness of the hotel. The quiet of the garden outside. The cadence of Jake's breath against my shoulder. The rhythm of his heart pounding against my back.

For the first time in months, I feel like I'm home, only a home unlike any I've ever experienced.

I relish the time I've spent with Jake on the farm, getting to know him, getting to know myself. It's like I've been given a glimpse at a different side of me. I'm still a city girl at heart, but I can't deny the farm has changed me. It's inevitably changed Jake as well. Just as I have to eventually return to Boston, I wonder when he'll head back to New York. To whatever demon he ran from that he'll eventually have to face.

He pulls me against him and places a warm kiss on the top of my shoulder. "Are you awake?"

I nod. My chest hurts in the most delicious way, following in a lazy dip down to my stomach.

"What are you thinking?" he asks.

"Isn't that supposed to be my question?" I ask with a smile.

"Women aren't the only ones who wonder things like that."

I adjust in his arms until I'm facing him. His jaw is slightly stubbled, considering the hour—I'm going to have some delectable whisker burns on my breasts—and his eyes convey his satisfaction. "You're quite proud of yourself, aren't you?"

His body shakes with mirth. Straight white teeth show under his sturdy lips. Lips that have obviously had a master's course in love making. "I have no complaints," he says.

I twist my hands around his arm that covers my chest. "Neither do I."

"So, really, what were you thinking about?" he asks again, his finger trailing down my cheek.

"What made you leave New York?"

He sighs and rolls onto his back. He flops his forearm over his eyes in a painfully obvious "I don't want to talk about it" manner. I'm not having it, though.

I run my hand over his chest, teasing his nipple for good measure. "Jake, don't shut me out."

When my fingers find the fresh scar on his shoulder, he shudders slightly. I know this is the key to his troubles. I adjust up onto my knees and lean over him. Softly, I layer a kiss over the puckered flesh that mars his otherwise perfect physique.

He reaches his hands up and takes my face. "You're amazing."

"I know," I say with a wink. Then I grow serious. I drag my finger across the silvery scar again. "Tell me about this. Is this what you're running from?"

Jake lifts my hand and places a soft kiss on my fingers. Then he clasps it to his chest and stares at the ceiling beams. "My running has to do with Grant's death."

I don't move my hand to get away. I merely sit still, mentally hoping to pull the story from him. From the way his heart is slamming away underneath my touch, I know we're at an important point.

Taking a deep breath, he says, "I got stabbed during a drug bust. It went down all wrong. The kid was hyped up on something he'd snorted."

His heart continues to drum, but I'm not stopping him. He needs this release.

"Grant got word that these kids were grinding up Ritalin prescriptions and snorting it like coke for one hell of a high. White collar kids, you know, not street kids. When they couldn't buy pills from their friends anymore, they started buying it on the street. Grant had a tip that a big deal was going down, so we moved in. I wasn't paying attention—or something—and I ran into a garbage can, knocking the lid off and causing a commotion."

I try not to wince at the picture Jake's painting.

"First, the kids panicked and took off running. Grant showed his badge and tried to reason with them. One kid—couldn't have been more than sixteen—pulled out a hunting knife and went ape shit. He went straight for Grant and sliced his throat open before I could even draw my weapon."

My body tenses at his words. "Jesus, Jake. That's horrible." My eyes fill with tears. I can't imagine the horror of witnessing anything that atrocious happening to one of my sisters. I can see in his eyes that Jake is reliving the moment, probably for the gazillionth time. I want so much to take the pain away. "You don't have to tell me more."

"Yes, I do." His agony is evident.

"I'm listening, Jake."

"I killed the kid."

My heart nearly stops at his admission, yet I understand. Of course he did. "You had to."

"No, Isabella, it wasn't my duty." His eyes are wild, understandably so. "I wasn't thinking clearly or trying to protect and serve. The oath I'd taken. I *wanted* to kill the little fucker. I wanted him to pay for taking my brother's life. The rage inside me was horrifying. I didn't recognize myself. He came after me, got me with the knife, as you can see, but goddammit, I killed him with my bare hands. I strangled the shit out of him until the drugs in his system couldn't fight back anymore."

I hitch myself up on my side and lay over his chest, kissing the tortured wound on his shoulder again. Loving him with all I can. "You did what anyone else would have done."

"Yeah, my sergeant agreed. Said I killed him in self-defense, but it was a mess. The kid was on the honor roll and had been admitted to Yale. Not a pretty picture, as you can imagine. So, it was best that I disappear while everything played out."

I bring my lips to his hoping to offer some tiny bit of solace. To let him know I understand completely and don't blame him for his reactions.

"It's more than that," he says. "Everything fell apart. My whole life. Melinda walked out on me. My father won't talk to me. And it's all my fault."

"What is?"

"Grant's death. It's my fault that he died. I blew it." Tears swim around the rim of his eyes.

"No it's not! That kid was strung out. He's the one who's at fault, not you."

"Tell my father that. He blames me."

"Oh Jake. You're not to blame. Sometimes really bad stuff happens to good people and we just don't know. I would never blame you for what happened to your brother."

"I didn't pay attention. I got distracted. I didn't cover his back and he—" I'm afraid to move or comment. I know he's taking a minute in his own mind to suss out the events of that horrible day. "It was all my fault," he says in a voice barely above a whisper.

"Jake, you can't torture yourself over something you couldn't control."

"Isabella, I know you're trying to help, but you weren't there. You don't know. You didn't have to see the look in his eyes as he died."

"I imagine it's the most painful thing you've ever experienced." Although death and violence are so much a part of being a cop, it would be hard not to be touched by witnessing people at their absolute worst.

His hands slide into my hair, rubbing and soothing. I feel relief seep from him as I don't stand in judgment over him. His eyes darken in the dimly lit room. "I can't go back."

Looking up, I ask, "To New York?"

"To New York. To being a cop. That part of my life is over."

"You don't have to go back."

"I do have things I need to face."

"You always have a place on the farm."

He traces my lips with his finger. "Thanks, *bella*."

"You need to mend things with your dad, though," I tell him.

"I know. I was actually on my way to see my father in Key Largo when my bike broke down. Dad didn't make it to Grant's funeral because he's too old to travel. I to need face *him*. I need his forgiveness."

"There's nothing to forgive."

He shrugs. "We'll see."

Another demon to wrestle.

I lay my head on his chest again. "What will you do if you're not a cop?"

Stroking my back, he says, "A friend of mine has a new security company and wants me to partner with him. It's not a rent-a-cop thing in a fake uniform. It's high tech. Satellites, fiber optic cabling, and using computers for everything. I could make a decent living off it, especially with everyone being so security-minded these days."

"Sounds promising. Good money." I pause for a moment.

"Maybe, I don't know." His smile returns, warming me to my toes. "Why, where are you going to be now? Are you going back to Boston?"

I honestly don't know the answer to this question so I shrug. Right now, the only place I want to be is by Jake's side.

"Where is this friend with the security company?" I ask.

"The Florida Keys."

"It would be nice if—"

For some reason I can't finish the sentence.

Laughter bubble from him. "What?"

I hide my face in his chest, not understanding my sudden shyness. The man's been inside me for heaven's sake. I guess it's because I'm letting him know I want him in my life. Such a bold thing for a woman of the twenty-first century to admit.

I drop my eyes. "I'd just like to be... near you."

My words are eaten up by his kiss. Aggressive and hot. Passionate and emotional. Laughter trickles from the crease in his mouth and no other words have to be spoken. He gets my drift. His tongue traces the inside of my mouth, mating with mine as we spiral, once again, out of control. He fills me up with the sense of him and I know I'll never get enough.

Ever.

CHAPTER THIRTY-ONE

I slip out into the dewy morning, being careful not to wake Jake as I go out into the courtyard. Over in the corner, a guy is reading *The Times-Picayune*, drinking coffee and smoking a cigarette. I sniff, capturing the tang of the nicotine that fills the air. Damn, I could go for a smoke. However, I gave up the nasty habit when I finished college. It sure would be good to top off an evening—and early morning—of full-out sex with a long drag on my good old friend, Virginia Slim.

Instead, I pull my cell phone out of my bathrobe pocket and dial the familiar number in Boston of a more important friend. Ten o'clock on a Friday morning, Vanessa should be at her desk.

"Vanessa Virtue."

"Hey be-atch."

"Griz! What's going on? How are things down on the farm?"

I adjust in the iron chair and tuck my feet underneath me. "I wouldn't know. I'm in New Orleans."

"What are you doing there?"

I pull my fingers up to my lips in a mock motion of smoking a cigarette. I breathe in deeply and then exhale the pretend smoke. "I needed a break."

"Why don't you just come home?" she pleads. "The wedding is next weekend and I could use some help with the final details. You've totally abandoned me as maid of honor."

"I thought you weren't going to make a big production out of this wedding."

"I'm not, really. Kyle's been great helping me out, but he's a guy, you know? He doesn't care that I'm having a hard time finding white hydrangeas to decorate the chapel. He's like 'babe, as long as you're there, that's all that matters.'"

My heart lurches in a sweet way at how wonderful Kyle is and how lucky Vanessa is to have him. Looking at the closed door to room 140, I'm feeling pretty fortunate myself. It's not every day a gal gets greeted by a hunk in leather, who drove over two hours on a motorcycle to deliver tulips.

And the best sex of a lifetime.

I close my eyes and hold the phone tightly to my head, reliving the precious memories of having sex—no, making love—with Jake. My skin tingles at the reminiscence and I long for more. Though it's deeper than that. It's him. Everything about him. His strength. His courage. His determination. All that he's been through and all he's battling internally. I've never met anyone quite so perfect inside and out.

Vanessa continues to prattle on. "My mother wants us to use Beethoven's 'Ode to Joy' for the processional but I want to use something less traditional." She stops for a minute. "Griz, are you still there?"

I snap out of my haze and smile like Vanessa's sitting right there with me. "I'm listening."

She snorts. "Like hell you are and I don't blame you. I'm a complete bore and self-centered. You called me. Was there something you wanted to tell me?"

I don't know if it's time to talk about this just yet. I'm still coming to terms with the emotions swirling through my system. My world changed overnight. For the first time in nearly a year, Isabella Perry has hopes for a happy ending.

"Jesus, this is serious," she exclaims. "You're never this quiet. Did a tornado destroy the chicken houses or something?"

"No, Double V, this has nothing to do with the farm."

And yet, it has everything to do with the farm.

With Aunt Stella's fortune, which wasn't in the form of money, but a special man.

Vanessa knows me like the back of her hand. "You sound weird. You're either drunk or... oh my God, you got laid!"

"Vanessa! Don't make it sound so crass. It was... *special.*"

"Hold on." I hear her set the phone down, get up and close the door to her office. Then she returns and scoops the phone up. "Dish it, bitch."

I do. I tell her everything from catching Jake fresh from the shower on Day One to our fishing lesson to him showing up here last night. Every detail. Well, most of them. I leave out the part about trying out the honey dust and feather last night.

She's silent and I don't know whether she's happy for me or pissed off that I've somehow been disloyal to Kyle's best friend. I know the inevitable question is coming.

"What about Rick, Griz?"

I adjust in the wrought iron chair and stretch my legs out to the empty one opposite me. "What about him?" *Hello... he dumped me.* Or do I need to remind her that? When in reality, I feel like he actually set me free.

"Don't you still love him?" she asks again.

Remarkably, I need very little time to think on this question. Yes, at one time I loved Rick dearly and thought I would for the rest of my life. In a way, I always will love him. Only not the kind of love it takes to sustain a long-term relationship. At the first sign of personal despair, Rick withdrew into himself, closing me off. When things turned around for him, he decided not to include me, but rather to "get off the pot," as he so aptly put it.

But Jake's been by my side through this whole farm ordeal, supporting me, helping out, and telling me I could do it. He's been my biggest cheerleader and my most supportive fan. Even though he's fighting his own inner turmoil, he's included me in his life, made a space on the shelf where I can sit and observe, offer advice and be there when he needs me.

For better or worse.

Vanessa breaks my thoughts again. "Do you love Rick, Griz?"

Bravely, I take a deep breath, exhilaration filling my body. "No, V. I love Jake."

"Who the hell is Jake?"

The man across the garden looks up and smiles at me, tipping his coffee mug in my direction. After I calm Vanessa down from her scolding me for not telling her about Jake, I regale her with the whole story.

I sit up tall and nearly sing out. "I'm *in love* with Jake."

"You just met him," Vanessa presses. I know she's got this allegiance to Rick because of Kyle, but I won't be daunted.

"It doesn't matter," I say. "It's like I've known Jake my whole life. Rather, I've been looking for him my whole life. He completes me."

"Who are you, frickin' Jerry Maguire?"

"I'm not kidding here, Vanessa. I mean it. This is it for me. I've found what you and Kyle have. Can't you be happy for me?"

I know she's struggling with this, but I also know she'll come around. That's what bestest friends do.

"Yeah. Okay. Of course I can be, Griz. I love you, hon. I want you to be happy, like I am. I want you to have love like I've found. You deserve it."

I nod into the phone. "I know I do."

"So, Jake Hansen, huh? You love him and that's all there is to it," she says.

Yeah, I do love him. I'd be a fool not to.

As if on cue, the door to room 140 creaks open and Jake squints up at the sunshine teaming through the lazy tree branches providing a canopy over the garden.

He grips the door and leans out. His bronzed torso makes my insides react, but my heart responds to the wink and smile he tosses my way. He mouths, "Hey."

I beam at him and stand up. Walking around the brick flower box, I steer toward my room, almost forgetting that I'm still on the phone.

"Um. Vanessa, I've got to go."

"He's there, isn't he? I can sense it."

"Yeah, you're right."

She giggles. "And he's naked, isn't he."

"Close to it," I say with an evil grin. "We'll talk soon."

"You better be at the wedding next weekend."

"Of course I will."

"Bring the Hunk-a-Hunk of Burning Love with you, why don't you?" she tacks on.

I reach out and lace Jake's fingers through mine. I look into his deep blue eyes that are focused on me and me alone. "I might just do that."

"Take care of yourself, Griz. And make sure that guy knows how special you are."

I pause in front of Jake as he stands there in the doorway. To Vanessa I say, "I'm all over it. Bye!" I click "end" and stash the phone in my pocket.

His smile crooks up in the corner. "You're all over what?"

"You." I wrap my arms around his middle and laze my tongue across his nipple. The sensation rocks me to my toes and my heart expands with the wonderful love I feel for him.

He hauls me into the room and back to the bed. Tugging me down into his lap, he says, "I like the sound of that." He pushes my robe aside and begins feasting on my shoulder. Man, I'm total putty in his hands. I don't know if I can feel any more joy. It's like I'm going to burst. From this man. This wonderful man who has changed my life.

"Oh, Jake, you've turned me into a nympho." His tongue lolls over my earlobe and the goose bumps break out over my skin. Oh yeah, he knows how to fine-tune me. I want to stay in bed all day and learn everything there is to know about him.

As if reading my mind, he pushes away slightly and looks into my eyes. "First, a late breakfast." He places a kiss on the end of my nose and says, "Then let's be tourists."

I cup his face and return his kiss. "Sounds like good outdoor fun. We'll need GPS."

"No, we won't," he says, nipping my lips again. "I've got it covered."

"How so?"

He nibbles my bottom lip, pulling it into his mouth. "I want to show you my city."

"*Your* city?"

"Yeah, I was born and raised here."

CHAPTER THIRTY-TWO

There's nothing like starting out the morning with a cup of creamy, chicory-flavored café au lait, a plate of powder sugar covered beignets, and a kick-ass handsome man who happens to have sugar all down the front of him.

Jake reaches for his fifth napkin. "It's impossible to eat these things without getting this stuff all over you."

The deep fried dough is sweet and airy and completely hits the spot for my famished body that has subsisted for the past fourteen hours strictly on items from the mini bar. Pringles, Planters (despite knowing how they're fertilized), and Snickers can only keep you going for so long. Same with sex. At some point, you have to come up for air.

Not too long, I hope.

"This is quintessential New Orleans," I say, looking around the crowded Café du Monde, the famed French Market coffee stand in Jackson Square. I pop the last bit of beignet into my mouth and smile at Jake. He leans over and kisses the side of my mouth. Then, he pulls his thumb across my bottom lip.

"You had a little sugar right there."

"Uh huh... sure..." I lean toward him for another kiss, this time a bit longer and more on the PDA side.

I don't know what's better, the French pastries or Jake. A girl shouldn't have to decide.

I drain the last bit of my coffee. "What's on the agenda?"

Jake wipes his mouth again and shifts in his chair. "We could be total tourists and take one of those." He points across the street to people lined up to take various tours of the French Quarter in horse drawn carriages. "Or we could do it my way."

"Which is?"

"Get off the beaten track. Take the streetcar—"

"—Named Desire?" I interrupt with a giggle. He drops a quick kiss on my lips to shut me up. "Well, it *was* based here."

He pulls his hand up to my neck and rubs gently. "As I was saying before I was so rudely interrupted is we can take the St. Charles Avenue streetcar out towards the Garden District and I can show you where I grew up."

I smile. "I'd like that." Seeing Jake's boyhood home will go a long way to showing me what kind of man he's become. Hell, in the two years I dated Rick, I went to his parent's house once. And they live in Massachusetts.

We pay our bill, wipe the excess powdered sugar from our clothing, and take off hand-in-hand down Decatur Street and past the Jax Brewery. After a bit of window-shopping and more PDA, we turn right onto Canal Street and head for the streetcar stop. When it arrives, it's just what I imagined. Old-timey, with wooden benches and big windows so I can get a good look at the city around me. The air smells of roasted nuts and a potpourri of flowers. A rich jasmine scent that coats my nostrils.

"The cars didn't run for a while after Katrina hit," he tells me.

I nod, remembering how horrible the aftermath from the vicious hurricane. I can see remnants of the storms fury even still here and there, as this city continues to heal.

Jake sits close to me on the bench as the streetcar lumbers down St. Charles Avenue, circles Lee Square, passes Emeril Lagasse's Delmonico restaurant and into the famed Garden District. Even this time of year, the atmosphere is alive with white flower petals floating off the blooming trees and scattering about like nature's confetti. Everywhere you look—in the trees, on power lines, on people's porches—Mardi Gras beads of all colors adorn the area as if a party takes place every night.

Jake reaches for the stop cord. "First Street. This is us."

I follow him off the trolley after making sure my day pass is tucked securely in the back pocket of my jeans. Jake takes my hand and pulls me along behind him as we cross the busy street and head down First Street. The houses are amazing. So large, deep, so French in design with black shutters, wrought iron railings and perfectly tended gardens. Each house and yard is unique, meant to entertain tourist with the fresh fragrance of flowers and the beauty of the Louisiana architecture.

"You grew up *here*?" I ask.

"We're almost there."

"Are you like a rich kid?"

He chuckles. "No. Not at all." He stops to face me. "Well, I guess you could say we did okay. Grant and I never wanted for anything growing up. See, my parents inherited the house from my grandfather, so it wasn't like they paid a fortune to live here. My dad made a hefty profit when he sold it to move to Key Largo."

We start walking again and I can't resist questioning. "Where's your mom?"

Jake squints ahead, but doesn't seem upset at my pressing. "She died during my junior year at Tulane. She battled cancer for a while. That's why I decided to go to school here."

My heart lurches for this man. Not only did he lose his brother in a tragic way, he doesn't have the comfort of his mother when he needs it. My mother can be a big pain in my butt at times, trying to run my life from Chicago, but at least I still have her. Makes me want to call her and tell her how much I love her.

"There it is," Jake says, drawing my attention back to our sightseeing.

I gaze across the street at the immaculately groomed green lawn, outlined with orange, red, and pink flowers. Some are azaleas, but the others look more exotic. The house is two stories with the traditional black iron railing and is a deep mauve color. An expansive porch circles the side, disappearing into a looming, wispy garden.

"It's gorgeous." I take a deep breath. "When did your dad sell?"

"About eight years ago. It was too much for him. Too lonely, he said, without Mom, Grant, and me." Jake glances wistfully across the street and I can read the emotions behind his eyes.

"Are you thinking about Grant?"

"Yeah. Hard not to." He points to the top level. "He and I used to shimmy down that drain pipe, onto the top of the front porch and sneak out of the house. We were hellions."

"I bet you were." Something tells me he wasn't just a hellion, but a heartbreaker, too, sneaking out to see girls. My cheeks flame at the thought of another woman enjoying Jake's company, his kisses, and his touch. I squash the inkling feelings because it's simply stupid. I'm the one here with him now. Changing my thought process, I say, "I hope it doesn't hurt you to be here."

He shakes his head. "I had a good childhood. I was taken care of, given opportunities, and I did my best with them. I only wish—"

He drops my hand and paces to the end of the block.

"Wish what, Jake?" That you'd never left here? That you'd never become a cop? That you'd never witnessed your brother's death?

"It's my dad. I wanted so much for him to be proud of me. He was a Crescent City cop for thirty years. Aside from doing what my big brother did, I wanted to be like my father. Strong, responsible, a family man." He looks into my eyes. "I've failed him on all accounts."

I try to gulp down the actual idea of starting a family with Jake—something I'd never seriously considered with Rick—and focus on his pain right now.

"You're not a failure, Jake. You've simply had something bad happen to you. You're reassessing your priorities and taking care of yourself."

He opens his mouth to speak, but instead takes my hand and leads me farther down the street, away from his glorious boyhood home and deeper into the magnificent display of stately manors. His mood shifts, like he's tucking the pain aside to deal with later. "Come on, let me show you where Anne Rice used to live and then I'll take you for the best cheeseburger of your life."

I smile, knowing that he is opening up to me and will do so more. I took Elements of Persuasion in college and I've gotten him to tell me this much. Share these parts of his life with me. I want to know everything about him and I want to help heal his soul. Just as he's healed mine.

Squeezing his hand and letting deeper conversations go for now, I say, "Can I get mine with relish and onions?"

He laughs. "Just don't expect me to kiss you afterwards."

⚜   ⚜   ⚜

Two hours later, after a walking tour of Lafayette cemetery and the Tulane campus, Jake and I are sitting on stools at the diner counter of The Camilla Grille, a landmark in New Orleans. The sizzle of hamburgers sparks the air and the scent of fresh-made pecan pie hovers overhead. Not like I can have any of it.

The waiter slides a small plate at me, filled to capacity with a meaty cheeseburger, topped with mayo and lettuce. I reach for the condiments and dabble on a healthy serving of relish and onions. On second thought, maybe I'll nix the onions. I take a bite and the juiciness of the burger oozes over my fingers. The taste takes me back to a childhood memory, of when I was a little girl in Chicago.

"You know," I say with my mouth full. "My father used to take us to this diner in Illinois that served food like this."

Jake holds his sandwich up next to mine and taps them together in a culinary toast. "To the perfect cheeseburger of childhood."

Now's the time to pry more. I reach for a deliciously greasy cheese fry and ask, "Did your family come here to eat?"

Swiping the napkin across his mouth, Jake says, "All the time. My mother was crazy about the omelets, Dad liked the pancakes and Grant and I always went for the burgers."

"Crazy red meat-eating men," I tease.

He points at my burger. "Speak for yourself."

This feels good. It feels right. Like I was destined to be here with Jake, learning about his life and seeing what molded him into the man he is today. He needs my encouragement, though. A little prodding to leap that hurdle looming in front of him.

"You should go see him, you know?"

"Who?" Jake asks, knowing damn well who I mean.

"Your dad."

"I know." He pauses. "I will... soon." He nabs a fry and pops it into his mouth. "I'm almost ready. It'll be hard to see the disappointment in his eyes. I have to face it eventually."

Laying my hand on his arm, I say, "I'm sure it won't be bad. He loves you, Jake."

So do I.

I quaff on the emotional knot in my throat. Jake gazes into my eyes and I almost feel like he can read my thoughts. A smile crosses his face and he runs his thumb over my bottom lip. Then he moves in and his lips touch mine and the za-za-zing shoots from my brain to my feet.

"Excuse me folks," the waiter interrupts. I pull away from Jake, slightly embarrassed. "Your purse is ringing, Miss."

"Oh, oh!" My cell phone. I grab the sleek silver device and look at the caller ID. My heart falls to my feet with I see the familiar number of someone I don't want to speak to. No, not the hated Boss from Hell, Claudia Coldren. No... it's Rick.

"I don't believe this." Myriad thoughts criss-cross in front of me. Do I answer? Do I send it to voice mail?

Another ring with Rick's Facebook picture staring out at me.

Jake's eyes widen. "What's wrong?"

How dare Rick call me right now of all times? "Sorry, Jake. I need to take this"

I press "send" and stand to walk outside. I don't even say hello.

"Isabella? Are you there?"

I clear my throat. "What do you want?"

"Nice attitude," Rick says sarcastically.

"What do you expect, Rick?" I ask.

"I expect you to tell me who the hell Jake Hansen is."

Really? *This* is why he called me? Not to say he was sorry or to apologize, but to get all alpha wolf or territorial. I can see it now. As soon as I got off the phone with Vanessa, she called Kyle and told him everything. And, of course, Kyle being Rick's best friend, he called him and told him that he'd blown it. Now Rick's ego can't handle that I've moved on.

"I don't owe you anything, Rick. So don't go getting all sanctimonious on me."

Rick's anger nearly crackles over the phone line. "You just hook up with the first grease monkey you meet in Alabama. Does he have all of his teeth?"

What an ass. "He's a cop. From New York, by way of New Orleans," I say, defending Jake.

"That makes no sense," Rick says. "What the hell is he doing in Alabama?"

I pace back in forth in front of the restaurant and shake my head in frustration. "Why? Are you writing a book?" I snark off.

"What if I am?" he tarts back.

I growl into the phone. "Then make it a mystery."

I am literally about to hang up when I hear him chuckle. "That's my girl. Always making me laugh."

My nostrils flare. "I am *not* your girl anymore. You made it abundantly clear that you wanted to 'get off the pot.' So what I do and *who* I do no longer concerns you."

"I can't believe that after all we went through together you'd just hook up with the first guy you meet."

Now it's my turn to laugh. "We're not seriously having this conversation, are we? You dump me in a bathroom and I'm supposed to just tell you what's going on in my life like you're my BFF? It doesn't work that way, Rick!" I stop and catch my breath.

Silence permeates the conversation.

Then Rick sniffs. Is he crying?

"I figured we'd cool it for a while, but that we'd get back together," he tells me. "You know, once we're both ready to settle down and start a family."

"You broke up with me!" So much for catching my breath. "But you know what? It was the best thing that ever happened to me because I realized what was missing from my life. I've learned so much about myself and what I can handle. I'm another person now, Rick. And I'm in love with someone else."

"Just like that?" he asks quietly.

"Yes."

He doesn't even say goodbye. He just hangs up.

That's okay. I made my point.

A bit shaken, I make my way back into the diner. I sit next to Jake and let my hands trail over his jean-clad thighs. "That was my ex," I admit.

"He can't have you back," Jake says firmly.

I drop my gaze coyly and enjoy the yummy thrill that tickles my spine. "No, he's certainly not. I'm happy with where I am right now."

"Good," he says. "So am I."

We meet halfway in a sweet kiss that tastes of burgers and fries, only adding to the memory of this treasure palace of his childhood.

When I pull back, I look at him seriously. "I want to find a way to get rid of the farm, but I want to keep the house. A getaway of sorts."

"I think that sounds great," he tells me.

"It needs some work—a coat of paint, cable, internet— but I think it's good move."

Jake turns and crams the last two fries into his mouth. Then, he wipes his hands on the paper napkin. "So, what's the next step? You want to get out of here or what?"

"Well, I'm booked at the Dauphine for one more night and then it's back to Dilligus Flats."

Jake picks my phone up from the counter and hands it to me. "Might as well get a head start."

I screw up my face. "What do you mean?"

"Who gives a shit what Esterhazy thinks? If you want to sell the farm, sell it. Don't let him scare you with threats of lawsuits or contracts. You know he's Double C's lawyer, too, right? He's just trying to manipulate you."

I flatten my lips and feel as if my eyes have completely bugged out of my head. "What? I did *not* know that little tidbit. What a bastard."

I reach into my purse for the business card of Westin Esterhazy and dial.

Isabella Perry's life is finally back on track.

CHAPTER THIRTY-THREE

Two days later, we reluctantly head back to Dilligus Flats. "Jake, pull off at the rest stop. I've got to pee."

He chuckles as he puts on the turn signal and steers the Chevy Shit off of I-10 and into the Alabama welcome center. His motorcycle rattles in the bed of the truck when we come to a stop in front of the large white building.

I move away from him to scoot out the door. "Be right back."

"You have the smallest bladder of any female I've ever known," he notes.

"Is that a particular quality you look for in a woman?"

"You have plenty of other qualities that interest me more."

I stick out my tongue and shut the door behind me. Making my way to the ladies' room, I squirm at the delicious memories of our final evening in New Orleans.

Jake doesn't need to elaborate on what he looks for in a woman I know. He pretty much listed all the areas that interested him last night when we tried out the position on page fifteen in the Kama Sutra book. And the one on page twenty-three. And the one on page twenty-eight.

I have no doubt of Jake's attractions or feelings for that matter. Whispered words in the darkness go a long way toward touching my heartstrings. Endearments I'd like to hear again in the light of day. Right now, I'm in assuming mode regarding our future knowing we'll iron things out before I leave for Vanessa and Kyle's wedding. There will be plenty of time to figure out our future when I get back to settle everything in Dilligus Flats.

I'm thinking positively... for once.

When I get back to the truck, Jake's on his cell phone. He jumps when he hears me quickly stashing the device in his jean pocket. The vein in his neck pulsates strongly and I wonder what I'm missing.

"Everything okay?" I ask, feeling it's okay to push.

"Yeah. Fine." He puts the truck in gear.

"If something's wrong, you can tell me."

"No," he assures me. "Just e-mails from people I no longer want to talk to."

"Melinda?" I ask immediately, my heart pounding hard in anticipation of his answer.

Jake shrugs. "I've ignored her for months."

"Do you still love her?" I ask with a pointed stare.

Jake turns and pins me with his eyes. "Do you still love Rick?"

Touché. If Melinda is e-mailing him, I guess I need to get over it since I didn't tell Jake that I'd talked to Rick on the phone while we were in New Orleans. None of that matters now, right? Jake and I are together. Melinda and Rick are both part of our collective pasts.

I try not to think about our exes as Jake turns us back out onto the interstate. Instead, I wonder how Jimmie's been doing with the chickens and how production is, considering the mister tragedy I walked away from.

"You know, I owe so much to Jimmie," I say to Jake. "I couldn't have survived this long without his help."

"Jimmie's a good guy."

"I wonder why Stella didn't marry him when she came back to Dilligus Flats?" I stare out the window, looking for answers to questions no one can provide to me.

Jake tugs at my hand to bring me closer to him while continuing to steer. "Who can understand other people's relationships? It's not for us to question."

Is that a reference to the earlier mention of our exes? I'm not sure, but I don't want to over-analyze.

I scoot over until our legs are touching and his right hand covers my knee. I don't move my hand to his thigh—like I want—since I want him to concentrate on the road ahead. I need to be serious. "I think it's important that you know about my relationship with Rick."

Glancing over, I see somewhat of a pained look cross Jake's face before he returns his gaze ahead. "Why's that?"

"I spent a lot of time with the guy. Two years of being a couple, thinking about the future, things like that. Then it all just disappeared. In a flash." More like a flush.

Jake removes his hand from my knee and steers the truck onto the exit that will eventually get us to Dilligus Flats. At least that s what I'm assuming and that he isn't pulling away from me.

"What I mean," I say, "is that I don't know if I can trust myself with relationships or what they mean because I mis-judged the last one so poorly." I'm an idiot. This is coming out all wrong.

"You can't condemn yourself because of the actions of another person," Jake says with assurance in his voice. "Besides, you said he broke up with you. That was his deci-sion and reflects on him, not you."

"I know," I say. "What I'm saying is how do you know to trust your emotions? To listen to your gut and throw caution to the wind?" Because I want to. With Jake.

"Sometimes you just have to lay your cards on the table, Isabella. And not think too much." His face softens and the side of his mouth hitches up. "Isabella... that's a mighty big name for someone like you. What does it mean?"

"Consecrated by God," I answer with a laugh. "My father's a Baptist minister."

He shakes his head. "Preacher's kids. The worst. Gotta watch out for them. They'll break your heart."

Mine takes a dip down to my stomach and back at his teasing. "I'd never break yours, Jake. I know what it feels like to be trampled on."

"Rick again, huh?"

"I'm sorry. It's not that I'm dwelling on it, it's just—"

He holds his hand up. "You don't have to explain. Remember, I've been there, too."

Crap, I'm no good at the whole laying cards on the table thing. I wish we weren't in the truck having this conversation. I wish we were lying in bed again. We're good in bed. Now, Jake seems to be a bit on the pensive side, and I wonder if it's something I've said or done, or whether he's thinking about his own future as I seem to be on the cusp of mine.

He's right, though. I *do* need to lay my hand on the table. In retrospect, I wasted a lot of time on Rick only to have my heart broken. The thing is, I needed that wake up call. I needed the cages of my world rattled. I needed for Rick to get off the pot. Because if we had been destined for each other, we wouldn't have been going through such a rough patch. We wouldn't have withheld our true feelings or emotions from each other. We wouldn't have turned away during career crisis and we would have consulted each other about our futures.

Jake's right. I don't need to think too much. I just need to tell him like it is.

And I will once we get back to the farm. Maybe once we're curled up together in bed.

Maybe just when the nerve strikes me.

We exit off the interstate and Jake maneuver's the truck through the country roads. We bounces along for a while in silence until I see the fence line of my property up ahead. A very fine fence line that Jake toiled long hours over. For Stella. For me. Perhaps for himself.

I reach over and rub his thigh. Now's the time. "Jake, I—"

"There's a car in the drive," he notes. "Maybe Esterhazy's found a buyer already."

"I don't care. This is about you and me, Jake. About the way I feel. I need to tell you something."

I can do it. Three little words.

Jake steers the truck in behind the white Ford Taurus that screams "rental car." He shifts the truck into park and turns to me. "Are you okay? You look really serious."

I wet my dry lips with my tongue, needing to find my voice somehow. The pounding of my pulse reverbs in my ears and I feel as if I might have a heart attack before I'm able to get this out. "I am, Jake. I need to say this. I've got to get the words out."

I'm going to burst with the love I feel for him. And I want him to know it. Now.

He takes my hands in his and smiles, no longer brooding. Maybe he can see in my eyes that I'm nuts about him, that I never want to leave him and I want to be with him always.

"Jake.. I... I—"

But he looks past me at whoever steps out of the car.

I tear my eyes from Jake's, from the moment of revelation, and glance across the yard and up onto the porch where someone bounds down the steps. In the twilight, it's hard to see clearly, but the woman marching toward us in designer clothes and high heels—that she's not managing well in on the lawn—is *not* happy.

Jake's head turns to follow the progression of my eyes. "What the hell is she doing here?" he utters like a curse.

He pulls away from me and the moment's lost. For a moment, I thought Rick had found me here. That I could have dealt with. This is worse.

The figure approaches the truck and my world teeters on its axis. Words collide in my throat threatening to strangle all the happiness from my soul. I gag them down, stuffing them into a place at the bottom of my stomach to digest later.

"Is that—?" I'm unable to finish the question due to the look on Jake's face. It's as if he's seen a ghost. A figure from his past. One he once loved. One he once pledged himself to.

"Melinda," he says with a bit too much emotion lacing his voice.

"Jake Hansen, you son of a bitch," she calls out to him, her silky chestnut hair highlighted by the setting sun. "I've been looking for you for months."

Not only is Jake's ex-fiancée here in front of me, but she's gorgeous. Like Fifth Avenue meets the Fashion District meets Victoria's Secret model stunning.

Jake drops my hand and moves away.

There's no way I can compete with such a goddess.

Chapter Thirty-Four

"What are you doing here, Melinda?" he asks her. Jake steps out of the cab of the truck and moves so I can get out. I'm pissed, with a capital "P." Just when I'm about to tell Jake how I feel, the altar-skipping bitch shows up looking smug and confident as if Jake still belongs to her. I notice there's a large, sparkly diamond ring on her left hand. Is she continuing to wear *his* ring even though she's the one who didn't show up for the wedding?

"Jake, darling," she says in a sexy voice. "I've been worried sick."

Melinda rushes forward, tripping up on the moist lawn. She reaches out for Jake with long, slender arms. The woman is totally oblivious to me as she throws herself into his arms. I feel like a complete idiot just standing here while these two reunite. She kisses him with her red-painted pursed lips. He doesn't exactly participate, but he doesn't push her away.

My mouth falls open. This woman left him standing at the altar, yet he holds her to him like a long-lost lover that he's missed. Tears immediately sting my eyes at the realization that I don't know Jake at all. Sharing a bed for a weekend doesn't mean that we share a soul no matter how romantic I feel about our union.

Then Jake, the Jake I just spent time with in New Orleans, pushes Melinda back from him, leveling his blue stare at her. "Worried sick? Really? You left me standing at the church waiting for you in a rented tux."

She lowers her heavily made up lashes. "I know, darling. I panicked, but only momentarily. It was your normal wedding day jitters. And then the limo got caught in traffic and by the time I arrived, you'd left. Everyone had left. I was devastated and heart broken."

To his credit, Jake rolls his eyes at her. "How did you find me... here?"

Melinda grabs his arm and hand possessively, tugging him toward her. "Jake, I've been frantic for months. No one knows anything about you. You don't answer my texts or e-mails or calls. You completely disappear from Manhattan. I had Daddy contact a private detective friend of his and—"

Jake snarls at her. "Your father? My *boss*? The one who demanded that I take administrative leave after what happened with Grant and that kid?"

"—Jake, stop it! Daddy's been just as concerned."

I pop to attention at this turn of events. Jake's captain is Melinda's father? He'd omitted that little detail out of the story he'd told me. I shake my head and wonder what my role is here in this tête-á-tête.

I want to scream out.

I want to wave my arms about.

I want them both to acknowledge that I'm standing here, shifting in place and wondering if the last few days in New Orleans are all that Jake and I have together.

I want Jake to see me.

I want him to tell Melinda to leave because I'm here.

Because I'm in love with him.

"Daddy saw that you used your credit card in New Orleans, which got his detective on the case. He tracked you down there and everything fell into place. I took the first flight out to get here." She looks around and pulls her face up into what I can only describe as perfectly disgusted disapproval. "You've been living *here*?" she asks.

And then she sees me.

Our eyes meet and I'm unsure what to do. I want to leap forward and claw at her face and pull her hair. That would be savagely, though. Not the way a Baptist minister's daughter was raised.

Instead I glance from her to him, waiting for Jake to say something.

Jake shakes loose from the seeming shock of Melinda's appearance. "Melinda, this is Isabella Perry. She owns the farm and is... a friend."

I wince at the verbal punch in the face. A friend, huh? That's all?

But I stand tall and extend my hand in a very friendly manner. "Nice to meet you, Melinda."

She ignores my hand and doesn't even make eye contact with me, clearly dismissing my existence. What a bitch! My mouth falls open and I'm about to chastise her for being a rude, rich, privileged Daddy's girl of a New Yorker, when she tugs at Jake's elbow.

"I'd really like to speak with you in private." Her eyes slice back to me. "Without an audience."

I cross my hands under my breasts, wondering if she notices my brand new Café du Monde T-shirt and the suitcase Jake set on the lawn indicating we've just come back from an intimate weekend. Doesn't this woman see that I have the glow of a woman freshly in love? Surely even she can pick up on that *something* is going on between Jake and me.

To Jake's credit, he hesitates. "I really don't have much to say to you, Melinda. Honestly, why are you here?"

Melinda flattens her lips in an unattractive grimace. "I came here for you, Jake. Daddy says you can have your job back. We can pick up where we left off as if nothing happened. We can get married as we planned."

Her words penetrate my soul, bursting the bubble of hope for a future with Jake. In one fail swoop, she's returned to give him her love, support, and a neatly wrapped return to work as a cop, thanks to her father.

What do I have to offer Jake? I'm unemployed, this farm is in financial ruins, and I'm not a glamazon goddess like Melinda.

I look over quickly at Jake. I can't exactly make out his expression in the dusk. He could be pissed, hurt, or amused, for all I know. He shifts his eyes to me, but I don't let him speak. He and Melinda need to deal with *whatever* is going on in private.

Without getting my purse, cell phone, or suitcase, I turn to walk toward the house.

Jake calls out, "Isabella!"

"Let her go," Melinda says.

Since Jake doesn't run to catch up with me, I assume he does as instructed.

Once inside the house, I slam the door and press my back against it, trying to will my insane heartbeat to slow down, but not stop all together.

I peek out the small window to the right of the door and watch as Jake slips into the passenger side of Melinda's rental car. She starts it up and together they drive away.

"Please let him come back to me," I say to my surroundings.

The fate of my heart is now in Jake's hands.

Two hours later, I knock on Jake's trailer, but there's no answer. Then, I walk through the orchard to the chicken houses where I see Jimmie's dirt-covered Dodge Ram.

"Jimmie?" I call out.

"In here."

I open the door to the house on the right and find him sitting at the belt cleaning a prodigious amount of goo off a large white egg.

I screw up my face and nearly gag. Never fails to do that to me, no matter how long I've done this. "Everything okay in here?"

"D'ain't it the funniest thing," he starts, pausing to scratch at his floppy ear. "Once we got all the dead bird out the other day, the production numbers went through the roof."

"You're kidding! How is that possible?" I walk over to the wall and note the large poster panel displaying our output. Sure enough, the bar graph has gone up over the last three days.

Jimmie places the egg gently in the crate and flips the conveyer back on to continue the flow of eggs. "Can't explain what's in the minds of these chickens. They ain't like people. Tragedy befalls us and we go to pieces. Chickens, they don't care. They go back to their lives. Laying and eating and shitting. Ain't nothing complicated."

I snicker at his analogy. He makes it all seem so simple. I wish human life was that simple. But we're the ones who mess things up with our self-doubt, neuroses, drama, and swirling emotions.

"I'm definitely learning that, Jimmie."

He smiles up at me, his nose upturned as he looks me over. "Looks like The Big Easy did y'all some good. You have a visitor there?"

The blush creeps across my face. "Thanks for telling Jake where I was."

"I knew you two would hit it off, you just had to get over yourselves."

I laugh heartily. Jimmie's a match maker.

"He didn't hurt you, did he?"

Not yet. "I think he healed me."

Nodding, he says, "I thought so."

"Have you seen him?" I ask.

"Ain't he with you?"

I hang my head and drag my foot across the dirty floor. "No, his ex-fiancée was here when we got back. They went off to… *talk*."

"You know that Jake, he's got a lot of demons to sort out," Jimmie says to me. Then he looks me in the face and narrows his already small eyes at me. "He's worth it, ain't he?"

A smile breaks out over my face. "I think he is."

"Then I say what are you doing here talking to me? Go find him. Tell him how you feel. Don't make the mistake I did so many years ago." He looks back at the belt and nabs three eggs that are approaching the end.

"You mean with Stella?"

Jimmie bobs his head up and down.

"No, I won't." I look around the wooden room, left bare without wood treatment, and smile. "I'm actually going to miss this place. I did a lot of thinking here."

"Miss it?"

"Yeah, I called Esterhazy yesterday and told him to put the egg business up for sale. He twisted the situation and information a bit to manipulate me into fulfilling the Double C contract, due to his own affiliation with them. I called him on it and made some threats of my own to let him know what I thought of the way he does business. I'm going to keep the house, though. We can still see each other from time to time."

Jimmie shuts off the belt and places the last two eggs in the tray. Then, he stands and scratches at his curly head. "You're selling the place? Stella's place?"

"I have to, Jimmie. It's what's best for me."

"Reckon I have to say you lasted here longer than I expected," he says. "I think you'll be able to sell, then you can get on with your life. With Jake, right?"

A grin crosses my lips and I dare not hide it. "That remains to be seen."

Motioning to the door, Jimmie says, "Don't waste no more time. Don't make the same mistake I did all those years ago."

Overcome with the need to connect with this precious man, I walk over behind the folding chair Jimmie is sitting on and hug him from behind. His chest jiggles with his mirth and he closes his meaty hand over my forearm. I lean around and plant a kiss on his cheek. "Thank you, Jimmie. I couldn't have done any of this without you."

"Quit wasting your kisses on an old man and go get your guy."

"Where do you think he is?

"Where he always goes to think..."

"Ah!' I pat Jimmie on the shoulder. "The lake."

CHAPTER THIRTY-FIVE

Even though it's pitch-black dark, the moonlight illuminated the figure sitting on the edge of the pier. Stubborn remnants of day's sunlight casts a dying haze over the top of the lake while burnt orange fingers reach out across the rippling water.

Jake looks so peaceful, so deep in thought, sitting there at the end of the quay with his fishing pole cast out into the middle of the lake. I almost hate to disturb his solitude.

Almost.

"Where's Melinda?" I ask, stepping onto the rickety wharf.

Jake tosses a look over his shoulder and then returns his attention to his fishing activity. "She's headed to Pensacola to fly back to New York."

To do what? I almost ask. I bite my tongue, though, and wait.

I walk up behind Jake, but I don't touch him. Not yet. "Catch anything?"

He looks down, unanswering.

I sit next to him and toy with a tear in my jeans, wondering what to say and how to say it.

"So that was the woman who left you at the altar," I say.

Jake nods. "According to her, she was merely late and I left too soon."

He reels in the hook and tosses it over to the left. He doesn't meet my gaze, but I can see there's a lot going on in his head. I have to speak now and let him know how I feel. Is it even the right time considering this new information from Melinda?

"What were you supposed to think?" I ask. "Most women aren't late for their own wedding."

"Melinda isn't most women," Jake says.

Jealousy burns from my stomach like acid reflux. Turning, he meets my eyes with his gorgeous deep blue ones so full of doubt. Does he still love her? Can I possibly compete with someone like her?

"She wants you back." It's not a question.

Jake nods.

"And what you do want?" I ask boldly.

Jake shocks me when he asks, "I should ask the same of you."

I scrunch up my face, "What do you mean?"

Reaching into his pocket, Jake tugs out my Android and places it on the dock between us. "So Rick didn't just call you while we were in New Orleans. He's been texting you, too."

I look down at the call log on my phone that shows Rick's number. A bit stunned by Jake's question, I say, "I'm not interested in Rick. I want *you*, Jake."

He snorts and stares out over the lake. "You don't want me. Hell, Melinda shouldn't want me. I'm a mess. Damaged goods. I have too much crap inside me that I still need to work out."

Reaching out to him, I say, "Oh please, Jake. That's not true at all."

His eyes sear into mine. "It is, Isabella, and you know it. I never should have come to New Orleans and gotten you involved in the vortex that is my life. And now, with Melinda back and her father offering me my job back... I don't know."

I lay my hand on his thigh. "I thought we did okay. We can work through it together."

"What are you saying, Isabella?"

"I know you've been through a lot of shit. So have I. We both have baggage and relationships that didn't work. That's life, though. We can help each other. Let me be there for you, like you've been here for me. Remember? The allergy attack, the alien invasion, dealing with the chickens, and the death and destruction. You've resurrected my soul, Jake."

He shakes his head. "Rick wants you back. And Melinda wants me back," he says. "Why should we keep screwing up our lives when we can just go back to the way things were for each of us?"

My pulse throbs chaotically at my temples. I so need three Excedrin to combat the pain searing my brain. "Do you believe that? Honestly?"

Not only can I not go back to Rick, I pretty much don't want to go back to Boston. I don't want to return to the life of rushing around in the morning to catch the train, to get to my cube in time to not piss out the powers that be, and all for what? For a pittance of a pay check that makes me a wage slave to the corporate douche bag men in charge? Jake and I had talked of possibilities. Of opportunities. And, what? It was all just something to get me in bed?

I can't believe that.

"Did you stop to think what I want?" I ask.

Tossing the line out once again, Jake looks so young, so vulnerable. He lifts his head, though, and meets me face on. "What *do* you want, Isabella?"

I look deeply into his eyes and muster up all the confidence I can garner. "I want you."

I can't take this anymore. I've got to cut to the chase.

Get ready.

Here we go.

I can barely hear from the hammering of my heart pounding out an eight-oh-eight beat on my tangled insides. "I love you, Jake."

His head snaps around and he almost looks angry with me. "You what? No, you can't love me. You barely know me."

I scoot closer and wrap my arm around his back. "I know enough to decide I want to be with you. I'm completely in love with you. I never felt like this for Rick."

"I'm totally fucked up, Isabella."

"Yeah, you are," I say with a gentle laugh. "So am I. I'm a complete flake and I know it, but with you, I feel stronger, more in control. You give me the strength to be a better person. Melinda's not right for you. If she were, you never would have fled from New York. You never would have found me. Haven't we both wasted enough time on relationships going nowhere?"

Jake hangs his head. So much turmoil boiling under the surface. I want him to let go. I don't want him to let Melinda manipulate him into doing something that isn't right for him.

"Are you still in love with Melinda?"

"I don't know what I feel anymore," he says in a whisper.

I cock my head to the side. "What did you say to me in New Orleans? 'Let us happen.'"

"It's not that easy," he says, running his hand through his hair. "I wish it were."

Now I'm annoyed. "You just said that to get me into bed."

"No, he snaps at me. "Everything's just fucked up. You. Melinda. The timing. All of it."

Time to lay my cards on the table. Go for it. I can't go through this pain again. I didn't have the strength to handle Rick's rejection last month, but I do have the intestinal fortitude to speak up now. I want Jake in my life. I can't pine for him while he wrestles his demons, though. Either we're in this together or we're not. Either he chooses me and an unknown future or he chooses Melinda and a future fill of the past he's already experienced.

Taking a deep breath for strength, I say, "I need to know if you're going to fish or cut bait."

A storm of emotion ripples across his face. My heart pounds furiously in anticipation of his response. Maybe I pushed him too far too fast. I need to know what my future holds and whether he'll be in or if I'm on my own.

Either way, I can face this. I'll have to.

Jake reaches into his pocket and withdraws a nail clipper. Meticulously, he folds it over and into place. With a long sigh that rips from his body, he leans forward and snips the end of his line off.

I watch it sink into the murkiness of the dark lake. I'm not going to cry—although my insides experience a feeling akin to a slow death—because I asked for this. I wanted brutal honesty. The truth. I've dealt with this before and I'll do it again. I'm a strong woman and I can make it on my own. I've already proven that.

I stave off the burning tears that brim on the edge of my lids. I'm going to take the high ground here, even as my heart cries out in pain and defeat. I lean over and place a chaste kiss on Jake's cheek.

He doesn't look up at me, though he does reach up for my hand. I resist and turn away. Clean break.

Isabella Perry will have her happy ending one of these days. Just not today.

CHAPTER THIRTY-SIX

I lay in bed playing with the strap of my tank top and listening to the tweaking of the birds outside the window. They seem to be bitching each other out about something. Probably some ultra, cool chick bird kicking the male bird's feathery ass for being such a jerk.

I didn't sleep that well, but that was expected after yet another break up. Hey, I asked for it with my "fish or cut bait" line. One of these days I'll find a man who's not afraid of that line of questioning.

I get up and pad to the bathroom to wash my face and brush my teeth. As soon as I run the belts this morning, I'm going back to Boston. Vanessa needs me to help out with last minute details, like the good maid of honor that I am.

As I spit out the last mouthful of Colgate, I hear Jake's motorcycle crank. I climb on top of the toilet and look out the window. He's wearing his leather jacket, his helmet, and his duffel is strapped to the back of the bike. I watch as he turns to look at the house as if seeking me out.

My heart pounds way in trepidation. "Come on, Jake..."

After about ten seconds, he smacks the visor of his helmet into place, revs the engine, and takes off in a cloud of red dirt.

I listen as the sound of his engine fades into the distance. And out of my life.

Back to Melinda. Back to New York. Back to being a cop.

I climb down and go to splash water on my face, quelling the tears that threaten. As much as I hurt, I know that Jake has to do what's best for him. There's a part of me, though, that hopes he's not returning to his former life, rather he's headed south to Key Largo to finally face his father and overcome the demon wrestling with him.

I look at my reflection in the mirror. My eyes look tired— so I cried a little last night after talking to William on the phone and coming clean on the whole sordid affair—and there's some puffiness.

Back in the bedroom, I call the airline and book my flight home for tomorrow. Since Jimmie agreed to tend to the chickens for me, everything should be smooth sailing until I can get back after the wedding to finalize everything. That is, if Westin Esterhazy can find me a buyer. Which might be easier than finding a man who'll stay by your side.

I move around the room, tucking away memories of my time here into the corners of my packed suitcase. I leave out my good travel clothes, as well as my Kenneth Cole wool coat since William said it's miserably cold in Boston. I glance at my hideous UGGs that I'd worn on my first day on the farm. The Boone Dockers sit next to them and I smile at the memory of being at Wal-Mart with Jake.

I squelch the ache deep inside at the hallow spot Jake left behind. He became such an important part of my life in such a short time. More so than Rick. Jake *got* me. Understood me. Even if he did walk away in the end.

I make my way through the house and into Stella's room. So many of her personal belongings have been packed up and given to the church to distribute to the needy. I gave Jimmie Stella's collection of homemade handkerchiefs to remember her. He seemed pleased with the gesture.

I look at the picture of Aunt Stella that she left for me and I smile. I hope I've made her proud with the way I've handled myself on the farm. Okay, so I wasn't so brave at all times, I made a lot of bad decisions, and made an ass of myself. No one can knock me for trying or putting my all into it. A part of me wishes I had the resources to keep the farm, pay a full-time staff to man the chicken houses, and maybe live here a couple months out of the year. As Jimmie says, "D'ain't gonna happen."

I cross to the armoire and pull out the white creation that was once Stella's wedding dress. It'll be perfect for the wedding this weekend. Of course, thumbing through Stella's handmade retro collection, I snag several more outfits to take with me, as well.

The phone trills down the hall. I tuck the gowns under my arm and run to my room. On the third ring, I snatch up my cell phone hoping it's Jake. He's calling to tell me what an ass he was and that he's coming back.

My pulse triples and knocks against my temple like a metronome. "Hello?"

"Ms. Perry. Westin Esterhazy here, attorney-at-law."

I roll my eyes at him introducing himself to me *yet again* and every time we talk. "Hey, Westin. What's up? Doing more dirty work for Double C? More lies and deceit to peddle at me?" I ask sarcastically.

He clears his throat. "Actually, Ms. Perry, you'll be happy to know that I have a perspective buyer for the farm with a very nice offer."

"Really?" My hope lifts. I see the proverbial light at the end of the tunnel. See, I had a feeling one of these Dilligus Flats farmers might pony up to take over this place. "Who is it? Anyone I know?" I joke.

"As a matter of fact, it is."

I jerk to attention with curiosity. "Really? Who?"

"James Ford Hemi."

Sitting in the 1970s decorated office—*is that Wainscoting?*—of Westin Esterhazy, Esquire, I stare across the expansive mahogany table at the prim and proper lawyer... and my good friend.

Jimmie's dressed in his Sunday best, complete with a fresh, clean Dale Earnhardt, Jr. #8, cap. He drums his chubby fingers on the table as Westin goes over the final details of the transfer.

The deal is, I get the house and the five acres surrounding it. Jimmie gets everything else, the other two hundred and fifty for twenty-five hundred dollars an acre. Then, on top of that, he's paying an additional sum for the egg business, which includes the houses, the inventory, feed, and those horrid chickens that I hate so much. Full transfer of the Double C contract goes to him. Proceeds from the sale will pay off the debt and after that, I'm looking at nearly over a quarter of a million dollars.

I keep sipping from the Dixie cup of water me as this sinks in. Something... anything to help me swallow what's being offered to me. I think I just had my first hot flash.

Westin pushes his glasses higher on his nose and harrumphs. "I seem to be missing a form. I'll be right back."

Up until now, everything has been terribly formal. Esterhazy acting as an intermediary. Jimmie and I staring at each other. Curiosity's about to kill the cat, though.

I clear my throat. "Jimmie, I can't believe you're buying the farm. Why didn't you mention this back in the beginning?"

He scratches next to his bulbous nose. "I reckon I didn't want go against Stella's wishes."

I lean forward. "You knew I wasn't cut out for this, yet you helped me all the time. Never mentioning you wanted the farm."

He sighs. "I owed it to old Hardwick for getting under her craw before she died."

Folding my fingers together and trying to understand everything, I ask, "What was it you said that upset her?"

He removes the bright red hat and tosses it to the table, next to the pile of papers. "I offered to bail her out and give her money for the business. I was willing to make sure she had enough capital to keep the place going. But she was too durn proud. Didn't want anyone taking care of her. Said 'I'll do it on my own or not at all, Jimmie.'"

I can understand why Stella's feathers would be ruffled. From all I had gleaned about her, she was an independent woman who marched to her own drum. So Jimmie had stuck around and helped me out of fierce loyalty to Stella and the memories of what they once had.

I respect the hell out of him for that.

I look at his face as the emotions ripple down his chins. Jimmie loved Stella until the day she died. They should've been together, not as friends, but as man and wife. Looking at him, I feel a kinship. Guess Jimmie and I are doomed to love people who run away and leave us.

He gets up for another cup of water and returns. "I wanted to offer to buy the place from you when you first arrived, but I figured it was some sort of test Stella had in mind for you, so who was I to buck that?"

"A test? Why? I'd never even met her?"

"You reminded her of herself. I suppose she wanted to make sure you knew what you wanted in your life. Maybe make up for some of the choices she did or didn't make."

It makes no sense. This dead relative orchestrating the course of my life. However, without Stella's foresight, I never would have met Jake. No matter how things look right now, I'm eternally grateful for that.

One question remains.

I pass the document across to Jimmie that sports the doozey of a bottom line digit. "I hate to be rude, Jimmie, but where exactly are you going to come up with this amount of money? I mean, I'm not so desperate that I want you to go into debt and mortgage your life. We could always work something out so you don't have to get loans or—"

"Isabella, now hush. I got plenty of money."

"Right," I say with a snicker. His suit is at least twenty years old, the collar on the shirt is faded, and I can see what appears to be soup stains on his paisley (hello, 1988) tie. "Jimmie, you don't have to—"

"Missy, I said to hush."

I sit up straight like a child who's been disciplined for having their elbows on the dinner table. My eyes grow wide with sudden realization. "You mean you *have* that kind of money?"

He reaches for his Dale Earnhardt hat and plops it back on top of his greasy curls. "Well, of course, I do. I made me a fortune on them there dot.com stocks back in the 90s. Clinton done told everyone to invest in the stock market back then, so that's what I done. Tech stocks, biomedical, you name it."

I toss my head back and laugh. I can't stop myself. "May I ask how much you're worth?"

"About four or five million. Cain't remember."

I nearly choke on the air. "Did Stella know this?"

He hangs his head. "Nah, I mean she knew I played around with my computer buying up stocks and stuff. I never told her how good I was at it."

"Maybe that's why she wouldn't let you take care of her. Thinking it might put a strain on you financially."

Jimmie rubs his double chin with his thumb and forefinger. "Never thought of it that way. Guess I should have come clean with her. Course, then I wouldn't have met you."

I truly do love Jimmie. Not like I love Jake, of course. But, I can't see not having Jimmie in my life now. For that matter, I don't know how I'll go on without Jake. There's a huge hole in my heart that's going to take a long time to mend. He's a tough act to follow.

Look at what miscommunication between Stella and Jimmie did all those years. Maybe they could have been happy... had a life together... or perhaps a more fulfilled one. Children, grandchildren, togetherness.

I reach across the table and take Jimmie's hand. "I'm sorry you lost Stella."

He pats the top of my hand. "Me too, sugar. Life goes on, though. And maybe I can honor her memory by making her business prosper."

"I'm sure you can."

Esterhazy bursts back in waving forms over his head. "These are typed up all wrong. I'm going to have to get my assistant to redo this one, so you two sit tight. We'll have this done and you can be on your way in no time, Ms. Perry."

I wink at Jimmie and then say, "Take your time, Westin."

When he leaves the room again, Jimmie says, "So what's next?"

"I'm going back to Boston for a wedding." I don't elaborate as to whose wedding it is since I've never told Jimmie details about my friends back home.

"Weddings are happy occasions," he notes, wistfully.

Noting his pain, I say, "They should be."

"So, I reckon you'll be leaving Dilligus Flats?"

"Yes and no." I'm so going to pull a Rhett Butler and pour some of my newfound fortune into the house to make it like Tara. A nice haven away from the frenetic pace of city life. A place to remember Aunt Stella, Jimmie... and Jake.

Jimmie must pick up on my thoughts. "What about Jake?"

I meet Jimmie's eyes for only a second. "What about him?"

"I didn't see his motor-sickle this morning."

I swallow deeply. "No, I don't guess you did."

"That boy's a fool," he says.

Westin returns to the room and slides the papers in front of me along with a classy Mont Blanc pen. I take it into my hand, feeling the heaviness on my fingers.

I lift my eyes to Jimmie's. "Yes, he is."

CHAPTER THIRTY-SEVEN

Vanessa sits in front of the mirror and sweeps blush onto her cheeks. "I'm so glad you came home. I couldn't have gotten everything done without you, Griz."

Two days in Boston running around like chickens with our heads off—*wait, bad analogy*—getting candles, making the candy bag favors, checking with the florist, making sure the ribbons for the pews were done, the place cards alphabetized, and the banquet sheets signed off on, we're finally taking a moment to relax in the minister's chambers of the Seaside Chapel in Hampton Beach, New Hampshire, while Vanessa puts on the finishing touches of her makeup.

My fellow bridesmaids, Marina Baye, the world's most efficient—and stressed out—PR lady, and Darcy Cressler an aspiring cellist, and Vanessa's sister, Victoria, are getting the final touches on their hair and makeup. The old wooden building by the ocean is the perfect place for the joining of such a special couple. My heart expands for the joy Vanessa and Kyle must be feeling, combined with a tad bit of jealousy over my friend having the man she loves standing up with her and announcing their love to the world.

I try not to think about Jake or what could have been. Dilligus Flats. New Orleans. It's all in the past. My future is here and now. With my best friend.

I smooth out the black trim hem of my sleeveless mod A-line gray dress, a la The House of Stella. My dress to wear for the all-white wedding is hanging on the back of the door to don at the last minute. My hair is not behaving in the heated chapel and I hope it won't be all flyaway. It's not my day, though. This is about Vanessa. And I'm glad to be here to help.

I come up behind her and smooth her gold-brown hair (that I know for a fact to be out of a Clairol bottle.) "I wouldn't miss being here for anything in the world."

She dabs a light pink gloss on her lips and smiles at my reflection. "Everything's perfect. The minister's here, my bratty sister is behaving, Kyle's parents didn't get lost on the way up here, the flowers are fresh, the candles are perfect, and you're here. Nothing's gone wrong that I know of."

"Well, you are an event planner," I say, pinning small white roses into her hair. "If anyone's wedding is going to go off without a hitch, it'll be yours."

A knock on the door interrupts our girly time. Vanessa's mom pokes her head in. "Sweetheart, may I come in?"

I turn toward Mrs. Virtue, who looks like death on a cracker. "What's wrong?" I mouth at her.

She holds up her hand and goes directly to Vanessa.

"What's up, Mom?"

"Sweetie, something's happened."

Vanessa gasps and grabs my arm. "It's not Kyle! He's okay, isn't he?" So much for the perfect wedding day. Me and my big mouth. Or maybe it's merely my bad relationship karma rubbing off. Certainly Kyle wouldn't pull a Stella or a Melinda and bolt.

Mrs. Virtue moves in. "No, dear. Kyle's fine. Looks mighty handsome in his Armani tux."

Somewhat relieved, Vanessa slumps. "Then what's wrong?"

"Well, dear. Sit down. Oh, you are sitting..."

She so does not need to mess with Vanessa right now. Is it possible that I know her daughter better? "Mrs. V, you might as well spit it out," I say.

The older woman pulls at the dainty handkerchief in her hand before she speaks. "Your father was getting everything out of the trunk of the car and he... well, he accidentally slammed it on your dress."

She shrieks. "My dress?"

"Now, Vanessa, it's not as bad as it looks."

The door opens again and Major Virtue, in full Air Force dress blues, walks in with the wounded wedding gown lying in his outstretched hands. He presents it to Vanessa like he's giving a folded American flag to a widow of a fallen soldier.

"Honey, I didn't mean to do it. Is it ruined?"

Vanessa's eyes are too clouded with tears to see anything, so I press forward. There's grease from the trunk lock on the front left hip and four healthy puncture marks in a perfect rectangular fashion. *Completely* noticeable.

"I'm not going to lie to you, Double V." I gnaw on my lip briefly. "It's pretty bad."

She waves her hands in front of her eyes. "I won't cry... I won't cry... I won't cry..."

Her mother moves in to hug her and her father hangs his head.

"Maybe you could hold your flowers over to the side." I mimic the action with her bouquet on my left hip.

Vanessa blots her eyes and shakes her head. "It's no good. It's so obvious. My wedding's ruined."

In the reflection of the mirror, I see Stella's white gown hanging on the back of the door and I know what I have to do.

"V?"

She looks up through glistening eyes. "Yeah?"

I cock my head towards the dress. "You and I wear the same size. It'll be perfect."

She looks at the dress and then back at me. "I couldn't do that. It's your aunt's. It belongs in your family."

I get the dress off the hanger and place it in her arms. Then I take her by the shoulders and hug her—being careful not to wrinkle Stella's creation. "*You're* my family, Vanessa."

She squeezes tightly. "Griz, how will I ever thank you?"

"By getting out there and saying 'I do.'"

"You're the best friend a girl could ever have."

Marina, Darcy, and Victoria bound in, unaware of the drama playing out.

"What's going on?" Darcy asks.

I smile. "A slight costume change, that's all."

Major Virtue leaves, awash with relief, and Vanessa's mother, Marina, Darcy, Victoria, and I tend to the bride. Preparing her for her long walk down the aisle to the man she loves.

I feel a sense of pride as I beam at my friend in the beautiful couture dress. Stella's design and I might not have any plans for the foreseeable future and somehow, I'm okay with it. I'm doing the right thing.

The dress is going to make it through *this* wedding day!

I walk slowly down the aisle to the strains of the string quartet playing "Pachelbel's Canon in D" or maybe it's "Jesu, Joy of Man's Desiring," I can't tell. Darcy's the classical music expert, not me. The music is pretty either way. If I'm ever lucky enough to be in this position, I'll have to get Vanessa to tell me her musical selection.

I have to stop thinking about myself. About what could have been. About what's lost. This is Vanessa's day. I'm here to stand up for her. Nothing more. All other silly thoughts aside.

However, my heart weeps momentarily when my eyes connect with Rick's where he's standing at the front of the church next to Kyle. The corner of his mouth lifts and I smile at him. Oh, how simple it would be to retreat to the pattern of being with Rick.

But it's not that easy.

I don't love Rick like that anymore.

I love Jake.

I wink at Kyle, who looks a tad bit nervous, and then I take my place on the front row of the chapel next to Marina, Darcy, and Victoria. The music transitions into "Here Comes the Bride" and the congregation rises. I twist around and watch my best friend float down the aisle in Stella's gorgeous creation. I beam with pride and wish that my great aunt could see how extraordinary Vanessa looks in the flowing gown. I look over at Kyle and see his deep love for his bride mirrored in his eyes. Vanessa steps up onto the altar and her father places her hand in Kyle's before kissing her on the cheek and taking his seat with Mrs. Virtue.

See, everything's perfect.

Just as it should be.

"Dearly beloved, we are gathered here today—" the minister begins.

When he gets to the part about anyone having an objection, the back door of the chapel slams open and I hear loud footsteps tromp in.

"No! Don't do it. Please..." the voice calls out.

What the hell?

CHAPTER THIRTY-EIGHT

Adrenalin coursing through my veins, I crane my neck to see through the crowd of people behind me—*what's with the big hat, lady?*—to get a good look at the intruder. Everyone gasps and Vanessa and Kyle both spin around to face the trespasser.

I step out into the aisle and my eyes sync up immediately with steely blue ones. Ones I know very well. My pulse accelerates and I find it difficult to swallow down my shock and my surprise.

"Jake," I barely manage to get out.

He looks right at me, taking in my gray and black attire. "What? You're not..." He stumbles over his words. "I thought... oh, my God."

I glance back to the altar. Kyle's brows crease as he looks between Vanessa and Jake. "Who the hell is this schmuck?"

Vanessa lays her hand on Kyle's arm. She smiles at me, then says to Kyle, "He's not here for me, sweetie."

Confusion crosses the plane of Jake's face. He looks at Vanessa. Kyle. Rick. Me.

"I thought... I mean," he stammers. "The dress. You're not..."

I shove my bouquet at Darcy and mouth, "I'm sorry," to Vanessa.

She winks. "It's okay. I get it." She shoos me away with an evil smile and then turns to the minister. "Kick it back up, Rev."

As the congregation laughs nervously and a collective sigh of relief skitters about, I drag Jake down the aisle with me toward the vestibule in the rear of the church. I'm so filled with joy over seeing him that I feel like my chest will split open. But, I hold back any emotional outburst, waiting to see what he has to say.

I mean, he *is* here, after all.

At the back of the chapel, we stand facing each other. Breathless. His face seems drawn and tired, but his eyes are alight with relief.

"I saw Stella's dress and thought..."

"Shhh, not so loud," I correct, hoping we're not detracting from the continuing ceremony inside.

Jake smiles and leans toward me, lowering his voice. "I thought that was you up there. I thought I'd screwed up for good and you were marrying Rick."

I try not to grin too broadly. "No, I'm not marrying Rick. Vanessa had a mishap with her wedding dress, so I let her wear Stella's. She would have been tickled pink, don't you think?"

Jake reaches out tentatively and takes my hand. My skin sizzles connecting again with his. My insides ache with warm delight while his fingers stroke the top of mine.

He looks up. "I think Stella would prefer that you wear it."

I shrug. "Maybe one day." Meeting his gaze, I can't help but ask, "What are you doing here, Jake?"

His eyes plead with me. "I'm an idiot. I shouldn't have walked away from you like that. I was just so taken aback that Melinda showed up. That she had our whole future mapped out and orchestrated. All the pain and guilt inside of me thought it would just be easier to follow along. Be the person everyone expected me to be."

"Not me, Jake," I say. Then I ask, "How did you know where to find me?"

"Jimmie told me."

I nod. Good old Jimmie.

"I came to tell you I'm sorry, Isabella. You didn't deserve what I said to you."

"Jake, I—"

He stops my words by placing his hand gently over my lips. I resist the urge to kiss his fingers; instead, I listen.

I steady my pulse with a deep breath. Gripping my hand tighter, Jake forges ahead. "I never should have acted like I did at the lake. Like I said, I was an idiot running away from the farm. Especially after what happened in New Orleans. After those amazing days with you."

I sense a blush creeping across my face, but I remain quiet, listening on edge. Rushed with relief at his apology.

"You brought me back to life after I'd lost to much. You gave me hope and made me see that I couldn't be buried so deep within myself."

I giggle. "I taught you all of that? I just thought we had really awesome sex."

His eyes crinkle in a smile. "That too. You're the best thing that's ever happened to me, Isabella," he says. "I told Melinda that."

"I'm sure she loved that," I say with a harrumph.

"I don't care," he tells me. "And Stella knew we'd be good together, too."

My brows furrow together. "What do you mean?"

"Esterhazy gave this to me when I stopped back at the farm." He reaches into the front pocket of his leather jacket and pulls out a piece of paper. "It's from Stella."

Man, that woman left a lot of notes behind. I read with great curiosity. "*Jake: I'm sending my Isabella to you. She'll be able to show you the way.*"

Wow, there's a real gut-punch moment.

"You did," he confirms.

"But how... when?" I'm stunned at how Stella orchestrated this from the grave, no less.

Jake takes the paper back from me. "Stella knew I had demons. She also knew I needed to get on with life. Get back on my feet. I just needed a swift kick in the ass."

I laugh quietly. "That you did."

"You're what I needed."

"I was? I mean, I am?"

He puts his finger under my chin. "And to think I almost lost you. I didn't, did I?"

I want to cry, but I don't, not yet. "No Jake, you didn't."

He pulls me to him and hugs me tightly. Whispering close to my ear, he says, "I had to get my life together before I could move on." He sets me away from him. "You helped me do that. You were what gave me the courage and strength to face the pain inside. When I left Dilligus Flats, I drove straight to see my father, like you told me to do. It was an over-due homecoming. He didn't blame me at all for what happened to Grant," he says with hope in his voice.

"Of course he didn't," I say, fighting my own emotional floodgate that threatens.

"You were right. Thank you for making me see the light."

I hold on to his forearms for strength and balance. So, everything's cool with his father. Now, what about us?

As if reading my mind, Jake looks back towards the sanctuary. Then, he takes my hand in his. "So where do we go from here?"

"The reception," I say, trying not to laugh.

"After that," he says.

I don't feel like being coy or playing games. "I just want to be with you."

He lets out a sigh. "Thank God you said that. I'm moving to The Keys to be closer to Dad. I'm going to do the security company with my friend. And I want you to be with me."

My chest aches in aching delight over his words. He's not running. He's not hiding. He's not getting off the pot or cutting bait. None of those things are options anymore.

Jake steps back and digs his hand into his pants pocket. Slowly, he withdraws a tiny diamond ring and holds it up between us, the white stone catching the light.

I move my hand to cover my mouth as my eyes fill with shimming tears.

"Jake, does this mean—"

"Jimmie gave me this. It's the ring he gave to Stella." Jake takes my left hand and slips the ring into place while my heart pounds away at my ribcage. "Just so you know, this is a *promise* ring for right now. Once I get the security business going and we make some money, then I'll get you something bigger and gaudier."

We laugh together, trying hard not to disturb the wedding behind us.

I hope Vanessa and Kyle can forgive me, for something as momentous as what they're pledging is happening to me, as well. I might not be able to hold back those tears after all.

In a whisper I can barely hear myself, I say, "This is perfect." Then, I look up into those shining blue eyes that reflect the glow of the afternoon sun bouncing off the nearby ocean. "So, what are you saying to me, Jake?"

I have to hear the words. I have to see them coming out of his mouth to know that it's true.

His eyes crinkle along with his smile. "I'm saying I can't fight this, Isabella. I want to fish... with you." He leans forward and softly touches his lips to mine in a whisper of a kiss. "I want to fish with you forever."

An electric bolt zaps me from my head to my toe as Jake's lips recapture mine in a breathless kiss for the ages. Our tongues tangle together and I breathe in the scent of him. Familiar. Home.

"I want to fish with you, too." I stop and chuckle. "I mean, I love you so much, Jake."

He squeezes tighter and says, "I love you, too."

Silently, I send up prayerful thanks to Aunt Stella, the wisest woman I never knew, the little matchmaker. She had both Jake and me pegged for certain. And as I stand here in this charming church, wrapped securely in the loving arms of Jake, I realize I'm not so unlucky after all. Stella's misfortune turned into my fortune.

Guess I get that happy ending after all.

COMING SOON!
BOOK 3 IN THE RESISTING TEMPTATION SERIES

CAN'T DENY THIS!

CHAPTER ONE

The receptionist looks like she's got one hell of a secret and she's dying to let it out.

I smile at her through the glass-front door as I punch in my security code and push into the foyer. "You okay, Janine?"

"Hey, Vanessa," she says, looking around to see if anyone's watching. "Actually, something's up."

I lift an eyebrow.

The telephone rings and she jumps in her seat. "Big announcement today. Big. Huge. The biggest," Janine whispers. She hits the button on the phone, turns her personality to instant perk and says, "DigitalDirection, how may I direct your call?"

I give her a sidelong glance. Since she's on the phone, I can't probe any further on this alleged huge announcement. So, I turn the corner and head down the hallway through the corporate ant farm to my cube. I pass the hodge-podge of office equipment that sits in the far corner. The printer is inactive Morning reports aren't churning. Are we still in business? Is this a federal holiday I don't know about?

The air is pungent with the smell of fresh toner. Hmm... at least the office manager's busy doing her job. I walk by the president and vice president's offices. The doors are closed. They're never closed.

Something big must be stewing indeed.

I stop outside my cubicle. I don't hear any lively chatter, more like a dull buzz of muted tête-à-têtes. The normal sound of fingers machine-gunning on keyboards has been silenced.

Just as I sit down, my work buddy, Isabella Perry, appears suddenly, hanging over the side divider of my cube. I slap a hand to my heart as my pulse pounds out of whack. "You scared hell and three dollars out of me, Griz!"

I'd dubbed Isabella "Griz"—short for Grizabella the Glamour Cat—when she'd share her obsessive love of the musical "Cats" with me over cocktails and scoping guys one night at a bar in downtown Boston. She'd seen the kids on "Glee" sing about it and now it's like her theme song or something. However, Griz is a lot like the down and out cat, trying to make a name for herself in the big city, just like me.

"Did you see him?" she asks.

"Him? Who?"

"The babe in the tight pants who was walking down the hallway."

"I just got here. What have I missed?"

Griz screws her nose up. "Nothing yet, but something's up."

"That's what everyone keeps telling me." Geez, I haven't even had my morning coffee and things are percolating here. I love when there's office intrigue in the air. "What's going on? Spill it!"

"I can't tell you more than I know," Griz says and then darts her gaze around the room.

"Which is?"

"Not a lick or a damn."

Frustrated, I mock at strangling her. "Don't make me..."

She raises an eyebrow and grabs a chair from the empty cubicle across from mine, dragging it into my small veal-pen space. "Well, I heard there's some shuffling in the higher ranks around here."

"No way!" Seriously? If the ax is falling, I hope it doesn't chop off my head. I start straightening things on my desk, like neatness will count if someone comes around to fire me. *Get real, Vanessa!*

Griz presses on. "Word is we've lost six clients because the new software version isn't ready. Change is definitely in the air. You can count on it."

In this sad-sack of an economy where so many people are on unemployment and trying to figure out how to pay their mortgages so the banks don't confiscate their homes and cars, losing one client is *not* an option. Clients leaving the company equals lack of profit. Lack of profit means cutting personnel. Cutting personnel means I'm updating my resume and e-mailing it all over town. My heartbeat triples at the thought of being dire, desperate, and downright panicked.

Instead of thinking about the heavy gloom of the nation's economy that surrounds us, I refocus on the cute guy that's been spotted in the hallway. "And this alleged babe you mentioned? What's his deal?"

"Don't know. He's in Jiles' office as we speak," Griz reports proudly.

Jiles Chancey. President and CEO. And pain in my ass. What kind of name is Jiles? I mean, I've heard of Giles— which means *baby goat*. No kidding. I looked it up one day on a name-your-baby website. Anyway, he's got this weird shape to him, like he wasn't turned enough as a sleeping baby, because his head isn't rounded quite right. His close-clipped blond beard hides how he talks out of the side of his mouth in a not-so-trustworthy manner.

He's top dog here at DigitalDirection. When I first started here, I quickly learned that Jiles is a control freak who doesn't take suggestions—especially from women. Especially a junior marketing flunky like me. He nearly snapped my head off the first time I dared to speak during a meeting. Definitely a victim of Little Man Syndrome. Standing a grunt over five-feet-five, he's someone I look down on...particularly when I'm wearing my trademark three inch heels, which put me up around five-eight on a good day.

Griz bounces in place. "Go walk past his office and look in the window. See what you can see."

I wave her off. "I don't think so. What if it's a negotiator they've brought in to do layoffs?" The one thing I can't imagine is losing my job, no matter how much certain people annoy me. I need the money, the stability, and the security. That's why I work my ass off, staying late and doing whatever menial tasks this Marketing Coordinator has to perform day in and day out to keep her health care, stock options, and subsidized MBTA pass when there are thousands of people in this city who don't have any of those things. I can't even begin to think about updating my resume, hitting the online job searches, or pounding the pavement. I love what I do. Great co-workers (a lot of cute ones), a good atmosphere and plenty of after work activities to keep my social calendar full. "Does your boss know anything, Griz?"

"She's not talking'," Griz says sternly in her nasally Midwestern accent.

Originally from the suburbs of Chicago, Isabella moved to Boston six months ago to work on the design team, enhancing our software's graphical interface. She's the cutest thing, too. And I don't mean that in a lesbian way. Since she's still fairly new to Boston, I've taken it upon myself to show her the ropes at work and around town.

"So what do you think?" Griz asks.

"It can't be anything too horrible," I say, fidgeting with the pens in my cup. "DigitalDirection is important. We develop state-of-the-art customer relationship management solutions for all businesses." *Whatever that means.*

"I'm so sick of hearing the CRM buzzword." Griz points her finger into her mouth and pretends to gag in an oh-so-twelve-year-old-girl way. "Besides, you helped write that marketing crap."

I can't help but laugh. I guess my minor in creative writing from American University sure is paying off. But I return to the serious, professional Vanessa Virtue. The Vanessa Virtue who has a stack of bills at home and a student loan teetering on the edge of default. I need this job. I don't want to be forced to throw in the white towel and admit to my parents—particularly my Air Force Colonel father—that I'm not capable of cutting it on my own...even at twenty-five. They've kind of been expecting me to fail and come running home. "Oh you know Vanessa...off chasing her crazy dreams." They can't understand that I'm a grown up now and can live my life on my own without the structure and strictness of the military lifestyle.

I expel the deep breath I've been holding and think about peeking into Jiles' office. The anxiety of what's to come is getting to me. I was thinking positively, but now I'm not so optimistic. Shit always happens in business when you least expect it. My heart is pounding out of control, my hands are sweating, and the tension in the air is palpable. "This could be really bad."

"Calm down," Griz says. "We don't even know what's going on. Lord Almighty, you take things so damn serious, Vanessa."

I snicker nervously at her. Griz is the daughter of a Baptist minister. Very strict, much like my military father. Only

Mr. Perry's general is God. Griz usually chastises herself for taking the Lord's name in vain, something instilled in her by years of churchgoing and sermons of fire and brimstone. I'm a terrible influence, though. She's turned into quite the potty mouth in her months hanging with me after work.

I run my fingers through my wavy hair, messing up the coif I worked so hard on first thing this morning before I left for work. "I should try to find my boss. Or at least check my e-mail." My BlackBerry has been silent all morning, so if someone knows anything, they're not talking—at least not to me—yet.

Griz peers over my shoulder as I stealthily input my password into the network system.

"There's something," she exclaims and points at my inbox.

"Back off, will you? There might be personal message in here." I never get anything but jokes from my marketing teammate, Jack, and an endless stream of SPAM inviting me to find singles in my area, start my career with a new adult undergraduate program, or purchase a new 4G Android online for only fifteen dollars. No thanks. I'm not *that* naive.

"There's an e-mail from Jiles announcing a company meeting at two today." I look at her. "Didn't you get this?"

"I haven't been at my desk. First I've heard of it."

Slightly relieved, I turn back to my friend. We have company meetings all of the time. "Okay. Until then, we need to chill and just get our work done."

Griz stands and fingers her hair behind her ears. "Right. Work. Let's meet up for lunch."

I snort at her one-track mind. I haven't even finished my chai soy latte and she wants a meal. All part of her charm, though. "Noon-thirty?"

"You're on. We'll go to that new place across the street. We can split one of their *huge* sandwiches," she says.

"How are you so skinny when all you do is eat?" I ask incredulously.

"Clean living," she says with a smile.

Frustrated as hell at the beginning of the morning and my friend who seems way too chipper than this day calls for, I lay my head on my desk and softly flail up and down a couple of times.

A quieter voice interrupts. "Vanessa, may I speak to you for a minute?"

I bolt upright at the sight of my very pregnant boss standing where Griz was moments ago.

"Oh. Hi, Aislin," I say as my cheeks heat.

Aislin Honan. Tall, beautiful red hair showing her Irish heritage, and thirty-eight. She's totally the woman I want to be someday. Smart, successful, mature…and married.

I watch as she rubs her distended belly. "Let's go to a conference room."

"Sure thing, Ais."

Aislin's my perfect mentor. Although I studied communications in school, I'd been flying by the seat of my pants with the marketing assignments at my first company out of college. Now I'm learning from Aislin and making sure the textbook knowledge I gained in school applies to real work situations. Instinct's one thing, but actually succeeding and helping the company's bottom line grow is another.

Okay, maybe Griz is right. I am too serious about everything.

I need a boyfriend. Something else in my life besides work. Something other than watching *The Food Network* when I get home, or playing Frontierville on Facebook into the wee hours.

I get no kicks from the online dating sites. The guys are after one thing and one thing only. What happened to getting to know someone or flirting or clicking? It's all about making the move, getting drunk, and falling into bed. I didn't even do that in college (not very well anyway), so why would I want to do it at twenty-five?

Besides, I have to be committed to my position here at The Compass. I want to make a difference. I don't want to do anything to screw up my chances here. Took me three interviews to get in the door here. I want to do a good job, get recognized for it, learn, grow, and support myself. (And keep the company management complaints to myself.)

I follow Aislin into the Great Barrier Reef conference room. All of our conference rooms are named after the Natural Wonders of the World. Since no one wants to sign up for the Iguassu Falls or Bay of Fundy conference rooms because they can't spell them, the HR department has devised a company-wide contest to rename the seven rooms, hoping for something more user-friendly.

My entry: The Seven Dwarfs. (To reflect the size of management.)

Once in the room, Aislin lowers her girth into the chair, which moans accepting her and her unborn child that looks overdue at this point. "I have some news for you, Vanessa."

My pulse accelerates and I silently send up a prayer that my job isn't on the line.

I sit opposite Aislin and lace my fingers together on top of the table in the most professional manner possible. My heart slams against my ribcage in a cocktail of anticipation, trepidation, and a bit of excitement when I see a smile break across her face.

She leans forward, her Irish green eyes bright like she knows a huge secret. "I'd like to congratulate you on your promotion."

I bite my lower lip to squash the desire to shout like I'm at a Patriots' playoffs game. I can't help but beam at her. "A promotion?"

"Yes. You've been doing a great job since we hired you. You're dedicated, trustworthy, creative, and very responsible."

It feels as if my skin is scorched from her amazing words. No one's ever complimented my work like this before. Prior to joining The Compass, I worked thankless hours at one of the big boy financial institutes downtown answering phones, making coffee, and doing other people's shit work that they didn't want to do. To get out of that mundane position, I reworked my resume detailing everything I did for the bubbly marketing chick—who had hair the color of whatever dye was on sale at CVS that week—and landed me the position here at DigitalDirection on Aislin's team. And now…a promotion!

"Since I'll be taking maternity leave in a few weeks, Jiles and I decided to split my responsibilities evenly between you and Jack."

Jack Daniels—not the guy who makes the whiskey—is my marketing teammate and resident webmaster. Jack—short for Johannes—is half Norwegian, half American. He spent most of his life in Norway, so he doesn't *get* that his name is the same as the God of College Alcoholics.

Jack's one of those hurly-burly, muscular Scandinavian speed skater types you see in the Olympics. But I don't flirt with him or have any interest in dating him. Or any of the guys at The Compass, although it's a virtual smorgasbord of hot men in business casual attire.

Company policy: *No Dating.*

It's in the employee handbook in black and white on page twenty-three. Even the mere hint of flirting with a co-worker can land you a starring role in the office e-mail loops and coffee machine gossip. I am focused on my career. No time for a quicky in the copy room with a co-worker.

Aislin continues, "Jack will work on promotions, handle ads, and manage the web design." She passes a piece of paper along the tabletop. "You'll be in charge of tradeshows and events, as well as the marketing budget. Nothing more than a few invoices and reporting to Jiles."

I gulp hard and read the title on the job description. "Marketing Events Manager." Me...a manager.

Aislin talks on about the bump in salary—*thank you!*— and the new responsibilities, but I barely hear her as I am still focused on the word *manager*. Sure, I can get ahead in my student loan payments and maybe buy that awesome Kenneth Cole carrier bag I've had my eye on, but more importantly, I'll get new business cards that I can send to my parents that read, "Vanessa Virtue. Marketing Events Manager."

Aislin clears her throat. "Here's everything you'll need to know about the Atlantic City show."

Taking the bright yellow folder labeled "CRM Strategic Conference," I await further explanation. I'm going to Atlantic City?

"You'll need to ship the tradeshow booth to the Taj Mahal Casino and Hotel," Aislin slides over a small silver key. "Don't lose that. It unlocks the booth and is our only one." I take the tiny key as she continues. "You'll be staying at the Taj Mahal with Ted Spencer, since New Jersey is his territory. He can teach you how to put the tradeshow booth together."

"Excellent," I say. Wait a sec. What do I know about building a booth? Do I need nails and a hammer? Should I not get a manicure beforehand? What are we doing at a casino? Will people be more interested in seeing software demos or gambling?

"So, just the two of us—Ted and me?" Ted is a bit of a corporate dork who wears attitude glasses and sports a closely-cropped goatee. I don't know how much fun a trip with him will be. Wait a minute...it's not about fun. It's about work. Must be a professional at all times no matter how much I want to celebrate right now.

"Well, I shouldn't say anything until the company meeting, but there might be a new person coming with you. More on that later. In the meantime, send Ted an e-mail. He'll need to give you a crash course in demoing the software."

I thumb through the paperwork. "What's the gist of this show?"

"It's all about CRM—customer relationship management, you know. And since our software provides such a huge client services function, we need to make sure we show up our competition."

"You mean SalesTracker?" I'll admit I don't know much about how our software works, but I do know who our competition is. Or SalesWankers as our British transplant sales person, Penelope Dunsbury coined them when she first started working here. They've been around a few years more than DigitalDirection and they're rumored to have just received a huge influx of venture capital and have vowed to put the rest of us out of business. True wankers.

"Exactly," Aislin stands and pushes her chair under the table. "I know you're going to do a great job, Vanessa."

"Thanks for believing in me." I crush the desire to scream for joy. Not professional. Or dance. Not the place. Or at least call Griz and give her the news. More doable.

And how cool is this? I'll be able to travel and meet new people and...

Oh God...

Travel. I gulp hard at the sudden lump of anxiety in my throat.

That means airplanes.

Security checks. Take offs. Landings.

The folder in my hand begins to shake. I think my blood pressure just went into the danger zone. Someone hand me a Zocor...no wait, that's for high cholesterol. I can't think.

Mentally, I shake it off, realizing I don't need to dwell on my insecurity at this moment. Not when all of this good news is still soaking in. I'll deal with it. I always have.

As we leave to return to our cubes, Aislin says, "One more thing. I've requested a company credit card for your travel-related expenses. You're going to be on the road quite a bit."

Nothing's better than traveling on the company's dime. I tamp down the apprehension of facing my biggest fear, forcing it to the pit of my stomach. This will be an adventure. More work experience to add to my resume.

The door to Jiles' office opens and I see the back of the mystery man Griz was talking about. If the front looks anything as nice as the back...*well...wow...*

The rest of him better not be good looking.

It doesn't matter. Company policy...no fraternization or cavorting.

And I'm not going to let anything—not even a cute ass—get in the way of my success.

AUTHOR BIO

Marley Gibson is a young adult, contemporary romance, and non-fiction author best known for her wildly popular GHOST HUNTRESS series. Gibson appeared on the premiere episode of Biography's "My Ghost Story," as well as being on episodes of the Travel Channel's "Paranormal Challenge," and "Ghost Adventures." A certified SCUBA diver, a closet gourmet chef, and an avid traveler, Marley lives in the Florida Keys with her husband, Patrick Burns from TruTV's "Haunting Evidence," and their two rescue kitties, Madison and Boo. When she's not crafting novels, she makes hand-crafted zombie baby dolls called DagNabIt Dolls that are all the rage! She can be found online at www.marleygibson.com, Facebook at marley.h.gibson, and Twitter @MarleyGibson. DagNabIt Dolls can be found on Facebook at www.facebook.com/DagNabItDolls/ or at www.dagnabitdolls.com.

ACKNOWLEDGEMENTS

Thanks so much to Deidre Knight, Jia Gayles, and TKA Distribution for helping me get this story out to readers. These characters have been a part of me for a very long time, so it's great to share their tale with everyone. More to come from the Resisting Temptation series.

Thanks so much to Jennifer Keller, Megan Bremer, and Wendy Toliver for reading and critiquing for me. Your support continues to bolster me up.

Thanks to Jessica Andersen and Charlene Glatkowski of the WACs for all the cheerleading.

Thanks to my husband and my love, Patrick Burns, for all of his encouragement and inspiration. You love me; I love you more!

And, to those of you curious about my research on this book, let's just say it's a venture my parents once tried and were happy to get out of. LOL…you'll see when you read the book.